"You are stul...
illogical and in....

"I am a...
behind a ...

"Exactl...
her. She g...

"I do not wish my readers to think that I spread falsehoods." She backed up, and some large potted plant stopped her progress.

"But you do," he insisted. "Don't make me prove it to you, Lady Somerset."

"Oh, you wouldn't dare."

"Oh?" he murmured, lifting one brow.

Her lips parted, against her will. *"Oh."*

Oh, hell and damnation, she was in trouble now.

Romances by **Maya Rodale**

A TALE OF TWO LOVERS
A GROOM OF ONE'S OWN
THE HEIR AND THE SPARE
THE ROGUE AND THE RIVAL

A Tale of Two Lovers

MAYA RODALE

AVON

An Imprint of HarperCollinsPublishers

This is a work of fiction. Names, characters, places, and incidents are products of the author's imagination or are used fictitiously and are not to be construed as real. Any resemblance to actual events, locales, organizations, or persons, living or dead, is entirely coincidental.

AVON BOOKS
An Imprint of HarperCollins*Publishers*
10 East 53rd Street
New York, New York 10022-5299

First Avon Books mass market printing: May 2011

Avon Trademark Reg. U.S. Pat. Off. and in Other Countries, Marca Registrada, Hecho en U.S.A.
HarperCollins® is a registered trademark of HarperCollins Publishers.

Printed in the U.S.A.

10 9 8 7 6 5 4 3 2 1

This book is dedicated to Denise,
who is also typically forthright.
Happy Birthday, D-bird!

and

For Tony,
even though I didn't take your suggestion
to name all the characters Tony.
Happy 25th Birthday, Baby!

Acknowledgments

This book would not have been possible without. . .

- ~ Coffee. Lots of good, strong, organic coffee.
- ~ My agent, Linda, and my editor, Tessa. Yea, team!
- ~ Jocelyn, for a clean apartment and thus a clear head and free time for writing.
- ~ Mark, for organizing my wedding so beautifully and so reliably so that I could be a relaxed bride who had met her deadline.
- ~ The folks at Rodale Institute for being awesome to work with and for understanding about this other job of mine.
- ~ The usual assortment of friends and writing partners.
- ~ My graduate school professors who enthusiastically supported my studies of

popular romance novels and tabloid–esque newspapers from the 19th century.

~ To the cowboy poet in Wyoming who gave me the idea for Roxbury's scandalous parking spot.

~ To my old family and my new family!

~ And Tony, for walking the dog so I could write, listening to me ramble about the book, for championing me when writing was hard, for reading more drafts than anyone, doing the dishes, reaching high things and most especially for marrying me. Hallelujah, I finally found a boy like me!

Author's Note

In every age, there are women who buck conventions and defy expectations. Those are the women I've found most fascinating and inspiring, and those were the characters I wanted to write. And so the Writing Girls were born.

Nothing like them actually existed in the Regency Era. However, at that time and earlier women were active in publishing. Mary de la Riviere Manley was the editor and founder of *The Female Tatler* (1709), and later of *The Examiner* (1711). Eliza Haywood launched *The Female Spectator,* the first magazine created by women, specifically for women, in 1744. Mrs. Elizabeth Johnson, a printer, published the first Sunday paper, *The British Gazette and Sunday Monitor,* in 1779. *La Belle Assemblee*, a Regency era women's fashion periodical, employed women.

Furthermore, virtually all articles in newspapers and periodicals were published anonymously, so who's to say there weren't women writing?

The London Weekly is based on papers like *John Bull* or *The Age*—very gossipy weekly papers—or, more contemporarily, the *New York Post*. Julianna's column draws on a long tradition of printed gossip (with a few having that same name, Fashionable Intelligence). For more information about women writers, my books, the Writing Girl world, and to sign up for my newsletter, please visit www.mayarodale.com.

A Tale of
Two Lovers

Part I

The Gentleman's Trouble and Strife

Chapter 1

London, 1823

The backstage of the Drury Lane playhouse was no place for ladies, but Julianna, Lady Somerset, had suffered enough of what proper women did and did not do. She adjusted the short veil slightly obscuring her face, clung to the shadows and kept her eyes wide open for scandal.

She had seen the notorious Lord Roxbury exit this way. Without a second thought, she followed him. In her experience, to rely on a man was the height of folly—unless it was to count on Lord Roxbury to get tangled up in a scandalous situation. He was a godsend to gossip columnists everywhere.

It was widely suspected but never confirmed that Julianna was the infamous Lady of Distinction, author of the column "Fashionable Intelligence" for the town's most popular newspaper, *The London Weekly*. Since that was, in fact, the truth, she was on a perpetual quest for gossip.

Thus, if Lord Roxbury went skulking off backstage at Drury Lane, she followed.

She sought a tall man who moved with confidence and radiated charm. His hair was black and slightly tousled, as if he'd just gotten out of bed. Frankly, he probably had. Many a woman had sighed over his eyes—plain brown, in her opinion. And his mouth was another subject of intense adoration by women who either had kissed this infamous, glorious rake or longed to do so.

Julianna Somerset could not be counted among the legions of ladies who fawned over him. Her heart and body belonged to no man—not after she had survived a love match gone wretchedly wrong. Like Roxbury and his ilk, the late Lord Somerset was a charmer, a seducer, a man of many great passions, and ultimately a heartbreaker.

Julianna had tasted true love once; it had a remarkably bitter aftertaste.

But that was all in the past. Julianna no longer had to sit at home wondering where her husband was, whom he was with, and how their love had faded to nothing. Other people's business was her focus now.

Hence the following of Lord Roxbury, backstage at Drury Lane, late at night. A man like that could only be up to no good.

"Ah, there you are!"

Julianna turned to see Alistair Grey, her companion for the evening. He reviewed plays for the same paper and they often attended the theater together. Tonight they had seen *She Would and She Would Not*, starring their friend, the renowned actress, "Mrs." Jocelyn Kemble.

"Have you discovered anyone in compromising positions yet?" Alistair asked in a low voice, linking his arm with hers.

"Everyone is on their best behavior this evening," Julianna lamented softly. "But I swear that I saw Roxbury dash off this way."

"I don't know how you see anything with that veil in this light," Alistair said.

"I see plenty. Certain things are hard to miss," Julianna replied. She had a gift for eavesdropping and an eye for compromising positions and drunken antics. Dim lighting and a black mesh veil did nothing to diminish her talents.

"This hall is desolate, Julianna. Let's go back to the dressing rooms where everyone is drinking and in various states of undress. Surely you'll find more to write about there than in this dark and dusty corridor."

"Yes, but I saw a couple go off this way, and the man looked just like Roxbury. You know how he is," she persisted. That, and she didn't particularly want to be in a crowded dressing room with a half dozen women in their underclothes and two dozen men ogling them.

"I know, but it's probably just some prop mistress and a third son of an impoverished nobleman," Alistair said dismissively.

"In other words, nothing remarkable," Julianna said, heaving a sigh.

The low rumble of a man's laugh broke the silence. In the dark, Julianna gave Alistair a pointed look that said, "I told you so." Together they crept closer, always taking care to remain in the shadows.

There was just enough light from a sconce high on the wall to discern a couple embracing. It was not the wisest position—in a corridor, near a light—she thought, when there were certainly darker and more anonymous locations here for a little romp. But one could be overwhelmed by passion anywhere. Her own deceased husband had been overwhelmed with passion while driving his carriage, and that was the last thing he ever did. In fact, he had been overwhelmed with passion quite frequently, though never with her.

Pushing aside bitter memories of her past, Julianna stepped closer, intent upon discerning their identities. The couple might only be theater underlings but if perchance one of them was a Person of Consequence, she would certainly need to report it.

What she saw shocked even her.

Two pairs of shiny black Hessians, *two* pairs of breeches-clad legs, *two* linen shirts coming undone, *two* dark coats hanging open.

"Oh, my . . ." Julianna murmured under her breath.

As her eyes adjusted to the light overhead, she identified their position: One—tall and dark-haired—clasped the other around the waist, from behind, pulling his partner flush against him. As for the other one . . . his hands were splayed upon the wall, supporting them both, arching his back, turning his head back to accept the kiss of his mysterious *male* paramour.

Julianna grasped Alistair's arm, giving it a squeeze.

This was beyond scandalous.

This was the sort of item that would cement her reputation as the very best.

It would be a serious blow to her archrival, the

infamous gossip columnist at *The London Times* otherwise known as the Man About Town. He would never be able to top this!

Julianna cursed her veil and stepped forward to gain a closer look. In the process, she tripped over a broom that someone had left carelessly propped against the wall. She swore under her breath.

It clattered onto the floor. The couple jerked apart and instinctively turned in her direction. One man's face was obscured, ducking behind the other for cover. Thanks to the light above she could see the other man's face clearly.

Oh Lord above! Lord Roxbury! With a man!

An earl's only son embracing another man was *news*. In her head she began to compose her column:

Has London's legendary rake, Lord R—so thoroughly exhausted the women of the ton that he must now move on to the stronger sex? Indeed, dear readers, you would not believe what this author has seen. . . .

Chapter 2

Carlyle House
A few days later

Like most gentlemen of his acquaintance, Simon Sinclair, Viscount Roxbury, was equally averse to both matrimony and poverty. His chief aim was to live and die a wealthy bachelor. He had succeeded admirably thus far.

However, his father, the lofty, prestigious, and esteemed Earl of Carlyle had vastly different expectations for his sons' futures. The eldest had expired, and now Roxbury's life, particularly his matrimonial state, was the earl's focus. It was a constant point of disagreement.

Whereas the son was a gallant and charming rake, the elder was a solid, reputable man who dutifully took up his seat in parliament, tended to his estates and gave his wife plenty of pin money but otherwise ignored her. As long as she had new gowns, jewels and a circle of friends, Lady Carlyle cared not for much else.

Roxbury lived in mortal terror that his life should be the same.

He craved passion and lived for the thrills of falling in love . . . over and over again.

Roxbury crumpled the note summoning him to his father's study for another lecture on the duties of a proper heir: not blowing through the fortune, getting married, and producing brats. He deliberately dropped the ball of paper onto the Aubusson carpet in one small sign of defiance.

They would always be father and son, but Roxbury was not to be ordered around like a child any longer.

"You are aware, of course, that I am able to receive correspondence at my residence," Roxbury began. "Sending a summons to my club is really unnecessary."

He had received the missive yesterday afternoon, as he was enjoying a game of cards with some fellows at White's. Roxbury only now found the time to venture over—after a soiree last night and a very leisurely lie-in with the delightful (and flexible) Lady Sheldon this morning.

On his way from her bedchamber to his father's study, Roxbury had paid call upon some of his acquaintances and paramours. None had been at home to him, which was deeply troubling. Not to be boastful, but he was a popular, well-liked fellow. No one ever refused his calls. He could not dwell on it now, though.

"It is necessary to send word to your club," his father said, with the sort of patient tone one reserves for toddlers or the mentally infirm. "Lord knows I could not possibly anticipate which woman's bedchamber you would be in. You certainly are never at your own horrifically decorated residence."

That was true on all counts. A series of angry mistresses had taken their vengeance by decorating the rooms of his townhouse in a uniquely wretched way, with each room worse than the last. There was an excessive amount of gold, and a revolting quantity of red velvet furniture. Roxbury vaguely understood that it was a desperate plea for his attention as the relationship wound down and his eye wandered to other women. However, he generally avoided thinking about it at all costs.

Thus, he preferred to spend his days at his club and his nights with other women. He'd been in three different women's bedchambers this past week alone. Or was it only two? It seemed ungentlemanly to keep count.

Funny, then, that he should have been refused by two or three women this morning. He frowned.

Roxbury loved women. Their lilting laughs, pouting lips, and mysterious eyes. The smooth curves and contours of a female body never failed to entrance him, as did their soft skin and silky hair. Most women were completely and utterly mad—but always to his endless amusement. Women were beautiful, charming, perplexing, delightful creatures, each in their own unique way. How could he limit his attractions, attentions, and affections to just one?

He couldn't possibly. He did not even try.

"I do not mind paying for your residence, and your allowance," his father droned on. He sat comfortably in a large chair on the other side of his desk. It was warm enough to go without a fire, but the windows were closed, too, lending a stale, suffocating air to the room.

"I thank you for that," Roxbury said politely, even though it was his portion from the family coffers, not some gift or charity. It went with the title—one he never asked for and would rather not have, given what it cost him to get it. The name of Roxbury was just a courtesy until he assumed the name and title of Carlyle—and all the responsibilities that came with it.

"After all, a gentleman must maintain a certain style and standard of living," the earl said as he reached for a cigar from the engraved wooden box on his desk, next to a letter opener fashioned from pure gold and studded with emeralds.

"I heartily agree," Roxbury said, wary of where his father's argument was going. He was fond of his fine things, too, but who wouldn't be?

The earl offered a cigar to his son, who accepted. Something strange was going on, he could just tell. First, those refused calls this morning. Lady Westleigh *never* refused him. And now this rambling from his father about living in style. Deuced unusual.

"Part of the duty of a father—a duty I take very seriously—is to provide for one's children. Fortunately, due to my intelligent management of the Carlyle estates, it's something I am able to do."

"I agree," Roxbury said. "Careful management of estates is essential. I am proud to report that Roxbury Park has been making a small profit of late." It was his own parcel of land that he'd been given at the age of eighteen as a future residence and independent source of income. That was when he'd been the second son, and didn't stand to inherit the vast lands and wealth of all the Earls of Carlyle.

Now, as was custom, he went by one of his father's lesser, spare titles—Viscount Roxbury. It had been Edward's name once, Roxbury thought, but then he shoved aside those memories. Now wasn't the time.

"Congratulations," his father said, and Roxbury did acknowledge a surge of pride at the accomplishment and recognition. It was dogged by a nagging sense of dread. This could not be the purpose of the meeting—there must be something else.

The clock on the mantel clicked loudly.

"You are going to need that money, I fear," his father said. Each word was heavier than the last.

The earl paused to light his cigar from the candelabra on his desk. The flame illuminated the slanting cheeks that puffed and pulled on the cigar until the end was aglow and the old man exhaled.

They had the same high cheekbones. The same black hair, though the elder's was graying. Edward, too, had shared these traits. And like his younger brother, Edward had also inherited a wild temperament and passionate nature from some long forgotten ancestor. How their staid and proper parents had raised such hellions was still a mystery to Simon.

They were down to one hellion, one heir, now.

The three of them had shared the same love of money, too. Money was freedom, comfort, and pleasure. It was a necessity and a luxury all at once. The scent of banknotes or the clink of coins did not excite him, but there was a way a man moved, lived, existed when he had an income—to say nothing of a fortune. He did not want to lose that.

Roxbury lifted one of the candles to light his own cigar.

Women. Money. Marriage. Something nefarious was underfoot, he could just tell.

"I have been fulfilling my duties as a father—providing for you, raising and educating you, etcetera, etcetera. However, you have not been fulfilling your duty as an heir."

Roxbury inhaled and exhaled the smoke in perfect rings, in defiance of the earnest and ominous direction of the conversation they'd had a thousand times before.

"I have given the matter much thought, and discussed it with your mother. We both agree that this is the best course of action."

Obviously, his mother generally agreed with whatever her husband suggested.

His father enjoyed his cigar for a moment, leaving Roxbury sitting and smoking in annoyed suspense.

"You have one month to take a wife of proper birth," the old man said. Roxbury choked on a rush of smoke. His father merely smiled and carried on. "In that time, if you have failed to marry a suitable woman, I shall cease to pay your bills."

"Poverty or matrimony?" Roxbury gasped.

"Precisely," the earl said, with a proud, triumphant smile.

"That can't be legal."

"I don't care. And you can't afford the solicitors to deal with the matter, so the point is moot." The smile broadened.

"This is a devious, manipulative, and—" Roxbury would have gone on to say it was repugnant, a violation of the rights of man, and generally an unsporting thing to do, but he was cut off.

"Frankly, I think it smacks of genius." His father inhaled and exhaled his cigar smoke in a steady stream of gray that promptly faded into the rest of the stale air.

Some animals in the wild ate their young. Apparently, his father would allow his only son to die of starvation or be henpecked to death. Poverty or matrimony indeed!

"It's sneaky, underhanded, and meddling like the worst society matron."

"We have a tradition in this family," the earl continued, his voice now booming once he hit upon one of his favorite subjects. "Roxbury men whore it up with the best of them until the age of thirty when they settle down, marry, and produce heirs. You are two and thirty and show no signs of reforming your behavior."

He could easily marry if he wanted to. Roxbury loved women and they loved him back. Honestly, he could have his pick of any of the adorable, ditzy debutantes because he had money, a title and was not hideous.

But he did not want to marry. He loved women, *plural*. Promising to love a woman, singular—forever and ever—was something he could not do. At heart, for all his rakish ways, he was a romantic. But he was also a levelheaded realist.

A wife would get in the way of his numerous affairs. A wife would get in the way of his life.

Instead of gallivanting backstage at the theater for all hours, he would have to escort the missus home at the conclusion of the performance. A wife, like his mistresses, would redecorate his townhouse in strange colors like salmon, periwinkle, and harvest gold. A wife would mean brats. And that would definitely be the end of life as he knew it.

Roxbury was quite fond of life as he knew it.

"To hell with tradition." Roxbury stamped out the cigar. Tradition hadn't given a damn about Edward. He was supposed to be the heir who would marry and make brats, and leave the way clear for Roxbury to be a reckless rake until the day he expired, which would ideally happen in the arms of a buxom, comely mistress. But Edward wasn't around anymore. He existed only in a portrait above the mantel in the drawing room and in a few poignant memories.

"I will not have my life's work passed along to one of your idiot cousins because you couldn't be bothered to consort with a proper woman for long enough to put a ring on her finger and a baby in her belly. I will not be failed by both of my sons."

"To hell with your ultimatum," Roxbury said in a ferocious voice before he quit the library and Carlyle House.

Chapter 3

White's Gentlemen's Club
St. James's Street, London

After that incredibly disturbing interview with his father—to say nothing of all those calls that had been inexplicably refused this morning—Roxbury proceeded to White's. A drink was certainly in order, either to toast his rebellion and impending poverty or to enjoy a last hurrah before submitting to the bonds and chains of holy matrimony. He was too blindingly mad to know what to do. Neither option appealed to him.

Marriage—never. Poverty—no, thank you.

He arrived at the same time as Lord Brookes, who arched his brow questioningly and sauntered past, declining to say hello. They frequently boxed together at Gentleman Jack's and had always been on good terms. How strange.

Roxbury sat down at a table with his old friend the Duke of Hamilton and Brandon and some other gents. They were all sipping brandies and reading the newspapers.

All the others left. Promptly.

There was a rush of chairs scraping the hard-wood floors as they were pushed back in haste, the sound of glasses thudding on the tabletop and the crinkling of newspapers as all the other gentlemen nearby gathered their things and removed themselves to seats on the far side of the room.

What the devil?

The Duke of Hamilton and Brandon, usually known simply as Brandon and a longtime friend, looked at Roxbury and shook his head.

Ever the attentive servant, Inchbald, who was approximately three hundred years old, brought over a double brandy and intoned, "My Lord, you will need this."

"For the love of God, what is going on?"

What had he done now? Or not done? Did this have anything to do with the ultimatum? The calls this morning?

Brandon merely handed his friend the newspaper he'd been reading. It was *The London Weekly*, a popular news rag that Roxbury wouldn't line his trunk with. In his opinion, the gossip columnist owed her entire career to him, for his antics so often appeared in her column.

He wasn't the only one, of course—she'd taken down Lord Wentworth with a mention of his visits to opium dens, then related the intimate details of Lord Haile's grand marriage proposal to all of London, and broken the news of Susannah Carrington and George Granby's midnight elopement—but Roxbury appeared regularly enough that he could refer to it as a reminder of what he had done the previous week, should he forget.

"At least you have a decent excuse for reading this rubbish," Roxbury muttered. Brandon had married one of *The Weekly*'s notorious Writing Girls—then known as Miss Harlow—of the column "Miss Harlow's Marriage in High Life."

Roxbury flipped straight to "Fashionable Intelligence" by A Lady of Distinction on page six.

Roxbury took a sip of his drink, thoughtful. He'd wager that if this Lady of Distinction were forced to print her real name, she wouldn't write half the things she did. Frankly, he was surprised her identity was still a secret. Speculation was rampant, of course, with most of the ton focusing on Lady something or other. That was the sort of drivel he didn't follow.

He possessed a sinking feeling that would soon change.

Roxbury began to read.

Has London's legendary rake, Lord R—, so thoroughly exhausted the women of the ton that he must now move on to the stronger sex?

Roxbury downed his drink in one long gulp, feeling the burn of the brandy and keeping his eyes focused on the page, not daring to look up. Inchbald stood over Roxbury's shoulder with the bottle and promptly refilled his glass.

Indeed, dear readers, you would not believe what this author has seen! Lord R— might have been embracing the lovely J— K—, fresh from the stage in her breeches role in She Would and She Would Not. *Yet for a man whose sensual appetites are notoriously insatiable, one knows not what to think.*

Inchbald poured a much-needed second brandy.

Indeed, it was clear what everyone did think. In fact, it explained all those uneasy glances from the other gents in the club and all those women who were not at home to him this morning.

He shuddered, actually shuddered, to think of the conversations currently raging in drawing rooms all over town. Roxbury took another long swallow, and damn if that didn't burn like nothing else.

Having just consumed two or three brandies within the space of five or six minutes, Roxbury could not see straight or focus on the ramifications of this salacious, malicious lie. That ultimatum . . . marriage or poverty . . . with a man? Or a woman?

One thing was certain: these things were not compatible, and they were not favorable.

How was he supposed to marry when no one was at home to him? How was he supposed to maintain his livelihood if his funds were cut off?

Even with all that alcohol muddling his mind and burning his gut, Roxbury knew beyond a shadow of a doubt that this was bad. This was the sort of scandal one never quite recovered from.

The stench of it would stay with him. Years from now—decades, even—whispers of this would follow in his wake, from club to ballroom and everywhere in between. He would not care so much, were it not for that ultimatum and a lifetime of poverty staring him in the face.

Roxbury set down the paper and Inchbald left the bottle beside it.

"I know it was a woman," Brandon said.

"But you do not doubt that it was me," Roxbury replied.

"I know you," his friend said. They'd been friends since Eton, where Roxbury's elder brother, Edward, had introduced them both to drinking, women, and wagering. At Eton, Roxbury had seduced every eligible female within a ten-mile radius. At university, he was notorious. There was no stopping him when he hit the ton.

Brandon had a point. Simon was well known for his romantic exploits, so it was believable that he would be caught in a compromising position. In fact, Roxbury was a legendary rake who was famously known to carry on affairs and intrigues with half of the women of the ton and they thought he was dallying with a *man*?

It was laughable. So Roxbury laughed.

He laughed long, hard, and doubled over in his seat, attracting even more uncomfortable and irritable looks. Brandon lifted his brow curiously and had a sip of his brandy.

"What, exactly, is so humorous about this situation?" Brandon asked.

"No one can possibly believe that story—not when dozens, hundreds, *thousands* of women could come forward and vouch for me," Roxbury pointed out. Perhaps not thousands but many, many women had firsthand knowledge of his abiding love and devotion to women and the female form.

"I hate to say it, Roxbury, but most of those women are married, and I daresay not one would risk her reputation to vouch for you."

Brandon was a stickler for facts, truths, honesty, and all those things. The burning feeling of rage, remorse, and panic in Simon's gut intensified.

"They weren't *all* married," he pointed out.

"Your reputation in the ton is not going to be saved by the word of women of negotiable affection," Brandon correctly and lamentably stated. Roxbury scowled because his friend was right— the word of an actress, or an opera singer or a demimonde darling was not going to carry much weight with the ton.

"There were some widows," he added. He did enjoy those women who were determined to enjoy what one of them had termed her "hard-earned freedom."

"They need their reputation, Roxbury. No one will confess to an affair with a man of questionable proclivities."

"Bloody hell," Roxbury swore, but the curse was insufficient. If there was no way to defuse this rumor . . . If no one would come forward to his defense . . .

It would be impossible to take a wife, particularly if this morning's rejected social calls were any indication. And if that failed, he was looking at a life of living on credit and dodging debtor's prison. His father, it should be noted, was in remarkably good health so his inheritance was far off indeed, not that he wished the man dead.

"I wouldn't worry. It should all be forgotten eventually," Brandon said casually, sipping his drink.

"I don't have the time," Roxbury said tightly. There was that ultimatum, and the clock was ticking. Granted, he'd just declared to hell with it. But that was when he had a choice and now that had been taken from him.

A life of leisure had been secure an hour ago. Now, he hadn't a prayer of finding a wife, and he could kiss his fortune goodbye, too.

Roxbury finished the brandy in his glass and then took a swig straight from the bottle. Life as he knew it was over. It was a sudden death, and he was reeling in shock, denial, regret, and bone-deep terror at what the future would bring.

And anger, too, because he was powerless to do anything. Marriage was impossible, and a refusal to comply meant little when he lacked the option of agreement. Of course, agreeing to his father's demands was something he didn't ever want to do, but the point of remaining a bachelor was to enjoy legions of beautiful women who probably would not have him now. And then he would be poor, too. Poor and alone.

He wondered if the earl had tried this stunt before, with Edward, and if that had been what sent him off to the navy and off to his death. If anyone thought Roxbury was a hellion . . . then they'd never met his elder brother.

Roxbury took another sip of his drink, silently cursing this impossible situation.

"By God, if it weren't for this damned column, all the debutantes and their mothers would be scheming to have me!"

"You have a high opinion of yourself," Brandon said.

"It's the truth and you know it, and it's not about me but my title, my fortune, and, well, I have been called devilishly handsome. Thank God for that. There's nothing worse than an impoverished lord, except for an ugly one."

"Roxbury, you are insufferable."

"Bloody hell, I'm going to be *poor*. When the old man delivered that ultimatum I never thought—"

Brandon merely took a modest sip of his drink. "What ultimatum?" he asked.

Roxbury explained. And then he lamented.

"I don't even have a choice, or a chance now! All because of a damned newspaper story! All because of that petty, irksome busybody who calls herself the Lady of Distinction! My God, if ever a title was unjustified! With just a few lines of moveable type she has annihilated my prospects, destroyed my future, and sentenced me to a life of poverty!"

"I'm sure someone will have you," Brandon said. "There is always Lady Hortensia Reeves."

Lady Hortensia Reeves left *much* to be desired. Miss Reeves was an agreeable woman; she was also firmly on the shelf, and a very proud collector of all sorts of items from embroidery to stamps, leaves, insects, and other rubbish. Apparently it was all neatly labeled and catalogued, so she was not some run-of-the-mill hoarder but a devoted hobbyist. Her other great interest was him, and her infatuation with him was quite painfully obvious.

Needless to say, Roxbury wanted to marry almost anyone else more than he did Lady Hortensia Reeves. While he did not want to marry at all, he *definitely* did not want to bind himself to just anyone if he had to take a wife. But that was all a moot point because the question of his marriage was now out of his hands and crushed by *The London Weekly*'s Lady of "Distinction."

Roxbury took another long swallow of brandy

straight from the bottle. He scowled at the older, stodgier lords that frowned in disapproval at him.

"Really, it is utterly unconscionable what she has done," Roxbury carried on. "It's thoughtless, inconsiderate, unchristian, and damned and downright wrong! This is my life at stake! My choices! My name. *My honor.*"

Roxbury stood suddenly, sending his chair tumbling backward and careening across the floor.

All eyes were upon him. With his hazy, drunken vision he saw the familiar faces of Lord Derby; Biddulph; that old dandy, Lord Walpole; Earl of Selborne's heir and a few others. With all their attention fixed upon him, Roxbury felt that he ought to make a statement. And so, with a nod of his noble head and a sweeping wave of his arm he grandly informed his peers:

"Gentlemen, you are all safe from my advances, though your wives are not."

The Lady of Distinction was not the only gossip in town. There was another gossip columnist on the prowl in London. His column had been printed in *The London Times* for forty years now. Alternately feared, reviled, celebrated, and adored, he was the archrival to the Lady of Distinction and an eternal man of mystery. In all of those forty years, for all the thousands of attempts to guess or discover his identity, no one had succeeded. He was known as The Man About Town, but that was all anyone knew of him.

With her story on Roxbury and his secret male lover, the upstart at *The Weekly* had won this week. It was all anyone spoke about in the clubs, or drawing rooms, or ballrooms or gaming hells. One by one, they'd raise their brows and lower their voices: *Have you heard the latest about Lord Roxbury?*

The Man About Town was immensely vexed that he'd stayed in the dressing rooms the other night instead of lurking around backstage. But what could he say? There were dozens of ladies in various states of undress.

He pulled on his cigar; his course was clear. He'd need to find Roxbury's lover, and he'd need to figure out whom that damned Lady of Distinction was.

But in the meantime, on the other side of the room, The Man About Town bit back a laugh at Roxbury's drunken declaration. Naturally, he'd seen and heard a lot in his time, and it took much to amuse him these days. With Roxbury, the latest "Fashionable Intelligence," and the Lady of Distinction, The Man About Town sensed that a fantastic scandal had only just begun.

Chapter 4

The offices of The London Weekly
53 Fleet Street, London

An infuriating carriage ride in an ill-sprung and stinking hired hack blackened Roxbury's temper further. After many starts, stops, hollers at insolent pedestrians, and unregulated traffic, the hack turned on Fleet Street and passed by four taverns, a few booksellers, coffeehouses, banks, and other shops before eventually halting before number 53.

THE LONDON WEEKLY was emblazoned in gold lettering on a massive wooden sign above the door. Subtle it was not.

Roxbury threw some coins to the driver, stormed across the road and through the door. First, there was arguing, blustering, and a bruising encounter with a gargantuan creature claiming to be the publisher. Roxbury was not fooled. Thanks to hours spent at Gentleman Jack's, one swift, deliberate blow to the man's temple cleared Roxbury's path, though leaving him with a bruised and swollen fist. Thanks to the copious amounts of brandy he had just consumed, he did not register the pain.

Undeterred, Roxbury charged toward the office door of one Mr. Derek Knightly: editor, publisher, and owner of that wretched rag *The London Weekly*.

Presumably Knightly was the man responsible for the nefarious lies of the Lady of Distinction and would be held accountable.

"Sir!"

"Stop!" People were shouting at him. He cared not.

"You can't go in there!"

Roxbury did not stop for the likes of those lowlife Grub Street hack writers.

Before he barged through the door to Knightly's office, Roxbury thought of nothing but the scandal, the lies, and the destruction to his life. His choices. His name. His honor.

A hot flaming rage got his blood boiling accordingly. He craved vengeance and would not rest until he had obtained satisfaction.

And yet, *after* he opened the door . . .

Roxbury saw the unexpected: a woman perched upon the corner of the desk.

She was a beauty. Auburn hair piled high. Her green eyes turned up mysteriously at the outer corners. Her skin was of the milky, creamy, want-to-lick-it variety, and she exposed much of it, from her smooth brow to her slender neck to the wide expanse of her décolletage.

There, or at the generous swells just below, Roxbury's gaze lingered, and though his blood still pumped furiously within him, his rage abated. Slightly.

"I was expecting you earlier," she practically purred, while taking a leisurely look at him, and practically giving herself away.

In an instant he knew who she was: that damned Lady of Distinction. She seemed familiar to him, from balls and soirees and the like. He had certainly seen her out, though they had never been introduced. But what was her name?

"Mr. Knightly, this irate man is Lord Roxbury," she said to the man reclining in his chair behind the desk. The proprietor of London's most popular and profitable paper was a youngish man with black hair and piercing blue eyes. She continued with the introductions: "Lord Roxbury, this is Mr. Derek Knightly."

This green-eyed she-devil who smoothly made the introductions like the best society hostess was the architect of his downfall. That she—whatever her name was—was so at ease in this impossible situation rekindled his anger. This was not a matter to be taken so lightly or discussed politely over tea.

She may have written his demise, but he would not allow her to enjoy it.

Roxbury focused his attentions solely on Knightly.

"Fetching secretary," he said with a nod in her direction, and he enjoyed the flash in her eyes and the hot flush in her cheeks. Irritation warring with vanity was such a pleasing expression on a woman.

"If you'll excuse us, we have important matters of business to discuss," Roxbury said patronizingly to her.

The ladybird alighted from her perch and stood

toe-to-toe with him. She was tall, and almost able to look him evenly in the eye.

"I am not a secretary," she said hotly.

"I beg your pardon?" He feigned shock. "What possible reason could you have for being here? Are you making the confession that I suspect you are?"

"Oh, how you wish I would," she retorted, stepping back. She resolutely folded her arms over her chest, which did marvelous things to her breasts. Because of the devastation she had inflicted upon his life, he felt no compunction to look away and instead he treated himself to a long, lascivious gaze until she unfolded her arms and gave him a look sharper than a thousand daggers.

"Women do have the gift of gab and excel at inane, idle chatter," Roxbury continued, speaking to Knightly and deliberately ignoring her. He was a quick study of women, and he knew that ignoring her would vex her tremendously. Plus, he could not afford to be distracted. "I'm sure that's what you were thinking when you hired a female to author the column."

"It was a brilliant decision on my part," Knightly agreed from where he sat behind the desk, his gaze alternating between them. There was an amused gleam in his eye.

Roxbury was surprised at the quick confession, but the evidence was damning: high society darling in a newspaperman's office, telling the most talked about man in London she was expecting him, and the flash of eyes when he accused her of such a lowly position as secretary.

"It was my idea," she said. Roxbury continued to ignore her. He knew this type: meddlesome, tyrannical, and always right. Probably prude, too. For all of his love of women, this kind was never a favorite of his.

"Sales have been tremendous. Her column is a smashing success," Knightly added firmly, and Roxbury understood him. Money was of more importance to him than the wounded feelings of lords and ladies.

"Yes, my *idle chatter* makes this paper the success that it is," she added.

"Your idle chatter destroys lives and reputations," Roxbury spoke sharply to her. For a second she seemed taken aback, as if she hadn't considered that, which was ridiculous because she was clearly not a fool.

What was her name?

"It's just gossip. You needn't have such a fit," she said with a delicate shrug, which infuriated him all the more. She could not possibly be ignorant of the consequences of her writing, and yet she couldn't possibly be so hard-hearted to the suffering her pen wrought.

"A fit?"

She could not possibly think a man, such as himself, would suffer from something so trivial, so missish, as a fit.

"Storming in here, slamming doors," she carried on. "I warn you not to cry, for that is surely newsworthy. What will the ton think of you then?"

A sissy, weepy, Nancy dandy.

Vaguely, he was aware of his hands balling into fists, and shooting pains in his right hand reminded him that he'd already used it for enough damage today.

"What will the ton think of you, *Lady Somerset*," he questioned, relieved to have recollected her name, "when they learn of your secret life?"

The lady paused. Then she blinked rapidly in succession, suggesting a slight panic. And then, with another one of those insouciant shrugs she replied.

"It's an open secret."

"That cloud of suspicion and mystery does wonders for you, I'm certain. But what happens when Lady Carrington has confirmation that you are the one that exposed her daughter's elopement? Or that you told the ton of Lord Wilcox's penchant for wearing women's undergarments? What of your reputation then?" He punctuated all this with a suggestive raise of his brow.

"You have no definitive proof that I am the Lady of Distinction." She smiled prettily at him, and he was angered to discover that her mouth was stunning, the way it curved suggestively yet sweetly at the same time. He was horrified that thoughts of kissing crossed his mind—here, and now, and with her.

She moved away from him. He blocked her, standing up straighter and squaring his shoulders to impress his size upon her.

Lady Somerset barely had to tilt her head back to look him in the eye—and she did, fiercely, daringly. His own eyes narrowed.

"I have been publicly humiliated. The repercussions are massive and irreparable," he said firmly. She blinked.

He took a step forward. She took a step backward. A few more steps back and they'd be up against the windows overlooking Fleet Street. For some strange reason, his heart was pounding.

"I sent you a letter prior to publication offering to withhold the information in exchange for a sum. You ignored it," she said.

Newspapers earned a fortune in suppression fees. He would have paid ten fortunes for this item to never see the light of day. But he never had the chance.

She must have sent it to his home, a place he rarely frequented. It was probably still there, unopened, with all the invitations and summons from his father and bills. For a meager sum, this could have never happened.

If the phrase "to see red" indicated anger, then at this moment he was seeing a violent explosion of crimson, vermillion, and burnt sienna.

"You've been out in society for quite some time now, Roxbury. You know these things just blow over in time," Lady Somerset said breezily, stepping away from him. Without a second thought he moved closer to her.

"I don't have time," he said through gritted teeth. Scarlet. Ruby. Wine. Blood.

"Oh? Why is that?" She tilted her head and peered up at him curiously. There was a touch of innocence to her, too, but he assumed it was feigned, given that she was a widow and a gossip and in a man's office.

"You mistake me for a fool, among other things," he told her.

"As much as I am enjoying this display of—God only knows what—I do have work to attend to," Knightly said, bored, from the other side of the room where he remained behind his desk.

Roxbury turned his back on the she-devil and addressed Knightly.

"I came here for satisfaction. My honor has been grossly insulted. I will not duel with a woman. That leaves you."

"A duel! You cannot fight a duel over this!" Lady Somerset exclaimed.

Knightly sat forward in his chair, his expression now intensely serious.

"I accept," he said gravely.

"I would almost respect you, Knightly, if we met under different circumstances. As for you," Roxbury continued, turning back to the buxom villainess, "you will print a retraction, and an apology."

"Oh will I?" she challenged, with a lift of her brow and arms akimbo.

Oh, yes, he definitely knew her type: The female know-it-all. Most often found amongst the married, mothers, and widows, though some females seemed to be born bossy. This variety of female was mostly just irritating, but when combined with wit and beauty—admittedly Lady Somerset possessed both, in spades—she could be incredibly dangerous.

From his limited experience with this type—he tended to the pleasure-seeking, carefree, fun-loving sorts—he knew that to tame this sort of female was a tremendous trial, though it could be well worth it.

In the case of Lady Somerset, he would not bother. That did not mean, however, that he would let her run roughshod over him—any more than she already had, that is.

"You will," Roxbury told her.

"Or what will happen?" she taunted. She stood

with her hands on her hips now, drawing his eyes to her hourglass figure. His mouth went dry. Her head was tilted slightly to the side, tempting him to feather kisses along her neck and shoulders, down to the full, generous swells of her breasts.

Tempting. So damned tempting.

But this was war, and he would be victorious.

"You will print an apology and a retraction, or your secret will be out, and I shall wish you the best of luck filling a column about the happenings of high society when you are no longer received."

Then he was treated to the rare experience of Lady Somerset speechless.

Even after Lord Roxbury slammed the door behind him on the way out, Julianna Somerset was still openmouthed and silent, and that was a rare thing indeed. She crossed her arms over her chest and turned to look out the window, as if pondering the view of Fleet Street it afforded. But she couldn't focus because her nerves were humming, her heart racing, and her thoughts were a tangled mess.

Roxbury's behavior to her was appalling, insulting, and deliberately provoking. She had never met him before, but she knew his sort, intimately, and did not care for it. He was a known rake, with a preference for other men's wives, merry widows, and the occasional actress and opera singer to liven things up.

There was, too, the possibility that he enjoyed other more unusual inclinations when women bored him.

She had expected Roxbury to come storming into the offices after he saw the item. Irate readers and embarrassed subjects of "Fashionable Intelligence" frequently came huffing and puffing to plead their cases and make demands of Knightly. But Roxbury had been one of the few to get past Mehitable Loud and the first to demand a duel.

Yet, Julianna had not been prepared for the tall, arrogant, tyrannical, strikingly handsome man that had stormed in. Oh, they had mingled at parties and she'd followed his exploits, but she'd never been in such close proximity to him.

Julianna now had an inkling of what legions of women felt around him: racing pulse, breath caught. He was a formidable presence with his height and his obviously muscled physique. His features were those of a peer—all noble and strong, though she had to admit he was particularly handsome. His eyes were dark, velvety brown—and the intensity of his gaze was practically palpable.

And Roxbury had spoken to her as no one ever dared. He made demands upon her, when she was the mistress of her own self. Julianna answered to no man—except for Knightly, some of the time, when it suited her.

Roxbury gave her orders, but she was under no obligation to him and delighted in pointing that out to him. It was oddly thrilling to be told what to do, and even more so to flagrantly disobey.

She turned from looking out the window at Fleet Street below to speak to her employer.

"I shall not write the apology or retraction," she told Knightly. He looked up from his work, editing articles for the next issue.

"You will," Knightly said, and then he returned to his work.

She scowled at him.

"I'd rather see your pride wounded than my person," Knightly added, setting his pencil down and giving her his attention.

"You cannot possibly mean to attend the duel. Over a little thing in the newspaper!"

"For the reputation of this newspaper and of myself, I will fight." Everyone knew that this newspaper was *everything* to Mr. Knightly. He had his mother, Delilah, but no other family and certainly no wife. More often than not, he slept in his office. He would fight for *The Weekly*, to the death, without a second thought or shadow of doubt.

"He's awful, isn't he? So very rude, storming in here like that and—"

Mr. Knightly laughed.

"Might I remind you, Lady Somerset, that is exactly how you made your entrance?"

A little over a year ago, Julianna had indeed dropped in uninvited and announced that she knew he was hiring women (for he had hired her dearest friend Sophie to write about weddings the day before) and that he ought to hire her as a gossip columnist.

Though she was not a shy, retiring person, to say the least, she had been quaking in her boots for that interview. It just wasn't done, she was unsure of the outcome, and she was desperate.

Most men left the bulk of their fortune to their wives, with small annuities to a favorite mistress or by-blows. The late, great Harry, Lord Somerset had little left over for his wife after providing for his numerous mistresses and bastards.

However, he had left her with a name so scandalous that it discouraged all but the worst suitors, which didn't quite matter since Julianna had no intention of marrying again. Her heart, mind, body, and livelihood were too precious to trust to another.

Thus she, a lady, needed to work. The opportunity to write a gossip column was a rare one indeed—it would allow her to supplement her meager annuity, while maintaining and improving her place in society. So Julianna brazened out the terrifying interview.

To her shock and relief, Mr. Knightly agreed. It was Mr. Knightly who had transformed her from Lady Somerset, the pitiable widow of one of London's more notorious cads, to A Lady of Distinction, the feared and awe-inspiring author of "Fashionable Intelligence."

Chapter 5

The outskirts of town, dawn

A duel! Over a little thing in the newspaper! After all, she hadn't said for a fact that he preferred his own sex. Julianna had even offered a more plausible explanation for why he appeared to be embracing a person in a gentleman's attire. Could she help what the ton chose to believe? No, she could not.

It was truly ridiculous that he was dueling with Knightly.

Men were *such* hotheaded idiots.

Thanks to her ever-faithful maid, Penny, and their network of housemaid informants—Penny's six sisters, all servants in the best houses in London—they were able to determine the time and location of the duel.

Julianna had not been invited, which had never stopped her from attending an event before.

The hack she hired stopped some distance from the dueling field and she alighted, followed by Miss Eliza Fielding, fellow Writing Girl and the only other woman daring enough to attend with her. Once upon a time, Julianna's best friend, Sophie, might have joined her on such an expedition, but now she was a married woman and a duchess, to boot, so she couldn't go gallivanting around far-flung corners of town at dawn witnessing duels.

Julianna and Eliza took cover behind a hedge-row and peered through the branches. The gentlemen would be livid to discover their serious business viewed by women, particularly the one who had caused it all.

The sky was already a pale, clear blue. The grassy field shimmered with dew. The air, crisp and sweet, promised a warm summer day. The sun was bright, the birds sang, and the breeze brushed over the trees.

"There's the surgeon," Eliza said, pointing to a man in black, leaning against a black carriage on the far side of the field. It was a jarring juxtaposition—something so dark and deathly on such a beautiful summer morning.

A small brown rabbit hopped across the field, blissfully unaware of the gruesome activity about to unfold around it.

A duel! The men might just stomp around and fire their shots into the air and call it a day. But there was a very real chance that one of them might get shot, or even die. Julianna had never considered that when putting pen to paper; she thought only of besting the Man About Town with delicious, exclusive gossip.

She had also considered Knightly's mantra of *scandal equals sales*, and she needed to keep her employer satisfied with her work.

But what if Knightly lost his life today? Julianna could not even wrap her head around it. She would grieve for a man who gave her an opportunity no one else would consider, and a man she respected. So many people depended upon him—the Writing Girls, particularly. If he died . . .

Julianna felt sick at the thought.

And what if Roxbury's life ended today? Her heart began to pound, which was strange because why should she have a care for him? He was nothing but a careless, carefree rake. That sort of man had never done her any favors.

"There is Mr. Knightly with Mehitable Loud," Eliza whispered. Their employer was calmly inspecting a set of pistols held by his second.

"What if he doesn't survive?" Eliza asked quietly, because the question was so grave. Who would take over the paper? Would the new publisher be so supportive of the Writing Girls? What if Knightly died because of something she had written? And then if they all lost their positions because of that? Julianna's mouth went dry, her palms became clammy, and the urge to cast up her accounts nearly overwhelmed her.

Julianna wrote because she loved to, but also because she needed the money. Eliza and Annabelle, too. It was an unspoken truth between the women that earning money meant they did not have to marry if they didn't want to. After her disastrous marriage, Julianna certainly had no wish to.

"I'm sure he'll survive," Julianna lied, to herself as much as Eliza. "Roxbury was too angry to see straight, let alone shoot straight."

At the far end of the field, a hunter green carriage emblazoned with the Roxbury family crest, gilded in gold and silver leaf, came into view. The impressive vehicle was pulled by a team of gray chargers and it came to a sudden stop, kicking up pebbles and dirt and punctuated by the whinnying of the horses.

Roxbury alighted from the carriage, in quite a rakish manner.

"He's deuced handsome," Eliza whispered, voicing Julianna's own thoughts. At liberty to stare brazenly at him from her hiding place, she took full advantage.

Handsome was insufficient. There was an air of strength and vitality about him, from his shiny black hair to the slightly tanned color of his skin. He strolled confidently over to the dueling field. His movements were quick and certain, but tense.

His breeches fit him to perfection, showing off well-muscled legs. She assumed his arms were muscular as well, and she idly wondered what it'd be like to have those arms embracing her . . .

She need only ask almost any woman in London for a definitive answer based on experience. He probably came to the dueling field straight from a woman's bedchamber.

Such thoughts aside, Roxbury seemed far too young and handsome and alive to actually die. He very well might this morning, and because of her and what she wrote.

Her heartbeat quickened, and remorse burned in her gut.

"Do you really think he was with a man?" Eliza wondered.

"It could very well have been Jocelyn. I know not."

It seemed so stupid now.

Julianna watched as the adversaries shook hands, and their seconds did the same. She did not recognize Roxbury's second—he was some average-sized man, in slovenly attire. After a quick conversation, pistols were taken in hand, the seconds moved away, and Knightly and Roxbury stood back-to-back.

It was Roxbury that she watched. Given the distance, it was impossible to discern his expression, but he carried himself as if fearless. This struck her with awe.

The men started taking their steps away from each other in anticipation of firing. Mehitable bellowed the numbers in his baritone, his voice easily carrying across the field.

One.

Two.

Julianna's heart pumped hard. Terror. It wasn't the threat of a stray bullet striking her, but that Knightly's aim would be true. How could that be? She cared nothing for Roxbury. She barely knew him. He was just another good-for-nothing rake, and this town had plenty of those. And yet . . .

Three. Four.

She was equally terrified that Knightly would not survive. It was unlikely she and the other Writing Girls would survive in the world without him. His death would be because of her doing, too. The bullet may not be hers, but at the end of the day, the fault would be her own. Her stomach ached with guilt.

Five.

Her heart was pounding heavily in her breast,

and she was quite overheated. With one gloved hand she undid a button or two at her throat.

With the other, she clasped Eliza's hand. What if they lost Knightly? What would become of them?

Six. Seven. Eight.

And what of Roxbury? He was too young, too beautiful to die. Knightly, too, but she was thinking of the enraged and wronged Roxbury and she did not know why.

Nine. Ten.

Julianna bit down on her fist to keep a cry from escaping.

Eleven. Twelve.

And then—so quickly she might have missed it had she blinked—the gentlemen turned, and fired.

The Man About Town hated reporting on duels. Getting up at dawn to travel to far-flung and desolate corners of town was not his idea of a good time, especially the mornings after what *was* his idea of a good time—late nights, fancy balls, and gaming hells.

Compounding his hatred was the fact that such effort was required for an event that lasted all of a minute. One had to count the time spent traveling to some remote outpost of London, skulking about in the bushes while awaiting everyone's arrival and then negotiating and confirming the terms, checking the pistols, etcetera, etcetera. For a minute of activity, if that.

Not for the first time did the Man About Town consider retiring.

Chapter 6

That evening at Lady Walmsly's soiree

"**D**ueling is a despicable habit," Lady Stewart-Wortly opined to her group of listeners. She approved of very little, other than modesty, chastity, piety, and, above all, complaining about the sins of others. One could read all about it in her book, *Lady Stewart-Wortly's Daily Devotional for Pious and Proper Ladies*, which she mentioned at every opportunity.

Julianna found her a tremendous bore at best.

"Some people think dueling is quite dashing," replied the young Lady Charlotte, sister to the Duke of Hamilton and Brandon.

"Some people are idiots," Lady Stewart-Wortly replied haughtily.

"Indeed," Lady Charlotte murmured, looking Lady Stewart-Wortly in the eye.

Lady Sophie Brandon, Charlotte's sister-in-law, bit back a smirk and Julianna did her very best to appear unaffected by the conversation or what she had witnessed this morning.

Lord Wilcox, with the penchant for women's undergarments, hovered behind her, nodding his head heavily in agreement. Lord Walpole smoothed back his gray hair, and bore an expression of disinterest, though Julianna could tell he was listening. Not for the first time did Julianna wonder if he was The Man About Town.

Apparently, she and Eliza hadn't been the only ones skulking about in the bushes. Word of the duel had spread around town as fast as the Great Fire of 1666.

There was no doubt that the Man About Town would report on it in his next column. He wrote for a daily paper, and his columns appeared three days a week. Because of that, he broke more stories than she. It rankled very, *very* much.

And because he was the *Man* About Town he also had access to sources of information that were forbidden to her. This morning's paper had featured the following scene about Roxbury at White's Gentlemen's Club:

Upon reading the latest "Fashionable Intelligence" about himself, Lord R—stood to make his advan—addresses to his fellow peers in White's. "You are all safe from my advances, though your wives are not." Ladies, you have been warned!

A few "little" lines in her column had sparked this rabid curiosity for all things Roxbury.

"To look at him, you'd never think that he'd risked his life this morning," Lady Sophie said, gesturing toward Roxbury. They all turned to look in his direction. He was standing at the edge of the ballroom, dressed in black save for the severe contrast of his white linen shirt. His eyes were dark, with a gaze suggesting utter boredom. His lips curved in a firm, wry smile. He stood with a glass of brandy in hand, tall and proud, and utterly ignored.

The sight took Julianna's breath away.

Typically, at a ball, Roxbury was to be found, charming and smiling and laughing, surrounded by bored wives and young widows taking full advantage of their freedom. A swarm of giggling debutantes was never far behind. Women and Roxbury went hand in hand, and it was ludicrous that the ton should believe the insinuations in her column.

But they did, and now this handsome charmer was receiving the cut direct from five hundred people simultaneously and still standing proud.

Definitely awe-inspiring and breathtaking.

And tremendously guilt inducing. A stroke of her pen, and the ton's darling was now an absolute outcast. She had thought only to best the Man About Town, and hadn't considered that a few lines of speculation would result in such an adored man standing utterly alone. He wasn't happy, but he was too proud to brood or hide at home. This had not been her intention, and she had never witnessed the devastating effects of her column so closely. Julianna felt quite sick.

"Lady Hortensia Reeves still seems quite interested in him," Sophie pointed out. Indeed, the lady was obviously and frequently staring at the outcast lord. It was nice to know that some things never changed: rain in England, the sunrise in the morning, and Lady Hortensia's deep and abiding infatuation with Roxbury.

"Did you hear about her newest collection?" Lady Charlotte asked. "Dung beetles."

"Oh, my," Sophie murmured.

"Well, everyone ought to have a hobby," Julianna said with a shrug. At least collections of insects didn't get anyone nearly killed. Well, except for the insects. Which wasn't quite as bad as nearly getting another person shot.

She wondered how Knightly was faring. Roxbury had not aimed wide, and now her beloved employer had a bullet wound and a raging fever because of her.

Julianna took a long swallow of her champagne. She had not foreseen these consequences and desperately wished she had. Knightly would be well, Roxbury would be flirting, and her stomach wouldn't ache with remorse.

Lady Stewart-Wortly was hitting the stride in her ballroom sermon and her booming voice distracted Julianna from her thoughts.

"Morals today are shockingly lax. The things the gossip columnists report! They are the scribes of the devil and authors of evil. Why, last week's "Fashionable Intelligence" reporting on the scandalous proclivities of Lord Roxbury has corrupted legions of youth across London. The author ought to be ashamed of herself."

Julianna studied the hemline of her gown.

"Lady Stewart-Wortly, you are remarkably well versed in the contents of numerous gossip columns, considering that you wouldn't possibly read them and expose yourself to such debauched literature," Lady Charlotte pointed out. For a seventeen-year-old girl she was quite astute.

"You are an impertinent girl," Lady Stewart-Wortly huffed.

"I know, everybody says so," Charlotte said, heaving a dramatic sigh, making Sophie purse her lips in an effort to restrain her laughter.

Julianna was still smoldering from Lady Stewart-Wortly's remarks, and too vexed to laugh. Scribe of the devil! Corruptor of legions of youth! Ashamed of herself!

She was, on the whole, damned proud, if anyone wanted to know—not that she could tell them, given that her identity was still somewhat of a mystery. She supported herself by her wits, talent and daring! She was making history and living a life of freedom that most women only dreamed of. She loved her writing and *The Weekly* and wished she could shout that love from the rooftops.

Not tonight, though.

Given the events of the morning, in which two men nearly lost their lives because of her writing, Julianna's pride was tempered considerably. She loved her writing, but it came with great responsibility to, say, not get innocent men injured or killed.

She dared another glance in Roxbury's direction, and found that his gaze was intensely focused upon her.

She needed to escape Roxbury's line of vision. The way he looked at her made her skin feel feverish, and she felt agitated in a manner she could not describe or understand.

Julianna excused herself from the group and walked away, with her dark green silk skirts rustling at her ankles as she wove through the crowds.

She passed by the Baron and Baroness of Pinner as they began a waltz, dodged an encounter with notorious talker Lady "Drawling" Rawlings, and nodded as she strolled by Lady Walmsly, the hostess, who smiled warmly.

"Lady Somerset." Someone called her name. She had her suspicions.

A quick glance over her shoulder confirmed them. It was Roxbury calling her—nay, commanding her—to stop.

Julianna faced forward, smiled blandly, and nodded politely at her acquaintances as she passed by them. Everyone nodded or smiled in kind acknowledgment. She had come far from the days after Somerset's death, when the name, and she, were tainted by his scandalous death. Now the ton thought her a respectable young matron. She was welcomed by one and all as a nice young widow, who may or may not write fiercely damaging things in the paper. Everyone took a precautionary approach and deemed it best to stay on her good side, just in case those rumors were true.

She was not eager for another rake to drag her down to the dregs of society, again, so she ignored the irate man trailing behind her, and prayed no one noticed that he followed her.

"Lady Somerset."

Julianna snapped open her fan and fanned herself with feigned ease as she slipped through the crowds. Lady Walmsly had really outdone herself this evening. She'd write all about it in her column . . . that is, if Knightly lived and the paper continued. Oh, Knightly! What had she done?

Finally Julianna stopped behind a pillar at the far

end of the ballroom, and was not surprised when Roxbury cornered her there. At least here they were out of sight.

His eyes were dark and his mouth was set in a firm, hard line. She was tall, but he towered over her. Much to her annoyance, Roxbury's mere presence set her heart aflutter.

The Man About Town watched Lord Roxbury follow Lady Somerset through the crowds. What business he could have with her, he knew not, though it did lend a certain amount of credence to the rumors that she was the Lady of Distinction. Then Roxbury absolutely would have business with her.

But how could that fun-loving, good-for-nothing rake know it when he, the Man About Town with years of experience in gossip and sleuthing, did not? How would one even confirm such a suspicion?

It was on his list of great mysteries to uncover.

He plucked a glass of champagne from a nearby waiter and forged ahead through the crowds, intent upon following the two of them. He knew a scandal in progress when he saw it.

Lady Somerset ducked into a discrete position behind a pillar. Roxbury followed. Then that damned old nag Lady Rawlings—otherwise known as the notorious Drawling Rawlings—appeared before him.

"Did you hear?" she asked slowly, fanning herself all the while. "Lord Roxbury fought a duel with that newspaperman this morning!"

The Man About Town fought the urge to sigh and say, "I know. I was there."

Chapter 7

"**G**ood evening, Roxbury," Julianna said smoothly, as if he did not affect her in the slightest. As if she wasn't backed up against a pillar with his towering, angry form looming over her. As if her heart wasn't pounding.

Yes, the man had a strange effect upon her, one that she did not care to explore. Part of it was certainly that gnawing guilt; part might have been attraction but she would be damned before she admitted to that. She thought it wise to keep this conversation short and light, and then make a quick escape.

"Lady Somerset," he murmured her name this time, and his lips curved into a slight smile as he gazed down at her. It was altogether too clear how he had seduced so many women. A half smile, a name murmured so it sounded like a caress. She would not fall for that. She would *not*.

"I trust you are enjoying yourself this evening," she said lightly.

"I most certainly am not." The smile vanished and his expression hardened.

If only he would just go away! She could more easily ignore him and her guilty feelings about this scandalous situation. Knightly, near death's door. Roxbury, an overnight social pariah. All of it her fault.

Fortunately, social murder was not a hanging offense.

Her every instinct, however, urged her to keep her guard up around Roxbury. Men like him were trouble. She knew that all too well. Often, she made sure the ladies of London knew it, too, so they might not suffer the same as she had done.

"Perhaps you'd enjoy yourself more if you were engaged elsewhere, in other pursuits," she suggested. Perhaps she could irk him into quitting her company.

"Witty, aren't you?" he remarked, seemingly at ease, but she saw the tension in his jaw.

Then Roxbury smiled once more, and in a way that made her insides quake. He pressed one hand on the pillar behind her head, and leaned in. Her cheeks flushed and her lips parted of their own volition. He smiled triumphantly.

"I might enjoy myself this evening after all," he murmured.

Trouble, indeed.

"Not with the likes of me," she said, ducking under his arm and slipping away. The last time a man had that effect on her, she married him. She'd been a nitwit of seventeen. She was older and wiser now.

Life with Somerset had been full of teachable moments and lessons learned the hard way. First: flirts, rakes, rogues, and charming men of all sorts are not to be trusted, especially when they smile at a girl so that her pulse begins to quicken and her cheeks turn pink.

The nearest escape from the ballroom was just ahead, so Julianna quickly exited through the double doors only to find herself in a long, empty gallery. Portraits of dead ancestors gazed down upon her in a dark, barely lit chamber. She shuddered.

It was a stupid direction to take. She hadn't been thinking. But now there was no escape.

Heavy, male footsteps echoed behind her. After a quick glance over her shoulder, she saw Roxbury pursuing her through the shadows.

"You're following me," she said. What had she been thinking about older and wiser? Perhaps she spoke too soon. She had to attend this party for her column, but she didn't think he would dare. She certainly never considered he would wish to speak to her.

"You are leading me on a merry chase. You do know how men love a chase." Roxbury continued to walk toward her.

The instinct to run was great. To be here, alone, with the likes of him could not possibly lead to anything good. Instead, with some idea of bravery, Julianna stood her ground and turned to face him.

"I confess I don't know what men love. A woman thinks it's this, when it's actually that . . ." She added a little shrug of her shoulders. Her heart pounded. She could not stop provoking him, dangerous as it was.

"Enough of the insinuations, Lady Somerset." His voice carried a whisper of a threat as he took one step toward her. She took one step back. "I can't fathom why you hold the opinion of me that you do. We'd never even met before yesterday."

Yes, but she was well aware of him, that he was like Somerset and that other women mustn't make the same foolish and uninformed decisions she had.

"That was not exactly a proper introduction," she replied coolly, standing her ground as he walked closer to her, stopping only inches away.

"You're not exactly a proper lady," Roxbury said in a low voice that sent shivers down her spine.

Her hand itched to slap him, but she didn't dare. It was dark, and she was alone with a strong, angry man. It was all well and good to spar with him in the ballroom or in Knightly's office, but in seclusion it seemed much more dangerous.

Fear: that was why her pulse was quick and her nerves at attention. It certainly wasn't excitement or anything of the sort. Definitely not an attraction, or so she told herself.

"I would think that is an insulting overture, if I did not know your preferences better," she said quickly. Fear made her speak faster, to match the pace of her racing heart. Fear made her speak more boldly than she ought to.

"You're mistaken to think you're safe with me, Lady Somerset," Roxbury said, and the warning tone of his voice was unmistakable, sending another shiver up and down her spine. Good God, what was happening to her?

"Am I?" she asked with a nervous laugh. "Well, then I ought to go. If you'll excuse me."

She walked away with only one thought: *escape*. She exited through the nearest doors, which unfortunately led to a conservatory. She swore under her breath. The room was too romantic, too secluded, too . . . lovely and wonderful.

A glass domed ceiling allowed the moonlight through to shine upon luscious plants and fragrant flowers. Lord Walmsly was a renowned collector of exotic plants from all over the world. Hundreds were in bloom now. The air was warm, fragrant. She could hear the sound of a burbling fountain and of Roxbury's footsteps pounding on the slate floor.

Ever since he'd stormed into the office, she'd been so very unsettled. When trying to sleep, she could not banish the image of his laughing, smiling face. It wasn't the way he looked at *her*, but the way he was around every other woman in London—the ones he liked, or fancied. When she finally slept, he haunted her dreams, with charming, roguish smiles meant for her. She'd woken up feverish.

Since then, her appetite had diminished. Any hour of the day found her jittery with some sort of nervous energy she could not control. At this moment, she was a bundle of nerves, and sincerely regretting drinking champagne on an empty stomach. She was not feeling quite like herself.

"What do you want from me?" she asked, exasperated now, and pausing next to a small potted orange tree. Roxbury stopped before her and folded his arms across his chest.

"I want you, Lady Somerset, as the Lady of Distinction to apologize publicly and print a retraction. I want you to tell all of London that you were mistaken."

In other words, confess to being a liar. Her pride would not allow it.

"My reputation for yours? The damage is already done. Why take me down with you?"

"Oh, my dear Lady Somerset . . ." He laughed and the sound echoed around the conservatory. She worried that someone might hear them, but then she recalled that they were very much alone, and quite far from the ballroom. Instead she worried someone might stumble upon them.

"I am not your dear lady."

"No, that you are not." His comment somehow made it an insult. As if she was not fit company for his harem. Her lips pursed, spinsterish.

"I understand that you are angry," she said, switching tactics and trying to reason with him. Roxbury laughed, and this time it was a bitter sound.

"*Angry* does not begin to describe it. What I am experiencing is a potent and seething mixture of outrage, fury, and indignation. For the first time in my life, I have a nearly unquenchable urge to throttle a woman."

Julianna smiled faintly.

Roxbury carried on, circling her as he paced. "I love women. If I am going to make a woman scream, it won't be from violence, but from earth-quaking, soul-shattering, life-altering pleasure."

She wished to fan herself, but would melt completely before giving him the satisfaction of knowing that his words affected her thusly. Aye, she hoped the moonlight disguised the deep flush of crimson in her cheeks. She did not know that kind of pleasure, but she did not doubt him capable of it.

"Tell them you were mistaken," he carried on.

"You know it as well as I do that I was caught with a woman, with Jocelyn Kemble, to be exact, still in costume from her performance that evening."

He stopped before her, and leveled a stare, as if daring her to disobey, which, of course, meant that she had to. And given the fact that he'd just made her very hot and definitely bothered by all that talk of pleasure meant that she had to do something to destroy any chance of experiencing it, particularly with him. That was the road to ruin, and she'd traveled it already.

"There was one woman dressed in breeches backstage, and over a dozen men. The odds are not in your favor," she pointed out. Somerset had always said she was tenacious to a fault.

At the moment, she desperately wanted to believe the rumors her column had started. For if they were not true . . . then she was alone, with a devilishly handsome man who made her warm and her knees weak, and who might, at any moment, either murder her or seduce her.

"You are stubborn, maddening, illogical, and infuriating," Roxbury grumbled, and she saw his hands ball into fists.

"I am a lady," she retorted, as she stepped behind a voluminous potted fern.

"Exactly. That's what I said," Roxbury said, following her. She gasped. He grinned.

"I do not wish for my readers to think me inconsistent, or that I spread falsehoods." She backed up, and some large potted plant stopped her progress.

"But you do," he insisted. "Don't make me prove it to you, Lady Somerset."

"Oh, you wouldn't dare." The words were out of

her mouth before she realized he probably would. If he was anything like her, a dare was never resisted.

"Oh?" he murmured, lifting one brow.

Her lips, against her will, parted to whisper *"Oh."*

Oh, hell and damnation, she was in trouble now.

Roxbury's palms closed upon her cheeks and she gasped. Few thoughts flashed across her brain: Roxbury. Rake. Somerset. Kiss. Ruin. Must stop.

Julianna protested by slapping her palms against his chest, as if to push him away. He only transferred his grip to her wrists, pressing them close to his heart. His chest was warm and firm under her palms and Lord above, she wanted to smooth her hands across his chest, exploring, owning.

Julianna watched his lips curve into a mocking smile, as if he could read her thoughts. As if he knew she wanted to indulge but would die before admitting it. Given that he was a legendary seducer, it was not impossible.

Instead, she gripped the fabric of his shirt and glared fiercely into his eyes. His gaze was equally dark, intense, and violent. Just when she thought he might ruthlessly shove her away, Roxbury lowered his mouth to hers.

Roxbury wanted to strangle her; he kissed her instead. The minute his lips collided against hers the violence of his anger transformed into pure, raw passion and he feared he might ravish the she-devil right here, against a potted fern in Walmsly's conservatory.

She murmured in something like protest or pleasure. He felt it all over.

It went without saying that he had enjoyed many

a kiss, with many a woman. This one was different. Was it the anger? Was it the challenge? Was it just the moonlight and the brandy he'd drunk earlier in the evening? Or was it perhaps how staunchly opposed she was to him and how quickly she had surrendered to him?

Aye, he could feel her melting under his touch.

Julianna knew better. Julianna thought *stop*. She thought to say no, to insist he quit, to demand an apology. Yet a surge of heat coursed through her as Roxbury impelled her to open to him, and not gently, either. She, who loved to disobey just because she could, did just the opposite. Julianna's brain shouted in outrage; her body sent up a prayer of thanks.

Roxbury's mouth was hot on hers, and his tongue expertly tangling with hers. He released his grasp on her wrists only to snake his arms around her waist and press her against him, and Julianna gasped as she felt the hot, hard length of him. She thought there was nothing, *nothing*, like this intimacy with a man, even if he was a completely disputable cad. Julianna had forgotten it. The memory came crashing back and she was powerless against it.

Again, she moaned. This time, he groaned.

Push him away. Her fists closed even more tightly around his shirt fabric.

Push him away. Her brain issued the command, and yet she pulled him closer.

Vaguely, she recalled that she despised him, and men of his ilk. But then her best intentions took their leave of her, along with her wits, good judgment, and common sense.

It was utterly frantic and wonderful, for a moment. Her body and his, her mouth and his all locked up together in a hot, passionate, tortured kiss. Roxbury's hands roughly caressed her and, devil take it, she liked it. Within minutes he had reduced her from a celibate widow who hated him to a panting woman inflamed with desire.

Roxbury ached to take this kiss too damn far. To run his fingers through her hair, to tug down the bodice of her gown and tug up her skirts, to leave layers of clothing on the floor. He wanted to leave Lady Somerset—this know-it-all, tightly wound, gossiping widow—ravished and thoroughly debauched. Roxbury wanted her to know, intimately, just the kind of man she was dealing with. This kiss was meant to demonstrate—exquisitely, and undeniably—his power over her.

But in the remnants of his brain left to coherent thought, Roxbury wondered about all the years they had attended the same parties, conversed with the same people, and danced the same waltzes but never with each other. He thought of all those evenings when a kiss with Lady Julianna might have been a sweet one, and not one of vengeance. That was a flicker of feeling, and it had no place in an angry kiss like this. He did not want to feel a shred of affection for this woman who had so thoroughly destroyed his world with just a few words.

Lady Somerset was surrendering to him, he could feel it. But he was, too.

That, naturally, was the moment that he abruptly broke the kiss and none too gently stepped back from her, as if she were too dangerous to touch.

Julianna stumbled back against the stupid

potted fern, holding on for dear life as she tried to catch her breath, and looking at Roxbury for answers. She saw that the moonlight made his cheeks seem higher. His eyes were black and his mouth was curved in a smile of triumph.

Aye, this was not just any rake, she thought, but a practiced and heartless one. She had quite nearly been thoroughly seduced—and she had no doubt that he would have done it just to teach her a lesson. Just to show his mastery over her. Just because he could.

"An apology and a retraction in the next issue," he demanded. His voice was raw.

It only took a second for her to understand and to plot her revenge.

"Very well, Roxbury," she said, smiling with pleasure at what she would write. He thought he'd won her over with one hot, illicit kiss. He quite nearly had—and that was intolerable, and dangerous, and simply not to be borne.

Roxbury thought he had a power over her— that, like any other woman, she'd trade in her dignity and do his bidding for a drop of his affections. He was mistaken.

Chapter 8

*Poverty or Matrimony? Twenty-six days
remain for Lord Roxbury*

The Offices of The London Weekly
53 Fleet Street, London

A few days later Julianna's pulse still had yet to subside! She attributed it to frustration at her inability to decide if she had enjoyed the kiss or despised it. It was clear that he didn't like her, which was fine, because she did not hold him in great esteem, either. But how could a kiss between two people who didn't care for each other be so . . . potent, intoxicating, and downright pleasurable?

She knew, too, that it was a kiss fueled with anger and frustration (she had felt her knees weaken—along with her resolve) and she understood all of Roxbury's women a little more now. In the end, after extensive thought, Julianna could only conclude that she hated that she enjoyed it.

It had been an age since her last kiss, and an eternity since last she was held in a man's embrace.

She had not longed for them until she got a taste of what she was missing. Damned Roxbury!

But that was not to be thought of, or discussed—especially not now, just before a meeting of *The London Weekly* staff.

All the writers and editors of *The Weekly* gathered once a week to pitch stories to Mr. Knightly, the publisher and editor. The Writing Girls routinely arrived early, claimed their corner of the table and gossiped shamelessly until the meeting began.

Though their backgrounds and temperaments varied, their unusual status of women who wrote bonded them together and genuine friendships had formed.

Miss Eliza Fielding, a dark-haired beauty, wrote anonymous columns about prominent social issues of the day—like the efficacy of Wright's Tonic for the Cure of Unsuitable Affections (Sophie confirmed it did not work) or a description of the Penny Weddings of the lower classes.

The ever-angelic Miss Annabelle Swift offered readers' advice in her column "Dear Annabelle." She also nursed a tender, constant, and unrequited passion for Derek Knightly. Julianna feared Annabelle's reaction when she saw him today—if he even arrived.

Her Grace, the Duchess of Hamilton and Brandon, formerly Miss Sophie Harlow, used to write about ton weddings in her column "Miss Harlow's Marriage in High Life." At the first opportunity she quit writing about weddings (which she had hated) and now she occasionally wrote about ladies' fashion (which she loved). The column lived on, with other authors.

Today, for the first time in her life, Julianna was dreading their usual chatter because, for once, she would be the subject. Like anyone else, she preferred gossip about someone other than herself.

"Why are we only hearing about this now?" Sophie demanded, waving a copy of *The Times* in the air. Owens and Grenville looked up from their very serious conversation and scowled. After a year, the men had largely accepted working with women. Every now and then, they did not.

"Shhh," Julianna urged.

"Oh, they've already seen it," Eliza said.

"We have," Owens confirmed, with a lascivious grin in her direction. She scowled at him.

"*Everyone* has already seen it," Annabelle said, to Julianna's dismay. She, too, had read it as soon as the newspaper hit the stands. She had to keep track of her rival, of course.

They were, of course, referring to a particular item from her sworn nemesis, The Man About Town. Eliza read it aloud:

"*Just asking: Which irate rake with questionable inclinations (if we are to believe the gossips, which usually we do) was seen following a certain distinguished lady (or so we occasionally assume with no proof)? They left the ballroom quite early. One returned to the party quite late. The other not at all.*"

"That's our Julianna. Always skulking around dark hallways and empty rooms," Alistair remarked with a grin.

"It's for my work. I take my writing very seriously," she explained, as everyone in hearing distance either snorted, rolled their eyes, or generally expressed disbelief at her excuse for being alone with an infamous rake.

"We know that. What we don't know is what happened once you were alone with Roxbury," Sophie prodded. "That man is notorious, so I'm sure it must have been *something*."

"Something wicked," Annabelle added in a hushed whisper.

"You don't believe that rubbish, do you?" Julianna asked dismissively.

"Aye, we believe the gossips," Alistair said, grinning. Sophie and the others nodded their agreement.

"So . . . Roxbury followed you out of the ballroom. Where did you go?" Eliza asked pointedly.

"The portrait gallery. We chatted about the artwork. I left."

"*And* . . ." Sophie prompted.

It took some wheedling and cajoling and finally out of frustration she confessed: "All right, all right. The wretched rake kissed me."

"Oooh," all the girls exclaimed and softly, under his breath Alistair said, "Pity, that."

"How was it?" Sophie asked.

"What was he like?" Annabelle questioned.

"Do you think he . . . you know?" Eliza wondered.

"Just tell us everything, darling," Alistair said.

"All I will say is that I am determined to find the Man About Town and silence him once and for all," Julianna declared. She'd often vowed as such and always kept an eye out for potential suspects.

"And Roxbury?" Annabelle prompted, but Julianna was spared from answering by the arrival of Mr. Knightly.

"Good morning," Knightly said as he strolled into the room. He was handsome and mysterious. His past was unknown, and his parentage uncertain. She had heard rumors that his father was the Earl of Harrowby but dared not mention it in her column, or at all. His private life—those precious few hours he spent outside of *The Weekly* offices— were just that: private.

Handsome. Mysterious. Brilliant. No wonder Annabelle sighed every time he walked into the room. And with his arm in a sling—thanks to the bullet he took in the duel—he was even rougher, more dashing.

Julianna couldn't look away from the white linen sling. It was a stark contrast against his dark gray jacket. At the sight of him injured, she felt her stomach ache. Yet she had to admit he wore it well. The pride with which he displayed his wounded arm was obvious; he had fought for his paper, and had walked away with his life, and everyone knew it.

Annabelle sighed upon seeing him, as she always did. Hopeless infatuation didn't even begin to describe her feelings for him.

"Ladies first," he said, grinning, and beginning this meeting as all others. That small measure of normalcy was much needed to slice through the tension.

When it was her turn, Julianna watched Mr. Knightly's reaction carefully as she said, "Roxbury has demanded again that I print an apology and a retraction."

Roxbury could demand whatever he wanted, she thought, but that did not mean she would provide it. The room hushed, awaiting Mr. Knightly's reply.

"This ongoing battle between papers and the scandal with Roxbury has been great for sales," Knightly remarked.

"Scandal equals sales," they all chanted in unison, although without their usual enthusiasm, because scandal had gotten someone shot. It was practically Knightly's personal motto, and definitely that of the paper.

"Aye," Mr. Knightly said with a grin.

That was all the permission she needed to write whatever she wished about the great rake, Lord Roxbury.

At the thought of him, she pressed her fingertips to her lips, as if she might still feel his own mouth there. That kiss . . . like Roxbury, it was dangerous to her sanity, her equilibrium, and her place in the world. It could not happen again, and she knew just how to ensure that it would not.

Chapter 9

The apartment of Jocelyn Kemble, actress
A few days later

"**O**h, good morning, Roxbury," Jocelyn purred. She sat in bed, under the pale blue covers and resting against large fluffy pillows. Her golden hair fell in waves around her pretty face. She wore a cinnamon-colored silk wrapper, and Lord only knew what else underneath. Had he not been in such a temper, Roxbury would have tried to find out.

"It is not a good morning," he corrected and then tossed that morning's issue of *The Weekly* onto her lap.

Every word the damned Lady of Distinction printed was worse than the last. He wouldn't really give a damn, either, except for that ultimatum. His father had sent a letter—to his club—in which he wrote that he dared not anticipate which lady's or *lord's* bedchamber he was in, but scandal notwithstanding he still expected a marriage in three weeks' time or access to family funds would cease.

Three weeks!

That letter was doused in brandy and tossed in the fireplace.

Something had to be done. Roxbury was not a man to stand idly by. He was beginning to understand why Edward had quit high society, his station, and his family obligations. Roxbury could always join the army, but he was rather fond of comforts and women.

Leaning against one of the mahogany posts at the foot of Jocelyn's massive bed, he listened as she read the Lady of Distinction's offensive and belittling words aloud.

"Lord R—insists that I owe him an apology and a retraction! As I am an obliging, kind-hearted Lady of Distinction, I shall offer the irate rake that which he desires. I'm so very sorry that my idle chatter has led the ton to the conclusion he insists is false."

Jocelyn giggled upon reading it, then recalling his presence, quickly schooled her features into an appropriately concerned and consoling expression.

"That is horrible," she said gravely. The corners of her mouth twitched, no doubt with suppressed laughter. He wished he could have a sense of humor about this whole thing.

"At least the Man About Town's column has me chasing after a woman, even if it is that demon Lady Somerset," Roxbury remarked dryly, referring to last week's column, which reported him following her.

"She's lovely, Roxbury. A little sharp, but that is to be expected after a marriage like the one she was stuck in. You remember old Somerset, do you not?"

"No."

"Any scandal, particularly one involving whoring, drinking, and gaming, and you could be certain that Somerset was involved."

"That's like half the men in the ton," Roxbury said with a shrug.

"Yes, but it's always particularly devastating for a young woman in love before the stars have faded from her eyes. An old lady like me knows what to expect."

"You're hardly old," he said to Jocelyn. She could not be more than eight and twenty. Lady Somerset, however, appeared young but had a smart look in her eye. She had seen and heard things about the world. She was not an innocent.

"In my profession I am," she said with a lovely, pitiable sigh.

He smiled, before launching into the reason he had called upon her.

"I need a favor from you, Jocelyn."

"Anything," she said. They had a long history together, from his early university days when she was the barmaid at the local tavern to just last week when they had been indulging in a bit of fun. He'd never been one of her formal protectors, but always the one she came to when she was in trouble.

"I need you to tell your side of this scandalous, salacious story," Roxbury said, carefully watching her response.

His grand plan: Have Jocelyn spill all the details that he was just an average rake, not one with peculiar tastes. Enjoy women flocking to him once more. Then he would consider taking some biddable, ignorable miss as a wife to satisfy the demands of the ultimatum, but carry on with pleasure as usual.

Roxbury found that social ostracism did not suit him—not exactly a surprising discovery. He was a creature that thrived upon laughter, the energy of a crowded ballroom, quick conversation, a woman's inviting gaze, her satiated body beside him in bed. He needed these things for a proper existence. As it was, he felt like an animal in captivity. Every need fulfilled except for the thrill of the hunt and the dangers of the wild.

"Oh," Jocelyn said with noticeably less enthusiasm.

"Oh?"

"I am in the process of negotiating an affair with Lord Brookes. I don't want to jeopardize that."

Confessing to making love in a hallway with another man was the sort of thing that would.

A tense moment of silence ensued.

"But you'll take care of me, won't you?" she asked, knowing the answer.

Roxbury only smiled because he wanted to promise her everything, but for the first time in his life, there was no guarantee that he would be good for the money. He felt sickened.

What had he come to—begging for favors from old friends to salvage his reputation so he could possibly do the second-to-last thing he wanted to do—get married? A life of poverty was the very last thing.

Not for the first time did he curse that ultimatum. He did not like the choices presented to him, and suspected that in truth the matter was out of his hands. No proper woman was at home to him.

How was he to marry one, then, when he couldn't get an interview to propose?

If Jocelyn would just print her story, and clear his name. . .

"I can make it up to you, Jocelyn," he promised. Somehow, some way, he thought, though he knew not how. There would probably be jewelry involved. But before he could mention that there might be a brooch or a necklace at the end of it . . .

"Oh, to hell with it," Jocelyn exclaimed. "Come, Roxbury, let's go spill all our secrets to the press."

The true identity of the Man About Town was and always would be a mystery. For forty years he (or she?) had been chronicling the lives, loves, scandals, and secrets of the haut ton.

In those forty years, he (for it was a he) had assembled a network of informants so vast, so disperse, and so efficient that little happened that did not come to his attention. He relied on servants placed in all the best houses, shopkeepers, waiters at coffeehouses, and orphaned brats on the streets trading gossip for a penny-a-line.

If a lady in Mayfair had a sneezing fit, he might wonder—in print—if she was consumptive. If a maid were ferrying secret love letters between a young lady and a forbidden paramour, the Man About Town would quote them. If a devilish lord were packing for a jaunt to Gretna, he wouldn't get outside London proper before *The London Times* printed the details, particularly the man's traveling companion. And if a footman should encounter a couple in a delicate position at a ball at midnight, it would be news by morning.

But it was the willingness of the ton to tattle on itself that never failed to amaze or amuse. Like the best hostesses, he kept calling hours. One could find the Man About Town at St. Bride's Church every Tuesday and Thursday afternoon.

This church was a particularly fitting destination for a gossip columnist's calling hours. Located on Fleet Street, it was known as the Church of the Press. It was the final resting place of novelists and poets.

The process of calling hours was simple. He wore a hooded cloak that obscured his face. He knelt at the altar as if in prayer, while his callers took their turn "praying" next to him, while really whispering all sorts of secrets. It was more like confession, actually.

Occasionally attempts were made to pull away his hood, and those were easily thwarted. Usually, however, people did not want to ruin the mystery.

It was here that Jocelyn Kemble found him and related her story. The hooded cloak concealed his expression, which was one of warring emotions: satisfaction to know the identity of Roxbury's scandalous backstage paramour and displeasure at who it was.

Nevertheless, the next morning, it appeared in print.

Chapter 10

That morning, Jocelyn's exposé in the Man About Town's column had hit the newsstands and breakfast tables all over London. At a ball that evening, Julianna was still seething. In the ballroom, she chatted briefly with Sophie and Brandon, then Lord Brookes, Lady Walmsly, and half a dozen others. All anyone wished to talk about was the Roxbury scandal, as it was being called.

All the while, Julianna glanced suspiciously from one elder gentleman to the next. One of them had to be the Man About Town, and she wished to vent her anger at him because of the trouble he caused her lately.

She ventured into the card room and sipped champagne and watched a high-stakes game progress. It was there that Roxbury found her and requested a waltz. The nerve. The audacity. That charming smile of his, tempting her to say yes and daring her to refuse.

Another woman might coyly murmur yes, with batting eyelashes and a simpering smile. She could never.

Music from the orchestra playing in the ballroom filtered in. The air was thick with smoke of men's cigars. The conversations were kept to a low hum as fortunes were won and lost at the turn of a card. Julianna took another sip of her drink and tried to ignore him, but he asked her again.

"You are demented if you think I will," she replied, after tossing him a sidelong glance and then dismissively looking away. She was too angry to look directly at him after that story in *The Times* this morning. Besides, she already knew about his velvety brown eyes, and slanting cheekbones, and his mouth—and that the women were right when they said it was made for kissing.

Jocelyn Kemble spilled everything to the Man About Town, and Julianna had no doubt that Roxbury was behind it. It glorified Roxbury's prowess as a lover with a level of detail nearly unfit to print. It mentioned an interruption from another couple—a spinster and a dandy—which made Julianna's color rise. Jocelyn described her boy's costume for the play. The long and short of it was that the Lady of Distinction was made out to be a liar.

Julianna was vexed that she herself didn't question Jocelyn sooner, and she was terrified of Knightly's reaction when he saw she had missed such a golden opportunity.

What had she been thinking? She hadn't. Actually, she'd been thinking about Roxbury, and his kiss, and more. Useless rubbish.

"Say yes, Lady Somerset. You know you want to," he murmured.

"I don't think I will, thank you."

She was in a foul mood, and he was too tempting. The man was just too damned handsome for his own good. She was a tall woman but his intimidating height made her feel small. And one could just tell that he was well muscled under his evening clothes. There was a reason half the women in the ton had slept with him, and the other half wished to.

"I do not *think* you will. I *know* you will," he replied easily.

"It would damage my reputation to be seen with you," she told him. Then he pointed out what she was afraid of—

"Everyone in this room is already watching us talk. Anybody nearby is listening. You can only imagine what they must be thinking of us."

She shrugged, as if she did not care in the slightest. Really, though, it was profoundly disturbing. Her reputation as a respectable matron—of one and twenty, mind you—was essential. Scandalous ladies were not invited out, and gossip columnists needed to be everywhere.

Being seen in a hushed conversation or waltzing with the likes of Roxbury would be damaging. There was no one more socially toxic than he at the moment.

But tongues were already wagging about the two of them—she could tell, just by looking around the room and catching all those lords and ladies quickly looking away.

"Waltz with me," he murmured quietly, and leaning in close so only she could hear. It made her shiver and that was really why she couldn't, wouldn't, and shouldn't do anything as intimate as waltz with him.

She always felt overheated and dizzy around him. Her wits were dulled and her judgment impaired. And then there was the chance that he might kiss her again—and that she would like it, which would lead to all sorts of trouble.

"I will not, thank you," she reiterated, though she truly meant *I dare not*.

"Suit yourself," he said, taking his turn to shrug. "I didn't want to tell everyone that you are the Lady of Dist—"

"*Shhhh.*" Julianna stomped on his foot to emphasize her point. He did not appear inconvenienced or annoyed in the slightest. In fact, another glance told her that he was clearly enjoying this exchange.

"But I could," he told her. Yes, there was definitely a spark of joy and mischief in his eyes. Her lips couldn't help but curve into a smile. That legendary Roxbury charm was still operating to full effect.

"You wouldn't," she confirmed.

"Right here. Right now." He taunted her and tempted her, and against all her wishes and better judgment, she was falling for it. Her cheeks felt hot and her heart was beating quickly out of nervous terror that he would just shout out her secret to the ton.

Frankly, it was amazing that he hadn't already.

"Never," she said.

"Ladies and gentlemen," Roxbury said loudly. A few people looked. She experienced a surge of terror. "This beautiful woman has agreed to waltz with me."

That she could not refuse. Roxbury offered his arm to her, and she accepted grudgingly. Arm in

arm they strolled from the card room to the ballroom, nodding and smiling faintly to the curious
glances from acquaintances.

He was a rake, she was a widow. The conclusion
was as obvious as it was false.

Roxbury smiled devilishly down at her as they
assumed the position: her right hand in his, her left
resting upon his shoulder. With his hand on the
small of her back, Roxbury pressed her close. She
felt trapped. Captive.

"Do not try to lead," he said.

"We haven't even taken a step yet," she pointed
out.

"Yes, but you look like the kind of woman who
would try to lead," he said with an air of authority,
as if he could read women like books. Given his
experience, he probably could.

"Why are you so desperate to waltz with me
anyway?"

"Oh, I have many reasons," Roxbury said, smiling. The first notes of the orchestra sounded and
they began to waltz. He led superbly, so there was
no need for her to.

"Enlighten me," she requested.

"So that my tarnished reputation might rub off
on yours," he answered.

"Oh, how lovely," Julianna said with excessive
sweetness and a smile to match.

One, two, three. One, two, three. They moved
along to the steps in perfect time, together. She was
surprised at how well they moved as a couple when
every other interaction had them at odds.

"And so that I might gloat about the Man About
Town's column this morning, while holding you so

that you cannot run away." To prove his point, he urged her just a bit closer, and those butterflies in her belly stirred to life and began to flutter off the dust on their wings.

"Splendid," she remarked dryly. He could not know his effect upon her!

"Lastly, thanks to you, it's been some time since I've held a woman. You shall have to suffer my advances."

"That's blackmail!"

"I'm not sure it is. Regardless, I'm only asking for one dance, when I could demand so much more," Roxbury said, but it didn't sound like a threat. In fact, it felt like temptation. What was happening to her? She was made of sterner stuff than this! One dance with a scoundrel who smiled and murmured would not be her undoing.

But the memory of that kiss—his mouth hot on hers, his hands through her hair, the length of her body pressed against his—lingered, so vividly she could practically feel it. He might not even be tempting her at all, and she could merely be suffering from wishful thinking! Dear Lord, did this man make a mess of her.

"Granted, I do have enough information to blackmail nearly any woman in the ton. One learns a lot after years in bedrooms all over town, you see."

"Yes, I see," she said tightly. She saw that this was why he was not to be trusted, and why she must not succumb to temptation. Somerset had spent years in bedrooms all over town—the years before and during their marriage, to be exact. And with her young, handsome charmer of a husband, Julianna had also experienced the fluttering sensation in her belly, the heat of pleasure and the dizzying effects of infatuation.

In his own way, Roxbury tempted her to experience all that again. She could never go back to that life. She did not think she could survive it again.

"I thought I would take exceptional pleasure in tormenting you," Roxbury told her. And he smiled, showing he truly did enjoy vexing her. Unfortunately, it was such a charming smile she couldn't help but return it.

"That is so romantic, Roxbury. I might swoon."

"Please don't. I should like to carry on with the gloating," Roxbury said joyfully.

Julianna made a move to go, but grinning all the while. Still, he held her close.

"It was a great maneuver to have Jocelyn speak to the Man About Town, was it not?" he began.

"Yes, it was. I am vexed that I did not think to speak to her first. Congratulations."

"How did it taste to say those words, dear Julianna?"

"Like vinegar," she replied pertly and Roxbury burst into a laughter that slowly faded into a big grin.

"Why are you smiling like that?" she asked suspiciously.

"I'm enjoying myself tremendously," he said, sounding a little bit surprised himself.

"Enough for the two of us?" she queried tartly.

"Admit it—you are enjoying this, too," he challenged, still smiling.

Julianna wanted to smile back, and to laugh, and to love being whirled around the ballroom in the arms of such a handsome and charming—if infuriating—young man. She wanted to savor this heat of pleasure, and the dizziness of desire.

"I cannot," she confessed.

There was too much at stake, though. There was the fact that they were engaged in a very public battle over very scathing rumors. Reputations were everything, and they were on the line. Her position at *The Weekly* was on the line. Last, but not least, her body and her heart were in jeopardy. She had seen this play before; she had lived it, and had no desire to do so again.

It was all too much to gamble on with a notorious man like Roxbury.

Was she enjoying this, too? She had her moments. But she didn't dare.

At the conclusion of the waltz, Julianna vanished into the crowds before Roxbury could whisk her off for . . . a kiss? More gloating? Another dance? An interlude on the terrace? She was obviously smarting over losing the latest round of their newspaper battle.

Roxbury knew not what his intentions were.

He did know she was not interested in whatever his intentions may be.

Roxbury had purposely limited experience with her type, but he was well aware what he was dealing with: a woman who had suffered a rake before. They were difficult ones to seduce, for they knew all the tricks and had experienced the consequences.

What did it mean that he was considering seducing her? Nothing. It meant nothing. He thought that about every woman. She was the only woman that could be cajoled into speaking to him at the moment and he had so craved the touch and the company of a woman. It had been too damn long.

It would behoove him to take a wife, though . . .

Jocelyn's public confession in *The Times* did not have the effect he would have hoped. Women eyed him coyly again, but none dared to speak to him and he knew that none would be receptive to his advances.

A life of poverty was staring him down. Just short of three weeks remained before the earl would cut off his funds.

"Lord Roxbury," a woman called his name. It'd been some time since he'd heard his name from a lady's lips. Other than Julianna's, that is.

It was Lady Hortensia Reeves.

"Lady Reeves, good evening," he said, bowing to her. He saw her blush.

"Good evening," she replied, and then, because he could see that she was nervous, he initiated a conversation on the weather, and then the party, to warm her up and bolster her confidence. Then when her cheeks were flushed and she was smiling, he knew she had gathered the courage to say what was really on her mind.

For once, it had nothing to do with her collections.

"I wanted to say how unfortunate it is that everyone has turned on you, Lord Roxbury. But now you know your true friends," she said.

He smiled kindly at her, and wished deeply that he owned a modicum of attraction for Lady Reeves. Because then it would be so simple—they would marry, he would be rich and . . .

No, she would love him and he would destroy her with his infidelity.

Roxbury smiled kindly at Lady Reeves, clasped her hand, and thanked her sincerely. But then he caught sight of Julianna on the far side of the ballroom—tall, gorgeous, aloof, and dangerous. . . .

Chapter 11

The offices of The London Weekly
53 Fleet Street, London

The mood at the next gathering of *The London Weekly*'s staff was more subdued than usual. A few days earlier the Man About Town had published that tittle-tattle tell-all with Jocelyn Kemble, thus upping the stakes in the ongoing battle between the two papers. It was the only thing London had been talking about.

Was he or wasn't he? Who to believe—the Lady of Distinction or the Man About Town? Should Lord Roxbury be received or not? Should the word of an actress be believed or not? *The London Weekly* or *The London Times*?

People avoided Roxbury in droves, just in case. Jocelyn's plays were sold out. Sales for both newspapers were stellar.

"You've seen the *other* column?" Eliza asked in a hushed, cautious whisper.

"Yes, of course," Julianna said sadly. It had come out the other day, and she had read it. Often.

But then she had waltzed with Roxbury and she had thought about that. A lot.

Between worrying about her writing and puzzling over her attraction to a man she despised and who was ruining her life, Julianna was exhausted.

Alistair made sad eyes at her, commiserating. "Poor darling," he murmured.

"I'm sure it will be fine," Annabelle said soothingly, but it was no consolation.

"I'm sure it will not be. Let me read it again," Julianna said, reaching for the paper Eliza had brought.

"No!" they all shouted at once.

Eliza held the paper away from her.

"Oh, I already have it memorized," Julianna said, and she began to recite the dreaded words from memory: *"This Man About Town has the pleasure to shed some light upon the proclivities of a certain scandalous rake—No, no, my readers, do not misunderstand me."*

And then another voice picked up the thread. It was Knightly arriving with a copy of *The London Times* in one hand—his other was still in a sling.

Julianna knew it was for his own reputation, and not for hers that he had fought. But she keenly felt it was all her fault—it could not be denied that it was—and the guilt at the sight of his injury, combined with the recent triumph of the Man About Town, made her want to cry.

She never cried.

Standing before his staff, Knightly read the dreaded words aloud. *"I will reveal the identity of Lord R—'s backstage paramour, and share her exclusive story with the readers of* The London

Times. *The great actress 'Mrs.' J—K—renowned for her talent and her beauty, has confessed to being the lover of Lord R—. She tells me that he is everything a man ought to be, and everything a woman could desire in a man. She had no doubts of his inclinations.*

Knightly set the paper upon the table. No one spoke. A dozen grave faces—none more so than Knightly's—stared at her.

That column made her look like a liar or an idiot for what she had written about Roxbury. It was so foolish of her not to have approached Jocelyn first. But she had been too muddled with something like lust for Roxbury that the thought did not occur to her.

"I did not risk my life for this paper, for your writing, so that you could lose stories to our archrival." Knightly spoke softly, but firmly. The controlled force of his words struck her more than if he had yelled, or hollered, or hit.

"Do not let it happen again."

The London Residence of the Duke and Duchess of Hamilton and Brandon

A few hours later, the Writing Girls had all gathered in Sophie's private sitting room, lounging on sofas and settees, gossiping, perusing the latest issue of the ladies' magazine *La Belle Assemblée*, and drinking tea.

"I wanted to weep, Sophie, and you know how I never cry," Julianna explained. She was sitting on a plush pink upholstered settee, enjoying tea and ginger biscuits but otherwise feeling sorry for herself.

"It was not good," Eliza confirmed and Annabelle looked up from her magazine and shook her head in agreement. There was no denying that today's meeting had been quite discomforting.

If she could go back to that night at Drury Lane, would she do anything differently? Julianna could still remember the shiver of anticipated triumph when she saw Roxbury backstage in that utterly compromising position. Who would have guessed it'd come to this—a battle between papers, with her integrity as a columnist having taken a hit?

"You did not *actually* shed a tear, though, did you?" Sophie asked from where she was lounging on pillows on the floor—so very unduchesslike.

"Absolutely not," Julianna said proudly. To reward herself, she ate another biscuit.

"Well, that is something," Sophie said, sipping her tea.

"Do you think Roxbury had anything to do with it?" Annabelle wondered innocently.

"Yes," Julianna conceded. "I cannot believe Jocelyn would go to *The Times* with this! We are acquainted! It must have been Roxbury's idea."

Given her position, Julianna occasionally—and discretely—socialized with the demimonde. She and Jocelyn had often laughed and conversed together at soirees and salons.

"She's an actress, courting admirers," Sophie reasoned. "She probably has her reasons."

"Being angry with her won't help you," Annabelle said wisely. Funny that wisdom was not at all comforting.

"But if I am not angry . . . Oh, nothing." Julianna changed her mind about what she was going to say and took a sip of hot tea instead.

"Oh *nothing*?" Sophie queried with a lift of her eyebrow.

"Now that sounds interesting," Eliza said with a mischievous smile. "It's definitely not nothing."

"I mentioned that Roxbury kissed me, did I not?"

"Ah, finally, the details! How was it?" Sophie asked, eagerly leaning forward.

"It was fine," Julianna replied and Eliza snorted with laughter. "But that's not the point. At a ball the other night, we waltzed together. He insisted."

"How romantic," Annabelle said, and Julianna was not sure if she was being sarcastic or not, because really, it could go either way.

"And now you can't stop thinking about him, etcetera, etcetera," Eliza supplied.

"And when you're around him your thoughts are all muddled and your heart pounds," Sophie added.

"And he haunts your dreams at night," Annabelle added wistfully.

They had it exactly right. Unfortunately. Day or night, Roxbury was somehow, in some way on her mind. Even when he was not around, he vexed her.

"How can this be happening to me? With him?" Julianna asked. "And in the name of anything holy, how do I get this devilish man out of my thoughts?"

"Distraction," Annabelle said confidently. There was a reason she was a professional advice-giver.

"Oh, that's smart," Eliza remarked, tucking a strand of dark hair behind her ear.

"It is, except then I think about the Man About Town, which makes me think about Knightly, who is angry with me. Which reminds me that I must discover something spectacular to print . . . before the Man About Town does so. I despise him," Julianna said, and she allowed a sigh and then helped herself to another ginger biscuit.

"You have the seven sisters. They must know of something scandalous. Someone in London must be up to trouble," Sophie said.

"I have the seven sisters, but he has his own vast network of informants, developed and cultivated over forty years. *And* he takes callers at St. Bride's. I ought to take callers."

"If only someone would elope," Annabelle said wishfully.

"Or be caught in a compromising position," Sophie added with a giggle.

"Or the Man About Town might be discovered," Eliza added suggestively.

"Do you know what rankles the most?" Julianna carried on. "Because the Man About Town is a man, he can go places that I cannot. Anyone can bribe a housemaid but he can go to Gentleman Jack's, or Harry Angelo's or White's."

"Who says you can't?" Eliza asked, with the lift of one brow. Roxbury did that, Julianna thought, much to her annoyance. But Eliza might be on to something. She was usually the one with the daring schemes. Julianna suspected this would be no exception.

"My dear Eliza, what *are* you suggesting?" Annabelle asked, with her blond curls bobbing as she tilted her head curiously.

"Dressing as a man, of course," Eliza answered as if it were obvious.

"Oooh!" Annabelle exclaimed, her blue eyes widening with wonder.

"Oh yes, let's!" Sophie cried happily. "We have plenty of gentlemen's attire here! Brandon's old things might work for you."

"Brandon's attire when he was my size will be woefully out of date," Julianna pointed out.

"We'll find something," Sophie said brightly.

As soon as she began to ponder the possibilities of going out disguised as a man, Julianna's heart pounded excitedly. Think of all the places she could go, like gaming hells and Harry Angelo's (well, perhaps not, as she had no experience fencing)! But she could certainly go to White's to lounge around and drink.

She could browse the infamous wager book. She could spy on high-stakes card games and eavesdrop on great matters of state. All she had to do was don a pair of breeches, stuff her hair under a cap, and find a chair in a dark corner from where she could watch all the action unfold before her, like a play at the theater.

Was it sheer madness? The risk of discovery was great. She would be utterly ruined if she were uncovered. High on the list of things that were just not done was dressing as the opposite sex and infiltrating a man's haven. For all she knew, it was a hanging offense. But Julianna had come too far in life, propelled by her own wits and daring, to care what was or was not done.

Within an hour Julianna was dressed as a man. The first thing she noticed was that she had very long, very shapely legs. Boots were much more comfortable than slippers. And she could *move* in this attire.

Her lips curved into a smile.

They had done their best to make her chest appear flat. A dark green waistcoat helped, as did a dark gray coat. Her auburn hair was taken out of its elaborate arrangement of pins and pulled back into a short queue and stuffed unceremoniously under a wool felt cap.

Brandon's valet, Jennings, had been enlisted to tie her cravat after neither Annabelle, Sophie, nor Eliza was able to do an even passably acceptable knot. The old man frowned deeply upon seeing her; he clearly did not approve, but dared not refuse the *look* from his duchess.

It was very clear that the duke would hear of this later, but that was not to be dwelt upon at present.

Julianna's smile broadened. Only an hour ago, she had been a properly dressed lady taking tea. And now she was an intrepid reporter, disguised as a man with all of London open to her now.

One hour after that . . .

Chapter 12

White's Gentlemen's Club
St. James's Street, London

"I shall be penniless before long," Roxbury mused to Brandon. "I will miss this place." He spent an inordinate amount of time here—in the mornings he paid social calls, afternoons were passed leisurely at the club, evenings were idled away at parties, and nights were devoted to women. Or so it used to be.

"Fortunately you have wealthy friends who are members," Brandon remarked and returned to reading his newspaper.

Roxbury appreciated the show of friendship. But his smile faded as he thought that he did not want to be dependent on Brandon for basic life necessities, like club membership and brandy. His mouth deepened into a frown as he thought about how he was, at the end of the day, reliant upon his father's largesse. It was just how things were done with sons in the ton, but it nagged to discover one was not as free as one had previously assumed.

That ultimatum . . .

Lately, Roxbury was leaning toward marriage for a reason he would never dare admit aloud: he was lonely. Near complete social ostracism would do that to anyone. He ached for the company and the touch of a woman. He missed card games, and joyfully, drunken camaraderie amongst him and his peers—wealthy, powerful men (or the sons of such).

And no, he did not mean that as the Lady of Distinction would take it.

Roxbury had even sent a letter to one of his favored lovers. It had been returned unopened. So if Roxbury wanted a woman, and if he wanted his fortune, it would have to be Lady Hortensia Reeves. Bless her heart, he just couldn't do it.

And his other option of poverty? Equally detestable, but attractive only because of the defiance and independence required.

He was down to just over a fortnight. Still undecided. Only one thing to do, he reckoned, and that was to have a drink and see what happened.

"What are you reading?" Roxbury asked. He did not want to be left alone with his thoughts. They depressed him.

"*The Times.*"

"I hope your wife doesn't hear about that," Roxbury said.

Brandon replied, "Me, too."

"Is there anything about me?"

"Not today. I should think you'd be happy with your two mentions earlier in the week."

"Ah, yes. The ones that had me consorting with women for a change."

"A particular woman," Brandon said pointedly.

Roxbury knew that Lady Somerset was the bosom friend of Brandon's wife. Which side would the duke take?

"It was quite sporting for Jocelyn to chat with the Man About Town," Roxbury said, preferring to discuss that column.

"And the other one . . ." Brandon suggested.

"I'm sure I don't know what you are talking about," Roxbury answered, suddenly deeply interested in a scratch on the table.

"Being a man, I take no pleasure in listening about your heartsick feelings or romantic intrigues, so if you don't care to talk about it I won't make you," Brandon remarked.

"You should know that being a man, I have no interest in discussing them," Roxbury said. He took a sip of his brandy. "I'm convinced that Lady Somerset is the devil incarnate."

"Because she is immune to your rakish charms?"

"No," Roxbury scoffed, even though that was exactly it. She showed no sign of being affected by his kiss. Not one letter, nor a suggestive, well-placed rumor reached him informing that she would welcome his advances. Her glances in his direction at balls were either nonexistent or lethal.

Getting the woman to waltz with him had been a trial and a half. In his heyday, he needed only to offer his hand. Ladies were known to carry smelling salts to parties when he would be in attendance.

It was mildly remarkable. It was as if she believed the rumors she spread, when she knew them to be false.

Lady Somerset, the tempting wench, did not occupy his thoughts for a significant portion of the day and an unseemly portion of the evening. Or so he told himself. She had to be the devil, to bewitch him so whilst being so unaffected herself.

"She is the devil incarnate because she has a poisonous tongue and pen and because she delights in ruining the lives of innocent men and because . . ."

Unless he was going mad and experiencing hallucinations, he saw Lady Julianna Somerset.

Dressed as a man.

In White's.

"She's here," he said, awed.

"How much have you had to drink? There hasn't been a woman in this establishment in three hundred years."

"She's a witch, and a woman disguised as a man and she is *here*."

Reluctantly, Roxbury broke into a grin. She may be the bane of his existence and a plague upon men, but the lady had gumption and he had to admire that.

Brandon glanced around and didn't see her, even though she was so obvious to Roxbury.

Those long, shapely legs could only belong to a woman, and for an instant he imagined her nude legs wrapped around his back while he buried himself inside her. His mouth went dry. Her own lips were too full and perfectly made for a woman's coy, mysterious smile to belong to a man.

Like most of the gents in the room, Brandon was focused on a newspaper. Some were undoubtedly reading Julianna's column, completely unaware that the authoress prowled among them, swaying her hips like a woman in skirts.

Roxbury sipped his drink and watched Julianna

investigate the club. She was probably trying to act like the bored gentleman who had been here a thousand times. For the most part she succeeded, except that he could see her biting her lip as if to contain pure, outrageous joy at her own mischief and daring.

This was no longer the same stuffy old club with the same old blokes, but a new wonderland, ripe for exploration and, for a gossip columnist, akin to a sweetshop for a young brat.

Lady Somerset took a seat in a chair by the fireplace with the portrait of King George III, and stretched those long legs out before her. Roxbury watched her laugh softly and he knew that she had seen the words some drunken smart arse had carved into the mantle years before: *Sorry about that unfortunate incident in the colonies.*

Good old practically blind Inchbald approached her. She ordered something. Wine? Water? Brandy?

He sipped his own drink, and settled in his chair, enjoying the show she was unwittingly putting on for him.

She picked up a copy of *The London Weekly* and pretended to read it. He knew she was only holding it above her face as a cover because he saw her eyes dart around the room—probably taking names and notes in her head.

He was half tempted to warn everyone that whatever they were doing was sure to become "Fashionable Intelligence." Yet this same crowd had believed the lies and rubbish printed about him, so he'd keep his mouth shut and let the fools expose themselves. Lord Sheldon would want to think twice about placing that wager and Lord

Borwick wouldn't want to order that fifth drink. Lord Walpole would want to hide his scribbling and Lord Brookes and his friend might wish to lower their voices as they discussed a new business venture so close to the Lady of Distinction.

It was only a matter of time before their gazes met from across the room. When they did, he discretely raised his glass in cheers.

Chapter 13

For Roxbury to discover her in such a situation—dressed as a man, in a gentlemen's club—seemed to Julianna like an occasion when a man would declare that a drink was in order. Thankfully, at that very moment the waiter—a man who surely predated the flood—brought her first ever brandy.

Roxbury's attentions made her nervous, and her hands shook as she tilted the brandy glass back for a sip. She took far too much and was sure her face turned bright red as the brandy burned its way down to her belly. Tears stung her eyes. But she could not reveal that she was a novice drinker.

Not here, and not with Roxbury watching.

She stood, intending to wander around the place, perhaps finding a room where he wasn't watching her. She noticed Lord Brookes deep in a conversation she ached to overhear, for it seemed so serious. Mitchell Twitchell was betting high on a very bad hand of cards in a game with Earl Sheldon and others beyond his league, and Lord Brandon was reading *The London Times*!

It was the sight of Lord Walpole filling up pages with an unfortunately illegible scrawl that piqued her curiosity like nothing else. That was quite a damning sight, considering he was her prime suspect for The Man About Town.

Because she was in disguise in White's, she didn't grin and laugh with glee as she wanted to do. Instead, she coolly made note of it and took another small sip of brandy, trying to seem like a man of the world.

That was damned hard to do when Roxbury was watching her. She knew it by the way her skin felt warm and exquisitely sensitive. Maybe it was the brandy instead of the smoldering gaze of a handsome man. She hoped so.

She hadn't gone far before she came to the famed White's wager book open and lying on an empty table, and a sigh of pleasure escaped her lips. Oh, the tales that had originated about the stupid bets and idiotic wagers recorded in this volume!

She traced her fingers along the spine and flipped it open, enjoying the pleasure of the pages fluttering along her fingertips. A shadow fell over the book. It was not her own.

Roxbury pulled out a chair and indicated that she should sit. It was such a gentlemanly gesture and years of training to be a lady forced her to accept, even though it was at odds with her disguise.

Roxbury availed himself to the seat beside her. For the sake of her disguise and reputation, she did not protest even though she wanted to howl at the unfairness of having waited so long to get near this book, and now he would steal her moment.

"It was your legs that I noticed and your lips

that gave you away," he murmured. Her cheeks flushed pink.

"That's a rather personal comment to make. Very ungentlemanly of you," she reprimanded. She was keenly aware that she was wearing breeches and a waistcoat, among other items of a man's attire, while lecturing him. She saw the mirth in his brown eyes.

"*I'm* being ungentlemanly?" he said with a laugh. She scowled because he absolutely had a point.

Ignoring him, she took another swallow of brandy, stifled a sputter, and focused upon the book.

Something was scrawled about Lord Alvanley and a raindrop and three thousand pounds. She would have loved to know more, but Roxbury was looming and leaning close to her, and it was distracting.

She felt overheated—the brandy, certainly.

"What you are is a tremendous bother," Julianna retorted.

"I could say the same of you. A monumental bother. An infernal nuisance. A constant pain in my ar—"

"I am bored of this conversation, Roxbury," she drawled.

"I have something that might interest you," he replied. He flipped through the pages until he found a particular one.

The gentlemen of White's had created a table rating the ladies of the ton on beauty, wit, sensibility, and principles.

"Oooh," she sighed, utterly delighted. This

was the sort of gossip sure to have Londoners in a heated, lively debate. When the news was discussed and argued about, more copies were sold. When more copies sold, Knightly was happy and she so needed to please him after getting him shot.

Julianna was not surprised to see that Lady Jersey was rated highly for beauty and received a zero for her principles. Oh, she would pitch a hysterical fit when she read that! Everyone whispered it, but never said so aloud in polite company. In contrast, Lady Melbourne had been rated very low for her figure (zero) and very high for her principles (fifteen).

"Do you think her principles are so high because she has a figure that discourages anyone to tempt her to misbehave?" Roxbury voiced her own shameful thought.

"I couldn't say," she deferred.

"I think it is," he replied, leaning in even closer. It annoyed her, because it was actually enjoyable in some way to be pouring over a book of secrets together. That, and he smelled good, and as a man ought to—like leather and soap and brandy.

"What is this on a scale of?" she queried.

"Considering the drunken louts that compiled it, I don't think there is one," he replied.

High marks went to Lady Barrymore for sense. Low marks for Lady Sefton's wit. She had to concur.

"Lady Stewart-Wortly has been rated very low for her principles," Julianna noted. "By whom, I wonder?"

"Well, that's interesting, given her work," Roxbury said, sounding genuinely intrigued. She had to agree; one would think the author of *Lady Stewart-Wortly's Daily Devotional for Pious and Proper Ladies* would have to be highly principled.

"I wonder what someone knows," Julianna mused. There was probably a story there for her to pursue.

"I cannot enlighten you. She's one of the few women I have not tried to seduce," Roxbury remarked as he perused the pages.

Julianna looked away, for he hadn't tried to seduce her, either, and it was mortifying to be lumped together with the likes of the aging and eternally evangelizing Lady Stewart-Wortly when it came to a rake's to-do list.

"I'm afraid to see if I'm rated in here," she whispered.

"I am as well. If you don't like what is written, you'll make me suffer for it."

"Why are you showing me this?" she asked in a whisper. The mere fact that he hadn't yanked off her hat and completely exposed her as a woman was an extraordinary kindness, given what her writing had done to his social life. In a word: murder.

"I'm giving you something to write about other than myself," he answered plainly. "It's not an act of kindness, mere self-preservation."

She smiled wryly. Given the lustful feelings this debauched and sinfully attractive man inspired in her, she could not afford to be wooed and wowed by kindness, so it was good he didn't provide any—other than not ruining her disguise in public. She owed him for that.

And yet, in the spirit of her own self-preservation—keeping Roxbury away from her and her traitorous feelings of desire—she spoke cuttingly.

"How clever. I had no idea there was a brain behind that pretty face," she said, smiling charmingly, and forgetting she was supposed to be a man. His eyes widened. She had insulted him by describing him with a feminine adjective.

"I'm not *pretty*, Lady S—" he said hotly.

"Shush!" She placed her finger over his lips. He mustn't expose her now!

The volume in the room suddenly dropped considerably, and they both froze in a very compromising position.

Chapter 14

Too late, Roxbury realized the error of being near her. He leaned back in his chair, putting as much distance between them as possible, short of leaving entirely. Something like gentlemanly concern kept him near her, for he could not leave her to be discovered by someone much more nefarious than he.

Or perhaps he did not wish to leave just yet.

It was so obvious to him that she was a woman dressing up as a man. But as he took a glance around at his companions—and not one of them would meet his eye—it was clear that they believed her to be a man.

A man who had leaned in close and touched his lips. In public. Dear God.

They had spent the past quarter of an hour perusing the betting book and conversing in hushed tones. It would not look good. In fact, it would look like the rumors were true beyond a shadow of a doubt.

But look at *her*! He wanted to yell. *Her*.

No man had a mouth like hers, with its ability to curve into a sphinxlike smile. Her features were too delicate. Julianna's green eyes were wide with wonder at her surroundings when every other man's gaze here was tired and jaded. And those legs—for the love of God, those long, luscious legs leading up to perfectly curved hips that could only belong to a woman.

At best, she could be passed off as someone's young cousin from the country.

He should expose her. Just yank off that cap and revel in her auburn hair tumbling down in waves. Laugh as jaws dropped on the stodgy old men and young swaggering bucks drinking unsuspectingly in the club.

By God, he'd like to run his fingers through her fiery hair, drawing her closer, to kissing distance. He'd claim that mouth of hers as his own, silencing her "witty" remarks until the only sound she was capable of uttering was a moan of pleasure. The jacket, the cravat, all the things of her boy disguise would go, until she was undeniably a woman, and a ravished one, at that. And his.

At some point, the fantasy had moved from club to bedroom. God, he needed a woman. It had been too damned long.

"You're staring, Roxbury. What will people think?"

Well, he wanted to say that it depended upon people's ability to read his mind. But that was not an avenue of conversation to pursue with her. Instead, he said, "I don't know how they are deceived by you."

"People see what they want to see," she said with a shrug.

"For example, you insist on seeing me as a rake with questionable tastes," he replied.

"And you see me as a complete harridan," she replied.

"And so much more," Roxbury said. "I see you as a complete and utter she-devil shrew who is destroying my life for no apparent purpose, other than to sell more newspapers."

"Tell me how you really feel, Roxbury," she retorted. "And I thought we were having a moment."

He would have never said such a thing to a woman he was seducing. But though he may have entertained lusty thoughts of Lady Somerset, he had no intention of seducing her. Frankly, he wasn't sure he'd survive.

"We might have been, in spite of myself. Everyone here thinks you are a man, which means they are thinking the worst of me right now."

Roxbury reached for her brandy glass and took a sip. She opened her mouth to protest but he gave her a sharp look and let it go. Amazing.

"It'll all blow over in time, Roxbury," she said softly. "Scandals always do."

"I don't have the time," he said tightly. Every day flew by, each more scandalous than the last. Marriage to a gently bred woman was unfathomable—no one would have him.

Never mind the fact that he did not actually want to get married. He just didn't want to go broke. It was quite the conundrum.

"So you've mentioned, Roxbury, but you have not explained why you don't have time. Will you tell me now?"

"No. But a great idea just occurred to me," he said, grinning devilishly.

"What is that?" she asked suspiciously, rightfully so.

"If I were to take that hat off your head . . ."

"You wouldn't dare," she whispered, holding on to said hat with both hands.

"I might. Or I might just taunt you with the possibility. I do enjoy having you at my mercy." Roxbury caught himself grinning in true amusement. There was nothing like taunting a tightly coiled woman like Lady Somerset. One day she'd open up, let down her hair . . . he probably wouldn't be there, but he would like to see it.

"Enjoy it this once. I'm going to go," she said, rising from her seat.

"Are you?" he queried, just after indicating to Inchbald that their glasses needed replenishing. Within a moment, they each had a full glass of brandy. Julianna looked at hers warily.

"Now that I think of it," she mused, "you are at my mercy as much as I'm at yours." Then she smiled, and he felt a mixture of terror and pleasure deep in his gut.

"Oh, the things I could do . . ." she began. "I could rest my hand upon your knee. Or higher."

She didn't actually do it, thank God. But the thought of her pale, soft ladylike hand on his knee, sliding higher and then higher . . . He took a sip of his drink.

"Perhaps I could clasp your hand in mine," she said, as she placed her palm over his hand resting on the table. This was high on the list of things that were just not done.

A few of the old windbags, unwinding after a session in parliament, took note. Who knew eyebrows could reach so far up one's forehead? Roxbury took a sip of brandy and pulled his hand away.

But that thought was fleeting. Instead, he thought of her hands upon other parts of his anatomy. Said other parts responded enthusiastically.

"At the end of it, when I unmask you," he said, "I'll be redeemed and you'll be the brazen hussy that dressed as a man and attempted to seduce me."

Julianna choked and sputtered on her sip of brandy.

"Or," he continued, with a grin. "When the brandy works its magic, and you unmask yourself."

"I shall do no such thing," she retorted. But already, she was beginning to slur her words. Her cheeks were very pink, and she was quite adorable. He was smiling at her, marveling, really, and feeling something like affection for this troubling, meddlesome girl dressed as a boy.

"You are handsome when you smile," she said grudgingly and that's how he knew for certain that she was tipsy.

"I know," he said. He knew that because everyone—ladies, mainly, always sighed so. But to hear it from the lips of such a lady termagant? He liked it.

"It is proper to say 'thank you' upon receiving a compliment," Little Miss Manners reminded him.

"It was a statement of fact as much as a compliment," he answered, just to vex her.

"You are impossible. I finally say something remotely nice to you and then—"

"I'm incorrigible, insufferable, etcetera, etcetera," he finished for her, for if she launched into a tirade about what an incorrigible, insufferable, vexatious good-for-nothing rake he was, then she would really give herself away.

"Assuredly," she muttered, taking another sip, and wincing. Another giveaway. It was impossible not to find her adorable. Her courage and effort at her disguise was admirable.

"I hope I am not interrupting anything serious," Brandon said, stopping by their table. Julianna nodded her head in acknowledgment.

"Not at all," Roxbury said. And then, quite loudly, he added, "I'd like to introduce my cousin Julian, newly arrived from Shropshire."

Roxbury grinned as Brandon and Julianna awkwardly shook hands, and obviously recognized each other—she was the good friend of his wife after all. She was also wearing his clothing.

"I had a jacket just like that one, in my Eton days," Brandon said pointedly.

Julianna only smiled faintly.

"Pardon him. He's not quite all there upstairs," Roxbury said loudly, and damn, did she scowl at him for that! He only smiled in return, thinking he'd never enjoyed himself more at White's—and what did that say?

It was why he did not reveal her disguise, because he wanted her company. She was a shrew, but she was a pretty one, and he was aching for a woman and hungering for company. Even if it came in the tempting, troubling, entertaining, and vexing form of Lady Somerset.

It was a troubling thought, quickly pushed aside.

"I wasn't aware you had a cousin, Roxbury," Brandon said, playing along.

"Neither was I. But you do know how poor relations have a way of coming out of the woodwork," he explained. Loudly.

Quite a few men in the vicinity nodded and grumbled their agreement.

"Come along, Julian," Roxbury said, clapping her on the back. "You've had your taste of London. Time for you to return to Shropshire."

Chapter 15

Once outside on St James's Street, the little minx attempted to walk away in the opposite direction than he—alone, and without saying goodbye. Roxbury grabbed a fistful of her coat, tugged her back, and chided her as if she was his slightly daft country cousin.

"This way, Julian."

"I'm not Julian," she grumbled.

Roxbury feigned shock.

"Oh, I am *terribly* sorry. Did you want me to announce you as Lady Somerset, otherwise known as the Lady of Distinction from *The London Weekly*?"

She pursed her lips, and her eyes narrowed. She was seething because he was right and she knew it. Roxbury paused to savor the moment.

"You are welcome," he said graciously.

"Thank you," she mumbled so quietly that if he had not been watching her lips move—her luscious, pink, undeniably female lips—he would have missed it.

Roxbury opened the door to his carriage and indicated she should join, but the maddening, stubborn, impossible woman stood her ground. She folded her arms across her chest.

It was immediately clear what this was about: she wanted to gallivant across London dressed as an idiotic country cousin all in some quest for "news" or "gossip" or "adventure" not at all realizing that people got killed for that sort of thing, especially when the person in question was a woman, a lady. Especially when the woman was drunk. He and his chaperoned ride put a stop to that.

"You do look remarkably mannish," he said, and he took pleasure in the way her eyes widened in shock and her lips pursed in vexation. "But it's getting dark, and we both know the streets of London are not safe for anyone. You haven't a prayer of defending yourself."

To his surprise, she did not immediately leap into the carriage and thank him for considering her well-being.

"Much as it would please me if you never wrote another word, I'm not going to have your death on my conscience," he said. "Are you coming or not?"

"I'm merely shocked at your chivalrous behavior," she replied, but they both knew she had wanted to go off alone in search of a dozen different kinds of trouble. "But yes, I'm coming."

He wasn't going to assist her into the carriage because it was at odds with her disguise. But out of habit she held out her hand, and out of habit he clasped it. Against all common sense, Roxbury made the grave mistake of looking her in the eye at this moment.

Lady Somerset did not flutter her lashes, or wink,

or lift her brow. She did not resort to any such tricks; instead, she looked him in the eye. That was the thing with her, she was direct and honest. So much of flirtation depended upon saying this and meaning that and he found her forthright manner intriguing.

In that moment he wondered how things might have been if they had met under different circumstances.

How had they not? How had he not tried to bed her?

He was probably chasing after light skirts and easy, lovely conquests. Lady Somerset was a challenge.

"Now you needn't worry for my safety," she said smugly, sitting primly and properly across from him in the carriage. Even dressed as a boy, she sat like a lady.

Wrong, he thought. She was alone in the carriage with a rake—and one nearly boiling over with pent-up desire. Perhaps he ought to let her wander the streets alone. But no, the dangers that awaited her there were far worse.

"I should be utterly distraught and sick with guilt if anything were to happen to you," he replied dryly. But the truth of the matter was that he was, occasionally, a gentleman. He could not, in good conscience allow her out on the streets in her state.

"Oh, the guilt," she scoffed. "I would hate for it to get in the way of your affairs."

"Naturally. You wouldn't have anything to write about if not for my affairs," he said, shocked at the note of bitterness there. "Unless there is another reason you protest them . . ."

"I don't care for what you are suggesting," she said, her hands attempting to smooth out her skirts, but not finding that volume of fabric there. There was only the light layer of her breeches. He forced his gaze back to her face and his attentions to the conversation at hand.

"Unless you have a tendre for me," he said. "Unless your bitterness toward my lovers—real or alleged—is merely jealousy?"

"You really ought to give up on thinking. You are truly terrible at it," she retorted.

"Indeed. Attempting the strenuous activity of rational thought gives me headaches. I'm sure you understand."

The words exchanged between them were sharp, and parried quickly. The glances were hot, searing and fleeting. It was all a method of protection, because if they did not trade cutting remarks . . .

The dimly lit carriage sheltered them from the rest of the world. The urge to kiss her was overwhelming. Her eyes, large, bright, and mysteriously upturned at the corners gave him another warm glance. Roxbury knew how to read a look like that: *It's dark. We are alone. Are you going to kiss me or not?*

"You know what they say is a remarkable cure for headaches?" he queried.

"Silence," she answered flatly.

Though that was not the answer he had in mind—he was thinking of lovemaking—nevertheless, Roxbury obliged her. One of his "tricks" with women was to give them exactly what they said they wanted . . . because usually it wasn't what they wanted at all and the sooner they established that, the sooner they could all move on.

If a woman said she could not see him anymore, he did not attempt to see her. It was never more than a few days before she wrote begging for his return.

Thus, with Lady Somerset, he'd wager that it was only a moment before she was chattering away again—on a subject of her choice, and he was very curious to know what that might be.

So they sat in silence as the carriage clattered through London.

As they passed the Burlington Arcade, she stared out the window and he enjoyed a good, long look at Lady Somerset in male attire. She'd done a fine job of it: Her boots were polished, her breeches were exquisitely fitted, her linen starched and white. The cravat was expertly tied. Her hair was tied into some makeshift queue—it would take only one tug of a ribbon to send it all tumbling down. Oh, how he wanted to.

What was it like to undress a woman in male clothing, he wondered?

That night at the theater with Jocelyn, he'd been about to. But that interruption reminded them to return to her dressing room where she had a potential suitor waiting.

The carriage rolled on through town and as they drove by the corner of St. James's Palace, he began to imagine undressing Lady Somerset, removing those boy clothes layer by layer. The starched cravat was the first to go. The jacket next. There were only four buttons on the waistcoat, significantly less than on a typical gown. The shirt would lift over her head and fall to the floor.

Aye, he knew how to remove clothing. That was

easy—and arousing enough—to imagine. But what would it be like with *her*? When the shirt came off, what would he see? Feel? That mystery set his blood on fire.

He'd already seen her creamy white skin, and her gowns showed off her figure exceptionally, suggesting full breasts and a narrow waist. But how soft was her skin? And how would the curve of her hips feel under his fingertips?

As they traveled along the strand, it did not escape his notice that he wasn't the only one looking. Lady Somerset was eyeing him just as much.

"You're staring again, Roxbury," she pointed out.

"You're a beautiful woman, Lady Somerset." He'd realized that long ago. Something about her bright green eyes, or her milky skin, or that outrageous mouth of hers. Something about the way she carried herself—strong, proud, and with her shoulders back (which showed off her décolletage marvelously).

"I'd say you are handsome, but you are already well aware of the fact. The last thing you need is another compliment to swell your head," she said, and he understood that to mean that she found him attractive but would rather expire than admit it to him.

"Bitter, bitter . . ." he said. And for the first time he wondered if he had said or done something to offend her once—so deeply and gravely because she was always having a go at him—or was it something else?

"I'm not bitter," she protested, which was ridiculous because they both knew that she was.

"Is it something I've said or done? Were you always this way or did old Somerset ruin a lovely young girl?"

Chapter 16

Julianna had not expected such a personal question and astute insight from Roxbury.

"Old Somerset" had actually been young, dashing, devastatingly handsome, and *hers*. Correction: Harry had been hers in name only. He was the folly of a seventeen-year-old girl's heart and the source of a woman's heartache.

Even now, she felt a twinge in her chest thinking of him. For the bright, fiery love they once had, and the dust remaining when the flame burned out.

Julianna glanced at Roxbury darkly and he was watching her curiously. But she could not explain any of it—not aloud and certainly not to him.

The same story had been repeatedly enacted in drawing rooms all over town—a pretty girl meets a dashing rogue. Romance, mystery, magic overwhelms. A mad and passionate dash to Gretna Green, with no thoughts whatsoever to the consequences.

Julianna recalled the night he had died. As was his habit, Somerset had gone out shortly after waking, which occurred late in the afternoon. She had sat by the fire, ever the stoic, restrained lady, wondering where he had gone, with whom, and what degenerate activities occupied him this evening. Rumors informed her that Somerset had turned to opium, and to orgies and the devil only knew what else. She was thankful for that, for how else would she know about her husband?

Occasionally, Julianna attended soirees with friends but the whispers and pitying glances drove her wild with anger. Usually, she had stayed in and attempted to puzzle out where it had all gone so wrong. They had been so in love once.

Late at night there had been an ominous knock at the door, and thus arrived the news that an accident had occurred. Somerset, some wench, copious quantities of alcohol, an overturned carriage.

Other than that grim revelation, it had been a typical evening.

The reading of the will was just as scandalous. Somerset left the bulk of his disposable fortune to various mistresses and his by-blows. For his wife, only a pittance remained in the form of a small yearly annuity, a small house in the once fashionable, now fallen neighborhood of Bloomsbury, a scandalous name in need of reformation . . . and her hard-earned freedom.

Julianna supplemented her meager income by writing, determined to rely on her own wit rather than request support from her family, who had always opposed the match. She vowed never to attach herself—her fate—to a man again.

Roxbury was mostly right. Once upon a time, she'd been a laughing young girl. She delighted in listening to her mother read to her from her correspondence with high society friends as bedtime stories. Growing up together, she and Sophie shared lessons, schemes, and wishes for dashing, loving husbands.

Somerset had wiped the stars from her eyes, after turning true love into a prison. It would make anyone sharp, bitter, and braced for soul-crushing and heart-aching disaster. But she did not wish to explain that.

Roxbury's question hung in the air, unanswered. *Were you always so sharp and bitter or did old Somerset ruin a lovely young girl?*

"What a quaint interpretation. That my late husband has anything to do with this, us," she mused, searching for a way to turn the tables on Roxbury. "I suppose it hasn't occurred to you that it is you that I object to?"

"It's unfathomable," Roxbury said flatly. "We barely know each other. Until the other week, we had never even met."

And what an introduction it had been.

"Oh God, or had we met before?" Roxbury asked. "Is that what this is all about? That I had never sought you out for an affair?"

Julianna lifted one brow. Really? He thought that was her problem?

No, she was just trying to do her job and live her life as a reputably respectable widow without a devastatingly handsome rake dodging her heels, making her heart race and muddling her thoughts. She liked sparring with him and she craved his kiss, and that would never do.

"Or did we have an affair?" he carried on, his voice lowering as if someone might hear, even though they were *quite* alone in this carriage. "I swear I'd remember you, if we had . . ."

Her lips parted in shock. They had not, of course. She liked to think that she was *not* forgettable. The evidence from her first marriage did not bode well, though.

"No, we have only recently met and we have never had an affair. I avoid the company of cads and rogues such as yourself, and you apparently labeled me as a bitter old shrew and never gave me a second glance. We both quickly ascertained that we could have no business with each other."

"You are a bitter shrew," Roxbury confirmed, to which she gasped. In certain instances it was not polite to agree with a lady. Then again, she was dressed as a boy.

He continued, "Old, I'm not so sure about. However, you are fetching."

The compliment in the midst of battle stunned her, and for a second, she was speechless. The rake thought she was fetching! Even more shocking was the rush of pleasure, and that left her tongue-tied. Then she recovered, because Lady Julianna Somerset never went long without something to say.

"It's the men's clothing you find attractive, is it not?" she said, smiling, and enjoying provoking him.

"If I find it remotely attractive, it's for the novelty and the fact that it's on a woman, even if that woman is you," he replied.

"You said I'm fetching," she reiterated.

"That doesn't mean I want to bed you," he said to her surprise.

"Why not?"

"Why not? *Why not?*" he echoed, flabbergasted.

She thought it a perfectly logical query. If he was a man of enormous appetites, she was fetching, why would he not wish to indulge?

Or did she not even want to know? What was *wrong* with her that two notorious, debauched rakes, generally indiscriminate with their affections, did not want to bed her?

No wonder she was a bitter shrew.

"Frankly, Lady Somerset, I'm not sure I would survive it," Roxbury remarked.

"That makes two of us. I would likely perish from boredom during the act," she said, because he couldn't know that she wished him to want her.

"If our lovemaking would prove fatal, we'd better not do it then," Roxbury said.

"On that, we are in agreement," she said.

"How strange," they both said at the same time. There was nothing to do but laugh—together for once, rather than at each other.

When the carriage stopped before her townhouse, Julianna experienced an unexpected rush of disappointment to be home. 24 Bloomsbury Place was a lonely house these days, and she felt it all the more after this afternoon's adventures—a damsel in disguise! Gossip galore! Even though Roxbury endlessly vexed her, it was good fun to spar with him.

Not that she would *ever* admit that to him.

"Thank you for seeing me home safely," she said politely, ever the lady regardless of her attire.

"My pleasure," he said, and she could not discern the ratio of sarcasm to genuine feeling in his tone.

She quit the carriage with Roxbury's assistance.

His hand was warm and strong around hers. Though she knew people were staring at the sight of what seemed to be two men, hand in hand, she didn't care, because for the first time, there was something in the way Roxbury looked at her that wasn't anger, or disdain, or immense frustration.

He did have lovely brown, almond-shaped eyes.

Lord help her, because she was beginning to understand the magic of Roxbury and how so many women had fallen under his spell. Most dangerous of all, when this handsome man looked at her, those hard-learned lessons from Somerset seemed to fade.

Perhaps he's different, temptation whispered, and logic told her all rakes were the same.

She would never sort all that out today, so instead Julianna indulged in the moment and offered a true smile to the man holding her hand.

Penny, Julianna's maid, let her into the house and did not bat one eyelash upon seeing her mistress dressed as a man and escorted home by her nemesis. Only once she was safe inside did Roxbury's carriage depart. He treated her like a lady even if she occasionally did not act like one.

Julianna collapsed onto the sofa in the little drawing room, and helped herself to the tea tray that Penny had thoughtfully laid out. There was a thick pile of correspondence that made her smile. She loved receiving copious amounts of letters from her vast array of acquaintances (and informants), and invitations to nearly everything happening in London—breakfast parties, afternoon teas, walks in the park, evenings at the theater, balls, soirees . . .

Julianna picked up the first letter in the stack and saw that it was from her mother. The Dowager Baroness Leighton took to her bed after her husband—a complete philanderer, Julianna noted disparagingly of her father—had expired. However, even from her bed the baroness was one of the most informed people in England. All morning she wrote letters to her wide circle of friends, and all afternoon she read letters sent to her.

No one saw the harm in confessing their secrets to the bedridden old lady in Buckinghamshire. Little did they know that she was a worse gossip than her daughter.

"My dear Julianna, I've heard things about you and Lord Roxbury," she wrote, ever direct and to the point. *"The stories have you two consorting in private rooms, in balls. Mind the rakes, darling; we both know the trouble they can cause a good woman. Roxbury, though, seems ripe for reformation, given the latest scandals about him, which I needn't bother repeating since everyone knows them."*

"I *started* them," Julianna grumbled. Telling her mother about her profession was not an option. The woman couldn't keep a secret if the fate of England depended on it. Also, Julianna feared her mother's heart might burst—literally—with pride for her daughter.

She reread the line about Roxbury being "ripe for reformation" and decided that her mother must have gone a bit batty after all those years in her bedchamber. The man was as ready to settle down as a rampant bull.

Her mother carried on with news about how

The Baron Pinner was forever bringing gorgeous bouquets of flowers to his lady. On the other hand, Lord Brookes was rumored to have ended an affair with Jocelyn Kemble after news broke that she was Roxbury's backstage, breeches-clad lover. The elderly Earl of Selborne had taken ill mysteriously. And Tuesday last, while deep in his cups, Lord Wilcox admitted to bedding "the last woman in England anyone would expect."

Julianna set the letter aside to save for her column, having decided to ignore the rest of the invitations and correspondence.

A melancholy mood seeped into her bones, settling in like a deep fog. Returning home to an empty house after a thrillingly adventurous afternoon with Roxbury was likely the cause.

It wasn't so long ago that Julianna and Sophie would sit on this settee, take tea, and chatter away amidst the clutter of their belongings. But now the room was neat, and there was no chatter because Sophie lived with her husband in a massive house in Mayfair, the center of the haut ton. Julianna lived alone in Bloomsbury, home to the professional class.

Why hadn't Roxbury tried to take a liberty with her? Why did he not want to bed her?

Because she was bitter . . . but fetching! Because she would bore him. Because she was a gossip columnist and any detail might make its way into her column.

Because she knew better.

Because she was *not* the sort of woman a man took liberties with.

Once, she had been. In those early days of her

great love with Somerset, she'd savored more than her fair share of stolen kisses from the handsome charmer. Why, then, for the first time in ages, did she wish for more?

Why did she catch herself daydreaming about that kiss with Roxbury? She remembered it all: the silvery glow of the moonlight, the fragrance of orange blossoms, the linen of his shirt clasped in her palms. And the especially delicious parts made her blush to consider them even now: the heat of his mouth on hers, the wide, warm expanse of his chest under her hands, his strong arms holding her captive, and the way hot, wild desire pulsed through her begging for release.

But it had only been one kiss.

One thing was certain: she could not afford for her column to be second rate, especially after Jocelyn's confessions to the Man About Town. And so, with a twinge of guilt in her heart, Julianna sat down at her desk and began to compose the next great installment of "Fashionable Intelligence."

Chapter 17

Gentleman Jack's
Bond Street, London

What would she write next? The question had consumed him for hours, for days. And now that he had the answer . . .

He'd been boxing at Gentleman Jack's for two hours now, and still Roxbury—sweaty, aching, and angry—raised his bruised fists, ready for another round.

Ever since their remarkably unusual, entertaining, and—dare he say it—pleasant afternoon together at White's, of all places, Roxbury had dared to hope Lady Somerset would not write something completely cruel, libelous, and otherwise horrendous.

She did.

He had dared to hope that his small acts of kindness to the evil woman—driving her home, not utterly exposing her at White's, or at all—would soften her heart and temper her poisonous pen. But no, she was a cold, heartless broad that would take any scrap of information and twist it around so that the bored, idiotic hordes in London would have some little tidbit to enjoy over a pot of tea.

After days of wondering what she might write, he finally knew.

Unfortunately, during those days in which he awaited her latest column, his thoughts of Julianna were not focused exclusively on her writing.

His mind strayed to the inevitable . . . Julianna in various states of undress (and it was women's dresses he imagined removing from her—*dresses*, thank you very much—one button, scrap of lace and stay at a time).

Roxbury knew that her kiss was a tortured mix of restraint and abandon, of innocence and experience. He wanted another taste. He just plain wanted her naked in his bed. He wanted her defenseless and in his power, and he wanted to *know* her.

If what she wrote was any indication, these were delights he would never, ever know.

"Oy, Roxbury! Did you come for a fight, or something else?" a young buck scoffed, adding a smirk at his own "wit." It was the sort just down to London after their first year at university, full of bravado, still learning to hold their liquor, losing at cards and the bane of many a woman. They were the ones that most delighted in taunting Roxbury with those rumors Lady Somerset had started.

Roxbury's store of patience with this sort was infinitesimal.

With blood at a low rolling boil, Simon raised his fists and narrowed his eyes. The fool accepted the invitation to fight.

They stood opposite, with fists raised and at the ready.

Roxbury would never admit it to anyone, but he felt the stirring of feelings for Lady Somerset. Those messy, inconvenient, confusing things that led to all manner of desperate behavior and heartache.

Feelings were no stranger to him. While most of his lovers were, admittedly, casual flings, he did have some passionate affairs of the heart. Those had sparked instantly and burned out quickly.

But this slow, smoldering interest in Lady Somerset was troubling because it was based on learning her rather than a sudden explosion of attraction, a passionate indulgence, and an interest that faded swiftly. All this, when by all rights he ought to despise her.

Around and around he and his opponent circled, fists at the ready. The buck had a vaguely familiar face, but he couldn't place it, or attach a name. His opponent, whoever he was, attempted a jab to Roxbury's jaw, which was easily evaded. Apparently, they were not playing by gentlemen's rules.

It was something about the way she strolled into White's dressed as a man, yet still accepted his hand when alighting the carriage. It was the sharp twists and turns of their conversation that were so enthralling that he forgot about ogling her . . . almost.

She had a marvelous figure, that Lady Somerset. Too bad she kept it covered.

In short, she appealed to both his brain and body. She might have been the first one to do so, and he couldn't remember a face or a name of one of his previous women. Only Julianna came to mind.

Roxbury's fists burned, and sweat beaded on his forehead but brushing it away wasn't worth the risk. Another jab evaded, another blow avoided.

This thing he felt about her was new, even though he was a renowned lover of women. He loved loving them, he enjoyed their company and delighted in bedding them. But when it came to an attachment beyond physical desire—well, that was uncharted territory that he did not intend to travel.

Of course, he also intended that he should never marry.

His fist shot out, blocking a potential blow from his opponent.

That damned ultimatum . . . it hung over his head like a blade from a guillotine. The clock ticked, the days passed, the sweat dripped into his eyes and his heart pounded.

All the while, his hands were bound, rendering him powerless, frustrated, and hopeless. He couldn't honor that damned ultimatum even if he wanted to. But he didn't want to.

Another punch blocked, another light step out of range, again dodging the onslaught.

Roxbury did not want to lose by default, either. He was a proud man, a wealthy aristocratic man. He did not passively accept his lot, but forged his fate with his bare hands and force of will.

Even if a woman did everything she could to destroy him. At the thought of her, and his fate, and the image of the guillotine and her voice—by God, her voice—reciting her latest "Fashionable Intelligence," Roxbury's blood hit the boiling point and spilled over.

His fist shot out, sure, quick, and steady. It landed solidly in his opponent's gut. The man doubled over, breathless, and then collapsed.

That's how he felt when he'd read Lady Somerset's latest column.

He thought of it now and heard it again in her voice. It was the sound of betrayal:

Lord R— was seen obviously enjoying the company of his 'cousin' from Shropshire—a fetching young man, by all accounts—at White's, where they spoke at length in a private tête-à-tête over the wager book.

And the contents of that wager book? Dear readers, I am delighted to share . . .

Chapter 18

Roxbury's house, the study
Later that evening . . .

With a brandy in his very bruised hand, Roxbury dwelled upon the rest of the bad news—there was more, beyond Julianna's column once again depicting him as having a taste for men, and now *young* men! He shuddered.

Though he knew they were not, it seemed as if Lady Somerset, the Man About Town, and his own damned father seemed to be conspiring against him.

The Times featured another tell-all from a courtesan whom he had not, in fact, bedded. Between these two gossip columns he had reportedly tupped most of London—female *and* male. He was exhausted just reading about it.

The Man About Town also reported the following:

Lady Hortensia Reeves was overheard saying of Lord R—, his lovers, and the rumors: she didn't care who, what, where, when, how, he bedded; she would have him as her husband any day.

He still had options: he could marry Lady Hortensia Reeves, secure his fortune, and carry on with his affairs while his wife pined away for him. All of her property—those collections of dung beetles, bottle caps, embroidery samples, four-leaf clovers, and assorted house pets—would become his.

The thought made his stomach churn—though not as much as the letter he received from his father.

The old man was writing from Bath, where he and the countess were visiting with relations and taking the waters. Rumors were reaching them about Roxbury's exploits, but the earl still expected him to tie the knot by the end of the week—or accept the consequences.

Seven days. He had a mere seven days to determine his fate.

It was tempting to say to hell with the ultimatum. With some concessions to frugality and economization, living off of the income from his own small estate was possible.

Here he paused, thoughtful, took a sip of his drink, and began to pace in his study, which was one of two rooms in his house that had not been violated by an angry ex-mistress.

The temptation to refuse marriage, to refuse to be manipulated, to refuse to participate in this ultimatum was more than great. It was a seductive, empowering course of action he didn't know why he hadn't thoroughly considered earlier.

He would not need to marry Lady Hortensia Reeves. He would not need to marry anyone.

He could afford to laugh off Lady Julianna's column and wait for the ton to forget. In time, they would. And, in time, he would inherit—that was a given. Until then, he would just make do with a little less and live on credit. That was not as horrendous a prospect as it had been before.

His pulse began to quicken. He hadn't been desperate enough to consider this earlier, but now that he was—

There was a knock at the door.

"Enter," he barked. It was Timson, his valet, who was discrete (had never uttered a word about his master publicly), and unflappable (never batted an eyelash when Roxbury returned the next morning in clothing that had spent the better portion of the night crumpled on the floor in a lady's bedchamber).

He was also anything but subservient.

It was as appalling as it was fiendishly amusing.

"My lord. Will you be needing to dress for the ball at Lord and Lady Rathdonnell's tonight?" Timson asked.

"Rathdonnell? Ball?" Roxbury echoed. It'd been some time since an invitation graced his home.

"You had replied favorably to the hostess when she sent her invitations out."

"When was that?"

"A few weeks ago," Timson said with a shrug.

"Ah. Before."

Timson wisely elected not to say anything. Like anyone else, he read the papers.

"Well, I don't know if I shall attend," Roxbury said grandly, sipping his brandy. Since he might not take a wife after all, that certainly negated any reason for him to go.

Yet, a glance around the study at the fire in the grate and all the fine things gave him second thoughts.

Timson leaned against the doorframe, utterly bored.

"The invitation has not been revoked, which suggests that Lady Rathdonnell is half hoping that I will come if only to provide amusement for her guests and fodder for the gossip columns."

Timson sighed.

"However, I also ought to take a wife, quickly."

Timson raised an eyebrow. He was not aware of the ultimatum shadowing his master's life. Should he refuse to comply? Choose poverty? He was not yet certain.

"Lord knows there are not any potential wives for me lying around the house."

"Aye, that there ain't."

"Are not," Roxbury corrected. "Yet, given my precarious social standing at the moment, and my experiences of the past week, I cannot expect that any sort of decent female would acknowledge me at the ball, were I to attend."

Other than Lady Hortensia Reeves or, possibly, Julianna. Both women were reasons to consider disregarding that damned ultimatum.

Back and forth, he paced, pausing only to occasionally take a sip.

"It's not a simple matter, Timson."

To his valet, it was just an issue of whether or not to attend a party. To Roxbury, this was somehow his future. To adhere to the ultimatum, or not? Poverty or matrimony? Subservience to his father, or the master of his own destiny?

While Roxbury paced and debated a decision that was now taking on epic proportions, Timson brushed imaginary lint off his jacket.

"Can you not even pretend to care?" Roxbury demanded.

"If you paid me more," his servant drawled.

"No other employer would tolerate such insubordination. You know that, do you not?"

"Aye, my lord," Timson said with a grin.

God only knew where Timson came from. He had been a valet for one of Roxbury's old Oxford friends who had no tolerance for his servant's surly, insubordinate attitude and fired him. Roxbury had found Timson vastly amusing, so he hired him.

"As I was saying . . ." Roxbury carried on before he was cut off.

"You were saying that you can't decide if you are going to the ball tonight because you are not certain of anyone acknowledging you. You are also making the error of presuming that I care. I only wish to know if you need proper evening attire, or if you are going to drink yourself into a stupor at home in your shirtsleeves."

"Well, when you phrase it like that, Timson, my course of action is clear."

Chapter 19

Three hours later
At Lord and Lady Rathdonnell's ball

It was abundantly clear that Roxbury's reputation had sunk to outrageously low levels when London's most notorious talker, Lady "Drawling" Rawlings, put her nose in the air and refused to look him in the eye as she passed by without uttering a word.

The only person who deigned to speak to him was Lady Stewart-Wortly, and that was solely for the purposes of attempting to convert him and, more likely, causing a scene that would land in the papers, thus gaining publicity for her book, *Lady Stewart-Wortly's Daily Devotional.*

"I fear for your soul, Roxbury," she said earnestly, clutching his palm to her chest, ever-so-slightly north of her bosoms. How tragic that lately the closest he'd come to a woman's breast was that of this overbearing evangelizing matron.

Roxbury thought of Julianna's marvelous breasts, and the way they swelled above the bodice of her gowns. His mouth went dry and he sipped his champagne. It went without saying that he would much rather have his hands pressed to Julianna's.

"Your God-given, eternal, immortal soul," Lady Stewart-Wortly pressed on. As she thought of his soul, he thought of a woman's breasts. That made him grin.

"Thank you for your concern, madam," he replied, extricating his hand. "You need not worry yourself. I am not concerned in the slightest."

Her brow furrowed, considering his lack of worry about his eternal salvation and other weighty matters. Roxbury took a sip of champagne, nodded, and began to walk away.

"But—" she began.

"Worry leads to wrinkles," he murmured with a suggestive nod, and her hand flew up to touch the fine lines in her forehead. Then Lady Stewart-Wortly recalled her reputation for deriding vanity and other earthly concerns.

"It is not only you, of course, but young people today!" she carried on. He winced as he recognized her sermon voice booming forth. 'There is an epidemic of wild and unchristian behavior!"

She adopted the tone and volume of a preacher and carried on about the morals of the youth today, of ladies led astray by novel reading, and of gentlemen engaged in all manner of debauchery.

"I wish," Roxbury muttered under his breath. He scanned the ballroom for Lady Somerset's telltale auburn hair and statuesque figure.

Lady Stewart-Wortly added that surely he was well aware of the evils she spoke of.

"Unfortunately, madam, of late I have not had

even the passing acquaintance with evil or even the merely naughty. I intend to rectify that as soon as possible," he answered, and grinned when Lady Stewart-Wortly's complexion took on the hue of an eggplant.

Those nearby—Wilcox, Count Forsque, and Lady Walmsly among them—were listening with varying levels of discretion. Lord Walpole strolled away, apparently bored, and asked a young lady to waltz.

Roxbury downed his champagne, wished he could do the same, accepted another drink from a passing footman, and entertained his own inner dialogue.

It's not true! he wanted to bellow. *I am not the sinner you think I am.*

I love women—I love making love to women.

"Such behavior is an affront to all that is sacred," Lady Stewart-Wortly persisted. She clutched his arm so that he could not leave. Again, he looked for Julianna; somehow this scene was all her fault and he wanted to complain to her about it—preferably in a dark, secluded place where the ranting might turn to something equally passionate, though much more romantic.

Nothing is as sacred to me as the pleasure between a man and a woman.

That was his church; that was the altar at which he worshipped.

"We have a duty to refuse temptation and to deny the fleeting pleasures they afford," she insisted in a bellow that disturbed the gossipy, trivial, and pleasant conversations in the vicinity.

Life was too short to deny exquisite, earthly

*pleasures like the smile of a beautiful woman; her
sigh when a man touched her just right; waking up
with a woman's head resting on your chest; lovemaking in the morning, or afternoon, or night.*

*Or a sweet, private glance in a crowded room,
of the heightened senses at the start of a new love
affair, of soulful pleasure of a good, deep, passionate kiss with a woman on the verge of utter
abandon.*

Roxbury was not sure which woman he was
angrier at—Lady Somerset for penning the fateful words that cast him out of his heaven or Lady
Stewart-Wortly for publicly taking him to task for
a supposed crime he did not commit, and for the
purpose of championing her own cause, namely
God, Christianity and above all, *Lady Stewart-
Wortly's Daily Devotional for Pious and Proper
Ladies.*

Roxbury downed the rest of his champagne in
one long, defiant swallow.

"I am praying for you, Roxbury," Lady Stewart-
Wortly said earnestly, with her enormous bosom
heaving.

A dozen rude thoughts crossed his mind. In
the end, he suggested that she save her prayers for
things that actually mattered more than idle good-
for-nothing rakes, like starving children or destitute widows. The list could go on, but he left it at
that. The point had been made.

As the Man About Town waltzed with a young,
talkative debutante, he listened for something
useful to his column. Young girls never knew what
to keep private, especially the ones on their first

year out. It was almost embarrassing how indiscrete they were.

Lady Charlotte Brandon was full of outrageous tales, but not one of them containing any sort of printable, verifiable gossip. Instead, he kept an eye on Roxbury who was stuck listening to one of Lady Stewart-Wortly's tirades. He couldn't hear, but he could see her posture, and it was that of a preacher in full swing. As the girl chattered on about some Miss Millicent Strangle or Strange or something, the Man About Town composed the item for the next column in his head.

Seen at a party: Lord R— drinking heavily while suffering through one of Lady S—W—'s tirades against debauchery, vice, pleasure, and other enjoyable activities worth living for. (We know you are reading this, Lady S— W—!). Our hats go off to Lord R— for managing to endure her for a record ten minutes. On behalf of gossips everywhere, we hope her efforts at reform are unsuccessful.

Chapter 20

Between the glasses of brandy Roxbury had consumed at home and the copious amount of champagne he drank at the ball, he was now good and drunk. Utterly, totally foxed one might say. Three sheets to the wind. Deep in his cups, etcetera, etcetera.

He almost entered the wrong vehicle, were it not for the excessive decoration of the Roxbury carriage—the family crest was emblazoned in gold and silver leaf—reminding him which was his.

Drunk as he was, one thing was clear to him after this evening: He was not going to marry anyone, ever. To hell with his father's ultimatum. To hell with the lectures of Lady Stewart-Wortly. To hell with Lady Somerset and her "Fashionable Intelligence."

He would live on credit, his own meager income, and his own damn wits rather than do his father's bidding, and let Lady Stewart-Wortly think she had reformed him. If he had nothing to lose, Lady Somerset and her loathsome column would have no power over him.

A surge of triumph coursed through him. To hell with it all!

But then his thoughts turned to Lady Somerset. She was supposed to attend the ball tonight, so he could express his frustration, disappointment, and anger about her latest column directly to her lovely face. He did not see her, and he had looked.

"Home, my lord?" his driver asked.

Roxbury thought about it for a second.

"To 24 Bloomsbury Place," he told his driver. He did not know what he intended to do when he got there. In his drunken state, it seemed imperative that he give her a piece of his mind.

Then he was going to celebrate his freedom— loudly and publicly. That was the thing about having no reputation to salvage, he thought drunkenly. It opened up all kinds of opportunities for scandalous behavior with minimal consequences.

To that end, he sent the driver to procure a bottle of champagne from a nearby tavern. Roxbury waited with the horses.

The neighborhood was quiet, for the hour was late. Everyone was either in bed or at a ball. Soon enough, however, people would start arriving home and the sun would rise not long after that. Servants would begin their chores, and deliveries from all over London would arrive. Gossipy housewives would open the curtains and survey the Square. Working men would leave for their offices. The city would come to life.

Everyone would see the unmistakable Roxbury carriage parked directly in front of the house of the respectable Lady Julianna Somerset.

He laughed softly to himself. An eye for an eye, or a reputation for a reputation.

Most, if not all, would tell a friend on the best authority, who would tell another friend in the strictest confidence, who would tell another friend . . .

By noon every person in London would *know* that Roxbury had spent the night at the home of Lady Somerset.

A woman's reputation was a delicate thing, vulnerable to the merest whisper of scandal. A gentleman took care of a lady's good name. That was a well-known fact. Roxbury knew all of that.

He also knew that Julianna had played fast and loose with his reputation—she had only suggested he was a lover of men, but that had been enough to destroy him socially. That was why he was going to very publicly spend the night at a woman's house, and why that lucky lady was Julianna Somerset.

And so, drunkenly and defiantly, Roxbury uncorked the bottle of champagne his driver had brought for him. And then he began to sing.

Chapter 21

Julianna awoke to the bizarre sound of a man singing in the dead of the night. At first she thought she was dreaming. After lying quietly and listening to the words, she knew the singing must be real, for never in her wildest dreams would she come up with such lyrics herself.

> *A country John in a village of late,*
> *Courted young Dorothy, Bridget, and Kate,*
> *And . . . Julianna Somerset.*

Her heart quite stopped at that. Her name was not an original lyric in the song; someone had squeezed it in. She had a sinking, irritating suspicion that she knew who.

After lighting a candle and checking the clock, she noted the hour was long past midnight. His voice, loud and clear, carried on:

> *He went up to London to pick up a lass,*
> *To show what a wriggle he had in his a . . .*

Appalling! She walked over to the window and peered out. The moonlight shined brightly, illuminating a carriage with the gold and silver Roxbury family crest. She would recognize it anywhere. It was parked in front of her house.

She saw Roxbury. In the middle of the street. Bottle in hand. Singing.

This was not good, and that was the understatement of the decade.

"Oh, blazing hell and eternal damnation," she muttered.

O when he got there it was late in the night
Two pretty young damsels appeared in his sight

Roxbury was either a massive idiot or this was a calculated attempt to ruin her. Either way, the result would be the same—she would be destroyed and it would be entirely his fault.

That she deserved it was a fleeting consideration. Nothing quite compared to drunkenly singing grossly inappropriate ballads in the dead of the night outside the window of a proper lady.

Said one to the other here's country John
I'll show him a trick before it be long

Some serenade!

The other houses around the square showed the telltale sign of alert residents—little glows of candlelight began appearing in quite a few windows. Julianna groaned.

Another man's voice pierced through the night air: "Quiet down, you damned fool!"

"Thank you," she said, though no one could hear her.

> *I'm as handsome a girl as any in town,*
> *Why dang it, says he, then I'll give thee a crown.*

She gasped. This was not to be tolerated. Julianna donned her wrapper and went off to find Frank, her man of all work. She found him in the foyer, already preparing to go out and do something.

"Don't you worry, Lady Somerset," he said, and she was comforted that her loyal—and large—servant was going to tend to the situation outside. She looked forward to watching the forcible removal of that infernal nuisance otherwise known as Lord Roxbury.

Julianna went to the window in the drawing room to watch. Except, like anything else involving Roxbury, it was not so simple.

If she hadn't been so blazing mad, it would have been laughable—indeed, she even heard a few neighbors chuckling loudly and cheering at the farce ensuing.

Being in an advanced state of intoxication, Roxbury's movements were wildly unpredictable. Frank was not quick and certainly no fighter, so while another man might have knocked the lights out of Roxbury, Frank tried to wrangle the drunken sot into the carriage. The driver had vanished.

As soon as Frank succeeded in getting Roxbury into the carriage, the drunk buffoon simply burst out through the other door and carried on with his song:

> *O where shall we go for to find a bed,*
> *That I may enjoy your sweet maidenhead.*

"Oh, you bounder!" she cried, but her voice did not carry far.

By now, every resident of Bloomsbury Square was wide-awake and half hanging out an open window to watch—and even participate.

They were not quiet. There were passionate calls for him to shut up and there were violent shouts for him to expire on the spot. A few louts added their own voices to the song, so when Roxbury got to the next verse, his voice was not alone:

> *Why dang it, says she, there's no bed to be found*
> *But I'll show you fine sport as I lie on the ground.*

Julianna thought that there weren't enough curses in the world to express the bottled up, choking, hot, burning, numbing, stunning *rage* she was currently experiencing. Worst of all, in the far recesses of her mind, she could see the humor of the situation—were it happening to someone else, that is. Oh, dear God, the glee that Man About Town would find in this!

The singers gained in number and in strength, drowning out the calls for silence.

> *Oh, then they were all in a woeful condition*
> *They sent up to London to find a physician.*

Julianna issued a strangled cry of mortification, frustration, and blazing anger. Carriages now began to roll into the square, bringing people home from parties. Roxbury's vehicle was parked directly in front of her townhouse, but at an angle that inhibited the passage of others.

A blockage of traffic ensued.

Roxbury continued to sing. His loyal supporters added their voices to his song.

Calls for his immediate death increased in number and in volume.

Everyone in Bloomsbury Square was surely involved now, and with his distinct carriage—thanks to that gold and silver crest—parked directly in front of her house, this fiasco was clearly linked back to her. Not to mention that he had included her name in this vile song!

And when Doctor Mendcock heard of their ills
He sent down amongst them a cartload of pills.

Enough was enough. Julianna did not pause to consider her state of undress—she wore only a dressing gown and wrapper—before opening her front door to confront the drunk, devilish, beast himself.

If there is one thing she'd learned in all her years, it was that men must be managed and if one wished for something done, she ought to just go and do it herself.

"Roxbury," she said in a low voice. He didn't seem to register her appearance. And then she said again, a little louder, "Roxbury."

She folded her arms across her chest. It was cold outside this late, especially when one wore so little. Her anger kept her warm, though. That, and the prickling heat of embarrassment as she realized that nearly all of her neighbors were witnessing her on the street, arguing with Roxbury, while wearing nothing more than a white silk dressing gown, and a silk wrapper of the palest blue.

"My lady calls me!" he cried loudly. She winced.

Some of the singers did not hear him and carried on with the song. Country John got exactly what he deserved, in her opinion.

"Quit your caterwauling, Roxbury, and listen to me carefully."

"I await your command with bated breath, my dear Lady Somerset!" he shouted. She wished she had brought a blunt heavy object or another weapon. A few onlookers shushed in order to overhear. Others kept singing. The calls for silence and death carried on.

"I am not your dear lady. You must leave at once. You are bothering the entire neighborhood." She spoke through clenched teeth, furious with Roxbury and angry with Frank for giving up and returning to the house.

"You break my heart, Lady Somerset," he said, stumbling toward her. Instinctively she took a step back. If there was one thing she loathed more than a rake, it was a drunk one, and one who claimed he cared for her despite all evidence to the contrary. Somerset, all over again. Just with more flair, she had to admit.

"You don't have a heart, Roxbury, and if you did it certainly doesn't beat for me," she told him. He couldn't possibly feel anything for her other than complete disdain and unrelenting hatred. Witness his behavior this evening.

His only response was to launch another ballad:

A wealthy young squire of Tamworth we hear
He courted a nobleman's daughter so fair

In another time, another place, and with an-

other man and a different song, it might have been
romantic to be serenaded outside her window.

The worst part of all—Roxbury was still dashing, even as he stumbled drunkenly toward her. He
treated her to that rakish grin of his that weakened
women's knees and made their hearts skip a beat.
She was not immune, which was the problem.

Oh, she was mad as hell, but she also had to
admit he was a handsome man. In another time,
and place, they might have . . . no, she corrected
her ridiculous train of thought. She and Roxbury
were no match—not in this lifetime, or any other.
Especially not after this escapade.

He opened his arms wide and sang:

And for to marry her it was his intent
All friends and relations gave their consent

Now that she was close enough to hear him
above all the others, she annoyingly noted that
he did have a very fine singing voice. No off-key
wailing from him, but a rich baritone singing of
fair maidens, marriage, and prostitutes. Oh dear
Lord.

The other singers finally caught on to the change
in song and joined him. Their voices filled the
Square and she wouldn't be surprised if they were
audible all the way in Mayfair.

The lady went home with a heart full of love
And gave out a notice that she'd lost a glove

Handsome as he may be, and however fine his
singing voice, what trumped them all was this:

Roxbury's carriage in front of her house. Roxbury causing a scene of epic proportions outside of her residence. Roxbury ruining her, one verse at a time.

She knew she deserved it. She could even faintly discern the humor of the situation. Regardless, Julianna was furious about it all.

It had been foolish of her to step outside and engage the enemy, but her rage had clouded rational thought. Had she known what he was about to do next, she would have never left the house.

Roxbury stumbled toward her, wrapping an arm around her waist. As she tried to disentangle herself, he leaned forward and drunkenly pressed his mouth against hers for a hot, fleeting, drunken, damaging kiss.

Julianna shoved him away easily, but it was too late. For this, all this, he would suffer. She would see to it.

It was too late to deny that any of this was attached to her. The only thing she could possibly do to salvage this situation—and her precious reputation—was to make it abundantly clear that this behavior was not welcome or encouraged by her.

She turned her back on him, and returned to the house.

"Don't go, my lady!" Roxbury called.

"Penny, the pistols please," Julianna said to her maid, who was watching from the open front door.

In the drawing room where she took tea and entertained visitors, Julianna calmly cleaned and loaded the guns. They were a lovely but mismatched set. One had belonged to her late father, the other her late husband. These were now the only protection those gentlemen offered her, not that they provided much more when they were living.

Taking the one that had been Somerset's, Julianna marched outside. Her silk wrapper billowed around her. It was not the typical shooting attire, but she did not have time to change.

From where she stood on her front stoop, in close range to the bane of her existence, Julianna aimed her pistol and pulled the trigger.

Chapter 22

Roxbury was enjoying this immensely. He was the ringleader of the Bloomsbury Square Singers! Their voices were rising in song to drown out the naysayers in perfect unison. Some of the more vocally ambitious had added a harmony. It was an exquisite event, the likes of which hadn't happened before and would probably never occur again.

And when she was married she told of her fun
How she went a-hunting with her dog and gun

Julianna did not seem tremendously pleased with the performance of his neighborhood serenade. No matter; with bottle in hand, jacket long gone, his cravat limp and waistcoat unbuttoned, he sang louder.

But now I have got him fast in a snare
I'll enjoy him forever, I vow and declare

No snare for him, Roxbury thought drunkenly. He would not marry. He would not surrender his freedom to his father and participate in that damned ultimatum.

When she reappeared, his singing stopped. Her wrapper and nightgown—pale blue and pure white in the moonlight—billowed around her as she stepped into the night. Ghostly. Hauntingly beautiful. His breath caught in his throat and he stopped singing.

The Bloomsbury Square Singers carried on without him.

Her hair tumbled down her back. In the daylight, he knew her hair was auburn, verging on red, and tonight it was purely dark and luscious.

Roxbury had wondered what it would be like to see her thus. Now that he did, he began to wonder what it would feel like to run his fingers through her hair, or to see those long, lovely locks splayed against his pillow or just slightly covering her bare breasts.

Roxbury stood admiring her, lost in fantasy, with the neighbors singing more of "The Golden Glove." She raised her hand, and he saw that she held something and squinted to see what, exactly. His vision was a bit blurry, but some things were clear: Lady Somerset held a pistol and she aimed it at him.

In fact, he saw about eight Lady Somersets holding eight pistols, every last one pointed at him.

She wouldn't dare shoot him! Very well, she would—but not here and now with every resident of Bloomsbury Place watching. That would be stupid and she was frighteningly intelligent.

Smugly sure that she wasn't going to pull the trigger, Simon lifted the bottle of champagne to his lips for one last sip and then he joined the chorus of singers for a repeat of the last line.

. . . I vow and declare . . .

The explosion of the gunshot was breathtakingly loud. In an instant, the singers quieted down, and those hollering for silence ceased their yells.

Simon dropped the bottle of champagne and it shattered on the cobblestones at his feet.

The lady's expression was calm and collected—which was as terrifying as it was beautiful. Glancing behind him, he saw that her aim had been perfect: her bullet hit the dead center of the Roxbury crest emblazoned on the side of the carriage. The wood splintered and the gold leaf chipped. The point was definitely made.

Strangely, his arm ached.

"My dear lady," he mumbled, stumbling toward her intent upon something like an apology and congratulating her for her outstanding marksmanship.

"I. Am. Not. Your. Dear. Lady." Julianna sauntered closer to him, her hips swaying ominously. His heart began to pound. The Square was quiet now, but everyone was probably watching.

They stood toe-to-toe, and she tilted her head back slightly to look him in the eye. He squinted, so that he would see the one and only Julianna and not the doubles and triples the alcohol made him see.

It occurred to him that they were within kissing distance, which was to say, not very much distance at all. But though the Square was now quiet, it was erroneous to presume all had gone to bed. It was best not to kiss her—not here, not now, not *again* and not when he was unsure how many bullets she had left to fire. But he wanted to.

"Roxbury," she said his name as if it were a warning. "If you are intent upon revenge and ruining my reputation, so be it, but at the very least—oh dear God you're bleeding!"

Chapter 23

The good news: it could only be a flesh wound. Julianna concluded that the bullet must have grazed or gone through his arm before piercing the crest on his carriage.

The bad news: her choices consisted of allowing him to potentially bleed to death on her front stoop, or to bring him inside and bandage him up. She had debated which was more scandalous. A dead rake in the night? Or a live one emerging from her home in the morning?

Reluctantly, she decided she ought to let him live. Looks and charm like his shouldn't be wasted.

Second thoughts swiftly followed. But nevertheless, she brought him into the drawing room.

"Remove your shirt, Roxbury," she ordered wearily.

"Oh my, Lady Somerset. How forward of you," he mumbled, stumbling around.

"Please, before you bleed all over the furniture," she said.

"Yes, madam, I shall remove my shirt. Breeches, too?" he asked with a rakish grin. She sighed impatiently.

His attempt to remove his shirt involved much drunken stumbling and strange contortions. Julianna gave up and laughed at him. That is, until he took it off.

The notorious rake Roxbury stood nearly naked in her drawing room, and what a marvelous sight it was. In the dim glow of candlelight, his chest appeared golden, taut and smooth, save for the contours and shadows of his muscles. Somerset was nothing compared to Roxbury, but Julianna did not want to think of her dead husband now. Not when a real, live man displayed himself thusly, intensely watching for her reaction, which was a combination of speechlessness and wide-eyed wonder.

Fortunately, he could not see the heat surging through her and rising to her cheeks. Or the way she was suddenly acutely aware of her silk nightgown caressing her skin. Or perhaps he could see these things—this was Roxbury, after all.

Then, again, she recalled the wound on his arm, which was up near his shoulder and bleeding quite profusely. Roxbury at least had the sense to press his shirt to it.

With Penny's assistance, she cleaned and bandaged the wound, which was not serious at all. He'd been a surprisingly docile patient, but only because the alcohol had finally claimed victory.

Julianna sat beside her wretched, undeserving patient alone with her thoughts, and the facts. The bane of her existence lay unconscious and in a state of undress on her settee. Outside, his damned carriage was parked in front of her townhouse. The driver had vanished. Nearby were the remains of a shattered champagne bottle on the cobblestones.

This was it, then—she knew social ruin when she saw it. Or, in this case, when it serenaded her with debauched ballads, parked in front of her house, and included compromising positions and gunshot wounds.

There would be talk, and it would be vicious and incessant. The ton would assume that he had spent the night and no one would believe it a chaste encounter. Yes, he'd been loud and kept the neighborhood up half the night. But the other half—after all of Bloomsbury Square saw them enter her house together—was unaccounted for.

Given that the man in question was Lord Roxbury—rumors of his partner preferences aside—who had spent his entire social life known as a tremendous flirt, scoundrel, lover of many women, and all-around rake, there was no way anyone would believe he and a woman hadn't spent the late night hours in sin together.

She was a widow. And she knew what the ton would think. It wouldn't be good. All those years of trying to make herself respectable after Somerset's exploits were now for naught. She was about to go down in a massive, flaming explosion of ruin.

Would she have to change her name and move to America? As long as she had her column to write, she would be fine. Julianna had weathered scandals before and was determined to do so again, but a tight little knot in her stomach suggested this would be no run-of-the-mill scandal.

Julianna gave one last glance to the idiot rake on her settee. He had the nerve to smile in his slumber. She went to her bed—alone—but she did not sleep.

Chapter 24

The following morning, it was no surprise to Roxbury that the lady of the house was not pleased to find him at her breakfast table. He gathered that his presence in her house had to do with the bandage on his arm. There was singing in the street, he recalled with a lazy smile. The gunshot was remembered less favorably. Clearly, he had caused a scene. Little by little details returned to him as he drank his coffee.

After he'd just poured a second cup, Julianna sauntered into the breakfast room, soft from sleep. First she glared at him, then her eyes widened and her lips parted when she noticed he did not have a shirt on, just his waistcoat. He hadn't been able to find his shirt or jacket.

She gave a sharp look to her maid, Penny, that asked, *What is he still doing here?*

"I'm sorry, milady. But he's a charmer," was all her redheaded maid said by way of explanation.

"Please find him his shirt. Promptly," Julianna ordered. Penny gave him a wink before she left him alone with the shooting she-devil.

Roxbury suppressed a smirk. He was glad to know his talents for charm hadn't gotten too rusty since he'd been out of practice lately. It was one of his rules of seduction and love affairs to always enlist a lady's maid to his cause. Success was impossible without her favor. It was something Edward had taught him.

Not that Roxbury had such intentions with Julianna. But he did recall that she looked like quite the temptress last night. A vision returned, unbidden, of her wrapper and silk nightgown, of the palest blue and nearly sheer white. She'd been magnificent. Had Somerset known what he had? Or had he been too terrified of such towering strength and beauty?

Roxbury knew not, and as he took a sip of coffee turned his thoughts to Julianna. It was a gross violation of etiquette to be at a table, shirtless, in front of a gently bred lady. But what could be done?

Julianna prepared a cup of tea for herself.

"Ah, nothing like tea to restore nerves, now is there," he quipped. It was remarkably effective. Since he had kept her up half the night with his neighborhood serenade, he suspected she would be in great need of it.

"I am remarkably calm," she stated. Her voice was still a little low and raspy from having just woken. He loved a woman's voice first thing in the morning. Suddenly, he was not sorry to be here.

"You are not fully awake and haven't yet come to your wits," he said. And when she did, those pistols would reappear. Hopefully he'd be long gone by then.

"Why are you still here?" she asked. "If you had any decency you would have left at first light."

He felt a fleeting pang of guilt, but ignored it. "I was in great need of coffee when I woke this morning. I slept in; it seems I was out quite late last evening." In other words, he was a drunken, lazy, good-for-nothing bounder who had wreaked all sorts of havoc on Julianna's life, just for a spot of amusement. That thought made him nauseous and he set down his coffee.

"You will ruin me," she whispered.

"My dear Lady Somerset, I already have." He tried to make his voice sound grand and carefree when that wasn't how he felt at all. Aye, she deserved it. But that did not bring him much pleasure.

A long silence ensued, in which she quietly sipped her tea. He noticed that her hand wavered—in anger or anxiety—and any feeling of triumphant revenge began to evaporate. His head began to ache and guilt began to burn in his gut. His arm started to throb in pain.

But it wasn't like she was an unmarried young woman—in which case he'd be obliged to offer for her, right here and right now. Since she was a widow, the same rules did not apply. So he did not have to beg her hand in marriage on bended knee in her breakfast room. While he had no intention of taking a wife, he did stand to gain—tremendously—if he married.

However, Roxbury suspected Julianna would accept utter social ostracism, change her name, and move to another country before she became his wife.

Roxbury sipped his coffee and dared a glance at her; she was glaring at him. Still, she managed to be beautiful.

Her hair was piled loosely atop her head. She wasn't as wide-eyed as usual—not when she was sleepy, and not when she was glaring—and it made her seem more mysterious.

He didn't know much about her at all, really, other than that she was always so tightly coiled and tense. She fiercely loved her writing and she was uncommonly daring. Her late husband had been a bad man. And she was the one woman in London who was not swayed by his charm.

What the hell was he doing here?

Playing fast and loose with a respectable woman's reputation and then sitting at her breakfast table, drinking coffee, uninvited. He had sung "Country John" outside her window, with the whole neighborhood joining in. She had put a bullet through his carriage and his arm.

Last night had been hazy and now that the pieces came together, he was beginning to grasp the enormity of the scandal that was about to clobber them both.

His behavior had not been gentlemanly. But Lady Sharpshooter in a nightgown hadn't been very ladylike, either.

What was it about her that reduced him to the behavior of an uncontrollable young lad, or provoked him to the most ungentlemanly outbursts? She incited his passions in the worst way.

Was it her beauty, or sharp wit, or the way she sipped her tea—obviously exasperated but still so very pretty?

Warily, he watched as she set down her tea and rang the bell. Penny returned quickly, with Roxbury's revolting, bloodstained shirt from last night.

He cringed at the thought of wearing it, but the alternative was to drive through London shirtless or request something else.

"The pistols, please, Penny."

"No need. I was just leaving," he said hastily, because Penny probably had them ready to fire.

"Pity, that," Julianna said dryly.

Roxbury stepped out of 24 Bloomsbury Place at midmorning, only to find an entire congregation filtering out of the church across the Square. More than a few people saw him, and pointed.

He winced, aware of what a spectacle he was, going out lacking a jacket or cravat. But the bloodstained shirt was so vile, he considered going without it. Pete, his driver, was missing, and the poor horses had been left there all night.

There was no choice but to drive his bullet-ridden carriage through London, wearing a bloodstained shirt and horrified expression as he began to comprehend the magnitude of the scandal that was about to hit.

Poverty or matrimony or defiance? Mere days remained for him to decide, but what choice did he really have?

Chapter 25

Fortunately, Julianna's friends would be there to help her weather the storm. They gathered in her drawing room later that afternoon. The curtains were drawn, blocking out the sunlight and the rest of the world. Penny provided tea and biscuits. Sophie brought issues of *La Belle Assemblée*. Annabelle and Eliza joined, too, with one providing optimism and the other offering the truth of the matter.

"The news is all over town, is it not?" Julianna asked, dreading the answer. Sophie nibbled on a biscuit and Eliza took a sip of tea. That was a yes.

"It has yet to be mentioned by the Man About Town," Annabelle offered consolingly. She brushed a blond curl out of her pretty blue eyes.

"That's because his column will not be published until tomorrow," Eliza answered before helping herself to another lump of sugar in her tea.

"And then it will be mentioned," Julianna said. "Prominently. In great depth. I am ruined."

No one knew quite what to say to that and they

all looked sheepishly away, uncomfortable by their silence.

To be fair, it was hard to fathom what a disaster it might be. No one could recall an instance of a gentleman acting so brazenly to a lady. Leaving his carriage parked in front of her home all evening! Singing a vile song like "Country John" in the presence of ladies, and in public! Not to mention how he knelt before her and wrapped his arms around her, or how he was seen entering her house at night, and leaving the next morning. And then there was the gunshot, too.

On the scandal scale, this could rank somewhere far above a third waltz, higher than a couple discovered in a compromising position but just a shade below a particularly gruesome murder of a prominent member of high society. Just. Barely.

The Baron of Pinner had once shocked an audience at a party by reciting limericks he'd composed as odes to certain parts of his lovely bride's anatomy. Fortunately, his lady had a sense of humor. But that was not quite the same as Roxbury bellowing naughty ballads outside her window for the whole neighborhood to hear. It wasn't followed by gunshots, either. And the baron and his lady were married.

Yes, the scandal would be as bad as she feared.

She prayed the scandal would fade quickly. Or perhaps the ton would take Roxbury to task, sparing her. But society was never kind to a woman of questionable morals. Her invitations were at stake—and with them, her livelihood. She needed her good reputation like she needed air or water— to survive.

"Any consolation? Any at all?" Julianna queried with desperation seeping into her voice. She could think of none herself.

"It'll be fine! The scandal will blow over in no time," Sophie said breezily.

"There will be no scandal at all." Amazingly, Annabelle declared such nonsense confidently.

Eliza set down her teacup and saucer with a clatter and a roll of her eyes.

"Oh, please," she said bluntly. "Everybody knows that Roxbury spent the better portion of the night here, and the Man About Town will write extensively upon it. There will be a scandal. The question is, Julianna, what do you intend to do about it?"

"Thank you, Eliza, for being the voice of reason," Julianna replied, even though her stomach began to ache at her friend's declaration.

"Well, what are you going to write in your column?" Sophie asked.

"Hopefully, I am going to cover someone else's news, which I prefer to be a shocking elopement or high-profile society murder or something that will make my news seem completely insignificant. Because nothing really happened."

"We could murder Roxbury," Sophie suggested, then calmly took a sip of her tea.

"Sophie!" Annabelle gasped.

"The idea has some merit, though I'd be the primary suspect," Julianna said.

"Julianna!" Annabelle cried out.

"I was jesting, anyway," Sophie replied. And then to Julianna she shook her head to say no, she was not joking. Eliza caught it and smirked.

"You must write about your own scandal, Juli-ana," Eliza said. "Otherwise you might risk reveal-ing yourself as the Lady of Distinction. You cannot do that, and certainly not over this."

"You have all the details that no one else has," Annabelle pointed out. "Particularly you-know-who."

Julianna nodded thoughtfully. "I think you're both right."

"But what are you going to do about Roxbury?" Sophie asked.

"What if he refuses to marry you?" Annabelle asked with a little line of worry above her blue eyes.

"Marry? *Marry?*" Julianna echoed. She would never marry again, and certainly not the likes of him. Annabelle, bless her, was far too romantic and optimistic.

"Everyone thinks he spent the night," Sophie stated. "Everyone is expecting a proposal."

Julianna looked around at her friends, and won-dered if they were lingering over tea and biscuits so they might be present when Roxbury recovered his manners and returned to propose on bended knee.

"I'm a widow. It's not the same as if I were a young unmarried girl," Julianna pointed out. Hopefully, enough of the ton would see it that way as well. "I refuse to marry him. Nothing could impel me to marry him. I have my column, a live-lihood, and a house of my own. I will not bind myself to another degenerate rake who will ignore my affections, trample my trust, and devastate my life."

Sophie reached out and took Julianna's hand. They did not speak of the late Lord Somerset. He'd been Harry to her once. Julianna had loved him, once.

Sophie had helped her elope—everything from whispered plans, to secretly packing her things and stealing off in the night. Sophie had lied to everyone about Julianna's whereabouts ("She took ill whilst staying with me, I'm nursing her") so Julianna and Harry could get a good start on their journey to Gretna.

As the marriage began its slow crumble, Sophie had been her confidante. Sophie, of all her friends, had to know that marriage to another great lover of women, plural, was utterly out of the question.

She could not trust that she would survive another marriage like her first.

Julianna sighed. "Well, I suppose I do have some 'Fashionable Intelligence' to share."

A few hours after her fellow writing girls had departed, Julianna rang for Penny.

"The pistols again, ma'am?" Penny asked, prompting Julianna's laughter.

"No, I have something more effective. This can be sent to Knightly." She handed her maid a sheet that had been folded and sealed.

It was the latest edition of "Fashionable Intelligence," short and sweet:

Given Lord R—'s recently discovered proclivities, first reported in these pages, I find it hard to believe that he spent the night at the home of a famously chaste widow, or that if he did, anything untoward occurred—other than his bellowing and warbling. Perhaps he was serenading some of her handsome footmen?

In other news . . .

"I'll see that he gets it straightaway. And here is the post for today." Penny handed her a slender packet consisting only of tradesmen bills and letters from the country, sent far before last night's scandal. Usually, Julianna received at least a dozen invitations and half as many letters from her friends in London. Any good spirit she'd felt from writing her column had vanished.

"Is this all?" she asked faintly.

When Penny nodded yes, Julianna's heart sank and her mouth went dry. Her social death was just beginning.

Chapter 26

White's

"**I** heard you had quite a night earlier this week," Brandon began the minute Roxbury took a seat next to him. They sat before a blazing fire—just the thing on a rainy day such as it was. It was not gentle late summer rain but a good, solid downpour raging outside.

For the past few days, since That Night, Simon had been laying low at his home, save for the occasional visit to Gentleman Jack's or the club. He was not particularly welcomed at either, but that had been the case for some time now.

"Wait till I've had a drink," Roxbury said, motioning to Inchbald.

"'Country John'?" Brandon queried. The song that had experienced a massive resurgence in popularity since his drunken, midnight rendition. One could not walk down any street in London without hearing someone singing or whistling the tune.

Lady Stewart-Wortly, ever the killjoy, reportedly fired her footman for humming it under his breath as he went about his duties. The Baron of Pinner had composed additional verses, and those broadsides were selling like hotcakes.

Roxbury only grinned sheepishly.

"You sang "Country John"—a song about prostitutes—at the top of your lungs outside the home of a respectable woman in the middle of the night. You even mentioned said lady by name, and drunkenly kissed her," Brandon recounted in a voice that expressed disbelief. Roxbury knew that it was outrageous and shameful. He also found it a bit humorous, but he kept that to himself.

Inchbald brought over a much-needed brandy and Roxbury thanked him for it.

Once the waiter was gone, Roxbury said in a very low voice, "She's the one that printed the salacious rumors that have destroyed me. We both know that she deserved it."

"I know she was not blameless, but I do know that she does not deserve the utter destruction of her reputation thanks to your serenade—if one could call it that."

"It wasn't *utter* . . ." Roxbury countered.

"The talk about the two of you is vicious. Haven't you heard any of it?"

"No." On his few ventures out, no one dared to speak to him. So he'd had a clue that things were bad. Very bad. But then again, he hadn't been spoken to in some time, thanks to her.

"They are saying that you two have had an affair gone horribly wrong, mostly thanks to talk that you left her house covered in blood. Since that is such a radical departure from the previous behavior of the lady in question, some are wondering what else she is hiding—more lovers? A few? A dozen? You can only imagine what sins they are attributing to her," Brandon said. Then he paused to take a sip of his drink before continuing. "We all know it's one thing for a widow to be discrete with one man, but if she is with many and publicly participating in scandalous scenes—well, that's another thing entirely. Never mind that she is a proper lady who was seen in public, in her night-clothes, and shooting a pistol."

Roxbury shrank down in his chair and took a sip of his drink. His friend showed no sign of stopping. Was this worse than a lecture from his father or not? Since the old man was staying in Bath, Roxbury had been spared a scathing letter—thus far. One had to account for the time it took the news to reach Bath, the old man to recover from the ensuing apoplexy, and then the letter to be delivered to London. He expected the missive any day now.

"And then given your recent rumors and factoring in your supposed tryst with Lady S, everyone is basically assuming you have an outrageous and insatiable appetite. You should see the cartoons, Roxbury. Lady Stewart-Wortly and the like are using you as an example for every ill . . . And calling for a ban on all vices—alcohol, tobacco, salacious literature—lest the next generation follow in your example and become unmarriageable drunks of questionable taste and no restraint."

"Ghastly. I despise being used as a reason to censor anything," Roxbury remarked insouciantly, as he casually took a sip of his drink. It was all to disguise the slow dawning horror he was experiencing.

"That's what you think is the worst of it?" Brandon queried. "What about Lady Somerset's reputation?"

Roxbury sipped his drink. His friend was a notoriously upstanding gentleman—the very finest and best England had to offer. Brandon wasn't overreacting now, though.

Roxbury was deliberately being flippant because to be honest and decent about this disastrous situation was a road he was not yet prepared to travel. There was only one way to possibly salvage a scandalous situation between a man and a woman, and Roxbury dared not consider it.

Because, given the timing of things, it meant that he would do the two things he wanted least in the world—get married, and in time to satisfy his father's ultimatum.

"You are a gentleman," Brandon said quietly, and Roxbury felt the force of the words in his bones.

"You live by higher standards of gentlemanly behavior than any other man could fathom, let alone aspire to," Roxbury answered tensely. Even Brandon's one big scandalous act—marrying a Writing Girl when he'd been betrothed to a duke's daughter—had been done with the utmost decorum and consideration for all parties involved.

"Someone has to set an example," Brandon said.

"Don't look at me," Roxbury replied. Because if he were going to act remotely like the gentleman he was in title . . . He couldn't think about that yet. Instead, he thought about *her*.

She was a complicated woman, that Julianna. Her beauty entranced him; her brash nature and sharp behavior drove him away. And yet he was constantly tempted to incite another battle, so that he may one day win and catch a glimpse of a vulnerable Julianna with her defenses down.

Such a sight was certain to be stunning, delightful and rare, like seeing a unicorn, or a woman in breeches.

Given his extensive experience with women, Roxbury had to wonder about her long silence and dark looks when he asked about Old Somerset. It was an unfortunate fact that there were awful brutes in the world who roamed free. Simon had known a few women who'd suffered thus; eventually they might love and trust again. But it took time. He wondered if Julianna was one of those girls.

Or perhaps she was just mean. Some people were born that way.

He sipped his brandy. Regardless of the reasons Lady Somerset was the way she was, she did not deserve the blacklisting, backstabbing, and general cruelty she was suffering at the hands of high society because of him. He knew as well as anyone that there was one—and only one—cure for such a malady: marriage.

Roxbury took another, longer sip of his brandy. In fact, he finished his glass and waved to Inchbald for more.

She would never accept his proposal, so there was really no point in asking.

Except for that damned vile ultimatum and the money he stood to keep if he were to marry within the week. His options were a very desperate Lady Somerset or Lady Hortensia Reeves. Or proud poverty. He had been so determined to refuse to comply.

Where the devil was Inchbald with the brandy?

And then there was the memory of Edward, laughing as he waved goodbye before galloping down the long drive of the family estate, never to return. Edward would have loved the scene last night, and he would have adored Lady Somerset. Which didn't really matter.

Roxbury wanted to be his own man, not a pawn in the earl's schemes or at the mercy of the haut ton. Would he trade his dignity for money? Just how much was it worth?

After a long silence, when he had been deep in thought, Roxbury announced, "I won't marry her."

"I did not suggest it," Brandon said, not even looking up from the newspaper he'd started reading. It wasn't *The Weekly*. Lady Somerset's "Fashionable Intelligence" had glossed over the events of the other night. The Man About Town, on the other hand. . .

"Yes, you did, in so many words. 'Ruining a lady's reputation, being a gentleman . . .'" Roxbury said.

"She is a widow. It's not quite the same," Brandon replied, using Roxbury's usual defense. He *wanted* to believe it, but he knew it was complete rubbish.

Nevertheless he replied, "Right. It's not at all the same as if she were a young, unmarried chit."

"It's completely different since her late husband was an embarrassingly notorious scoundrel. She has plenty of experience with degenerate rakes disregarding her reputation. I'm sure she expects exactly this sort of behavior," Brandon said casually as he perused the paper.

Ah, Old Somerset. Roxbury took a sip of his drink and recalled, again, her long silence and darkened expression at the mention of her dead husband. Was *he* like Somerset? How bad was her marriage?

"I can't tell if you are saying I'm boring and predictable or the worst sort of scoundrel," Roxbury replied.

"In the mind of a lady, are those things mutually exclusive?" Brandon mused.

"What's with all the philosophizing?"

"We can talk about something else, if you'd like," Brandon offered.

"Yes. Very much," Roxbury said emphatically.

"How about that ultimatum? Any progress on finding a wife?" Brandon asked.

He was obviously fighting a grin.

"Your point is taken," Roxbury said, downing the rest of his brandy.

He should marry her. He ought to. He'd get his money. She'd get her reputation. And, he thought with a derisive smirk, they'd all live happily ever after.

Chapter 27

The offices of The London Weekly

When Julianna first encountered Derek Knightly, it was after she stormed into his office, uninvited or unannounced. Once she had his attention, she told him he ought to have a gossip columnist and it ought to be her.

That brazen spirit and gumption had left her now. She paced and fretted outside of Knightly's office door, gathering her courage to go in. But her thoughts were all jumbled and her nerves were utterly frayed.

Dear merciful Lord above, did the social downward spiral advance at a ghastly speed. There were no more invitations. She had called upon Lady Fairleigh, only to be told that the lady was not at home, even though her laugh drifted from the drawing room into the foyer Mortified, Julianna did not attempt another social call again.

As if it could not possibly be worse, the Man About Town had published a series of horrendous columns exposing her and Roxbury and the scandal she was desperate to dust under the rug. Just one paragraph had her in a mood for days. Her rival had written the following:

We haven't seen Lady S—out since Lord R— caused a commotion singing romantic yet ribald ballads outside her window . . . all night long. Perhaps she is sitting at home awaiting a proposal?

She was *not* waiting for a proposal. Although, it would have been nice to have one so that she could refuse it. When Somerset's body was being lowered into the ground, she swore that she'd never suffer another husband.

But that was neither here nor there because there was no proposal, and no invitations. In a way, it didn't matter because as Lady Somerset she really ought to lay low. But as the Lady of Distinction it was imperative that she be out and about in the social whirl.

She took a deep breath and smoothed her skirts. She wore red, for courage. It was a bold choice with her auburn hair, but that, too, was neither here nor there since a change in attire was out of the question. She'd made it to the offices and it was raining too hard to venture out of doors unless absolutely necessary.

But if she did not go out, how else was she to glean the best tidbits—who was seen waltzing too closely, or walking off with, or discovered with whom? Who was overheard saying something scathing about a rival, or how could she compose reviews of ladies' gowns and reports of men's wagers? Sophie did her best at finding information for her, and she had her network of spies, but Julianna was a professional. She saw it all, stored it in her memory and composed it into lovingly crafted exposés.

Her secret network and the people of London did continue to send their gossip to her at *The London Weekly* with the hopes that she would, as she always did, claim, "a reader from Mayfair provided the following intelligence:" whatever that may be. But they all wrote about her! And they were all false!

A reader from Bloomsbury reported that she had sobbed for two days straight. Another claimed they saw her lurking outside of Roxbury's home.

Another report had her buying a new gown at Madame Auteuil's—as if she had the occasion and the money for such a purchase! The reader suggested the dress was supposed to tempt Roxbury into proposing.

It was all lies, speculation, and complete hogwash. She'd once delighted in just that, but now her heart wasn't in it.

"Come in, Julianna," Knightly called out and she entered his office and stood before his desk as he finished editing another writer's article. The rain lashed against the windows. A fire dwindled in the grate. She shivered, and not necessarily from the cold.

Knightly tucked his pencil behind his ear and focused those vivid blue eyes upon her. Annabelle frequently waxed poetic about his eyes. He leaned back in his chair.

"As you know, Julianna, I am fond of saying—"

"Scandal equals sales. I know," she said, and she marveled at how quiet her voice had become. She was not a tired little mouse, but oh, how she felt like one!

"This equation has always been a reliable one. I've built my empire upon it." Knightly's voice was low and quiet. He didn't need to speak loudly to assert his authority.

"The Writing Girls owe their livelihoods to it," she said.

"Yes," he said, pushing his fingers through his hair thoughtfully. "However, for the first time, the equation has failed."

"Whatever do you mean?" She blinked a few times, perplexed.

"I'm going to read to you from the Man About Town's column," Knightly said, looking her in the eye. Her heart began to sink slowly.

"Oh, that's fine. I've already read it," she said. Read it a dozen times at least, actually. Really, she could not endure it another time.

"No, listen," he insisted, and then he picked up *The London Times* and read the following aloud:

"News from the Man About Town

Every so often a scandal comes along that is so shocking, so delicious, so wildly unexpected that this Man About Town can hardly contain my glee long enough to write.

Glee? Glee! Her life as she knew it was crashing down all around her, and he found it amusing? Not for the first time did she vow to find the Man About Town and expose and ruin him.

Knightly continued reading:

"I hear you all are desperate to know the latest, greatest scandal. Lord R——, whose romantic tastes have been in question of late, has gloriously, publicly, spectacularly given London an answer. The facts: Lord R——'s carriage parked outside of the

*home of Lady S—. All night. Dear readers, there
is more! He sang bawdy ballads, 'Country John,'
in particular. She fired a shot right at the family . . .
crest on the carriage (you thought I was going to
say jewels, did you not?). Lady S—, as we all know,
is the widow of the late Lord S—who set the bar
high on horribly impolite behavior, so this little she-
nanigan of R—'s is nothing to her, we presume."*

Julianna bit her lip to keep from protesting. If
it wasn't one scandalous man in her life, it was
another—and then another reporting on it all!
This time, though, there was so much more on
the line. And they thought it was nothing to her.

In the back of her mind was the nagging thought
that she might deserve this, for hadn't she composed
such gossip and lies herself? Hadn't she also taken
glee in the downfall of others because she knew it
was going to bring in large suppression fees or sell
even more newspapers?

She fought to keep one lone rebellious tear in its
place. She would not cry in front of Knightly. Not
here, not now. He didn't seem to notice. He kept
reading:

*"But why? Ah, that is the question. I, for one,
wonder about those rumors that have been swirl-
ing and circulating around this town for some
time now. Is Lady S—The London Weekly's Lady
of Distinction?"*

The Man About Town was good; she had to give
him that. Except it was so very bad for her. It was
beyond merely *bad*, and completely disastrous, utterly damaging, and absolutely devastating.

"In contrast, this is what you have reported on
the most talked about topic in London," Knightly

said, setting down *The London Times* and picking up an issue of *The Weekly*.

Her knees began to wobble; here she thought the saying "quaking in one's boots" was just a phrase. Unfortunately this was the moment she discovered the truth of it.

Knightly read her words—so few of them on the most popular subject of the moment.

"Given Lord R—'s recently discovered proclivities, first reported in these pages, I find it hard to believe that he spent the night at the home of a famously chaste widow, or that if he did, anything untoward occurred—other than his bellowing and warbling. Perhaps he was serenading some of her handsome footmen?

In other news . . ."

Knightly looked up at her, and his gaze was positively glacial.

"I won't even begin to review the Man About Town's other columns from this week," Knightly said. *Thank God,* she thought. Each one was worse than the last.

"I understand, Mr. Knightly. I will drag my own name through the mud for the benefit of this paper," she said. The hint was taken. Eliza had been correct, and Julianna ought to have listened to her. Her attempts at avoiding the issue weren't doing anyone any favors. It had been an optimistic strategy.

"Julianna . . ."

"It's just that I fought for this name I'm stuck with to mean something other than . . ." She managed to bite back the rest of the words she ached to say: she gave a man her heart, her body, and she took his name and accepted his protection. It was the worst bargain of her life.

Knightly looked uncomfortable at such a personal revelation. She couldn't fault him for it. She decided not to attempt to complete her sentence on the matter.

He cleared his throat and began again. "Julianna—"

"Very well. I'll write more about this scandal. Lord knows that nothing else is happening," she said with a little laugh that was obviously forced. Knightly even winced.

"But when something else does happen, will you be there to report it?" he questioned. His eyes were so blue, and it was disconcerting when he leveled a stare and awaited a good, honest answer.

"Whatever do you mean?" she asked, and her voice sounded high and hollow to her ears. She knew, just knew, where this was going.

"Your position requires you to be a fixture at ton parties. If your reputation is such that you are not invited . . ."

Her heart began to pound so hard she feared Knightly would hear it. Under her gloves, her palms were damp and clammy.

Oh please, don't let this be happening to her! Not now!

"This will all blow over in no time at all," she said breezily. "Why, anything more exciting could happen tomorrow and everyone will forget this rubbish between Roxbury and myself!"

"And if it doesn't?" Knightly asked, skeptically lifting one brow. Her heart pounded harder, if such a thing was possible.

"I have my network of informants and—" she started, but her voice began to falter. And then, she just gave up.

"Lady Somerset, I don't have a family. I don't have a wife or a mistress. I don't have anything that I give a damn about in this world, other than the success of *The London Weekly*."

Once upon a time, she'd brazenly stormed into his office and forged her own fate. It felt like a lifetime ago—a lifetime that was slowly, achingly coming to an end.

Chapter 28

Roxbury had no intentions of proposing, but he could not get the thought out of his mind. He thought about the money and he thought about being the knight in shining armor that rescued the damsel in distress. But then he thought of Edward's last words to him: "A man's life is his own" and he thought of complying with his father's wishes. God, did it rankle to do so.

As he was brooding over this and gazing out the window of his carriage on his way home, he spotted her.

"Speak of the devil," he murmured to himself. The madwoman was walking quickly—stomping and storming one might say—and roughly dodging through slow-moving pedestrians in her path. All of this in the pouring rain.

Roxbury opened the window and shouted her name.

"Lady Somerset!"

She looked up, around, and kept walking. He hollered her name again as raindrops lashed against his face. She was insane to be out in this weather with nothing more than a bonnet and a spencer as protection.

"Lady Somerset!"

He called her name again, and his carriage slowed to her pace, holding up traffic behind him.

"Get in the carriage," he told her, ever the gentleman.

"Go to hell." She snarled the words with a viciousness that surprised him. It might have even wounded him, slightly, but now was not the time to dwell on it. With the window open while he argued with her, rain was getting in the carriage.

"I was already planning on it. Get in the carriage."

"No." It was a heartrending sound.

"Are you mad? It's pouring rain, you are soaked, and I know you are miles away from your home."

"I'd rather walk to France and back than spend five minutes in your presence," she sputtered and then she furiously pushed a soaked strand of hair out of her face.

Roxbury declined to point out the impossibility of walking to France from England. For a moment, he was thoughtful, and then he saw his error. He'd been trying to use logic and reason with a woman. He grinned; she glared and stormed away.

Roxbury shouted to his driver to halt the carriage—ignoring the shouts and protests of those traveling behind them. Then he opened the door and stepped into the storm. Julianna quickened her pace; he did as well.

At the first convenient moment, which was rather soon, he scooped up Lady Julianna Somerset in his arms, as if she were a princess.

"What are you doing? Put me down!" she protested. How shocking.

"I'm saving you, my lady," he replied gallantly.

"Help! Somebody help me!" she cried. He felt sorry for her, truly. But he was acting for his own good. Perhaps even both their good.

"Lover's quarrel," he explained to a few mildly curious onlookers, and this answer seemed to placate them, which was slightly disturbing and further evidence that she should not be walking the streets of London alone. What possessed her to in the first place, he knew not. He got the sense something quite awful had just occurred.

Lady Somerset did not struggle as much as he'd expected, which he interpreted to mean that she really did want a ride in a warm, covered carriage but her pride would not permit her to accept the offer.

Once they were safely ensconced in the carriage Lady Somerset looked at him furiously, and then she removed her bonnet and pushed her wet locks away from her face.

"Are those raindrops or tears upon your cheeks, my fair lady?" he asked. The look she gave him made his insides cold.

"The raindrops are, obviously, from the rain I was recently walking in before I was kidnapped against my will, you wretched, horrible jackanapes. I was walking in the rain, rather than taking a hackney, because . . . because . . ." Lady Somerset couldn't seem to manage the words. She held her fist to her mouth, almost as if she was biting back sobs or trying not to hyperventilate. But that could not be so of the strong and formidable Lady of Distinction.

"As for the tears, well," she continued, once she

found her voice again. "Let's just say that every-thing is your damned fault, Roxbury. I hate you deeply and passionately right now and I am not your lady."

"Brandy?" he offered.

She accepted the bottle and took a small, lady-like sip. She did not sputter and turn red as she did upon her first taste at White's. The lady had been practicing, perhaps?

Roxbury reached down under the cushions and brought out a second bottle. He hadn't quite gotten around to fixing the splintered wood from her bullet, but he did make sure the carriage was appropriately stocked with necessary supplies.

"I'd like to propose a toast," he said grandly. "To ruining each other's lives."

"I did no such thing," she said witheringly. "Not like you've destroyed mine."

"Oh? Oh really, madam? I beg to differ."

"Go on then, beg," she retorted. The brandy must be taking effect, for the spark in her eyes and the flush in her cheeks were returning. There was nothing like brandy on a cold, wet day.

"I'll be damned if I beg to you," he replied. Even though she had something he could very much use. The marriage. The money. The ultimatum. He ruined her. He should offer. Or live and die a poor bachelor. He sipped his brandy and considered his options.

"Of course. How did I ruin your life, Roxbury? How did one little woman wreck the life of a wealthy English peer?" she asked.

"Do you really think I will confide in you? If I wanted all of London to know my business, I'd tell them myself rather than leave the message to be twisted by your malicious pen."

Honestly, she was not to be trusted.

"Thanks to you and your stunt, I no longer possess that pen," she cried.

"Get a new one," he retorted.

"It's a metaphor, you fool. I've lost my damned column thanks to you, you evil, demented blockhead!"

"Lost it? How negligent. When did you see it last?" he asked breezily, before the implications of what she said fully dawned on him. Before he realized that she was no longer the Lady of Distinction. That she wasn't a threat anymore, but just a woman in desperate straits.

That changed everything. *Everything.*

"Lost it? How negligent?" she cried in frustration. "Oooh!"

She raised her palm at him, open and ready to fly at his face. He caught her by the wrist and then gently let go.

"Am I to understand that you no longer write for *The Weekly*?" he questioned.

"That is correct, you vile, despicable bounder. I no longer write for it, because I am no longer invited anywhere, all because some demented drunken idiot thought it would be great fun to sing revolting songs outside my window."

She was furious, but he was intrigued. A devilishly genius idea was taking shape in his head.

Let go? Lady Somerset let go from *The Weekly*? If there was one thing more scandalous than a woman writing publicly, it was a writing woman, publicly disgraced.

And if he were to marry her . . .

If he were to take as his bride a pistol-slinging widow who was plagued with the most outrageous rumors about her—that she wrote for a newspaper, that she was relieved of duties from said paper, that she'd been having a secret affair with him and Lord only knew who else—it would satisfy the terms of the ultimatum. But by God, would it rankle the earl to have to accept her and that would satisfy Roxbury.

They would marry for the sake of her reputation, and because she would certainly need funds. In fact, unless she had some dark secrets, she had no fortune and no prospects. Thanks to their marriage, he'd have funds to support them both.

Roxbury imagined the look on his father's face as he brought home one of the most scandalous, brazen, and brash women this town had ever seen—as his future countess.

In his mind, that was what made it acceptable for Roxbury to marry her.

In that moment, he experienced a swell of affection for her and could have kissed her.

"If you're trying to think of something to say, I suggest beginning with an apology," Lady Somerset said. Roxbury smiled at her, seeing her differently now. He needed her, and it was essential she understand she needed him, too.

"I'm sorry that all of London thinks you are a trollop because of where my carriage parked one evening," he said, relishing the opportunity to give an apology like the one she had written for him.

"And I'm sorry that you were ever born," she replied, not at all taking kindly to the taste of her own medicine.

"And you are also sorry that London thinks I like to bed men because of what you wrote. But you're not sorry you wrote it," he said pointedly.

"If I had my column . . ." she said threateningly.

"But you do not. I cannot tell you how relieved I am." Honestly, he really was. It was an entirely different experience simply being near her now. He needn't be on guard as much. He needn't fear that every wink, word, grin, or glance would end up cast in a salacious and unflattering light for the whole of London to read.

"Speak for yourself," she muttered. They fell silent. The rain beat down on the carriage.

If they were to marry . . .

Still, a marriage wasn't something he wanted. But he could set aside his feelings of doom long enough to see that it would solve some very pressing problems.

But would she see that? How on earth could he make her when it would be useless to employ logic and when her pride had to be considered? It was a daunting task.

He thought of Edward again. *"A man's life is his own."* And in this moment, Roxbury understood why Edward wouldn't settle down, either. Because it was a damn tricky thing to live one's own life when it all depended upon the whim and the word of a woman.

Second thoughts began to creep in, but he made a pointed effort to ignore them.

Roxbury took a deep breath and casually asked, "Have I mentioned that you ruined my life?"

"Perhaps once or twice, fleetingly. You certainly didn't harp on and on and on and on about it in some vague, melodramatic fashion," she replied, and he grinned. Her sarcasm was sharply accurate. He had been saying that line with an unnecessary frequency.

That was the thing with Lady Somerset—she would never sugarcoat a thing, or agree with him for the sake of it. He was used to the opposite with women—they either wanted to be his lovers or wished to stay, thus he'd heard nothing but agreement. No one ever challenged him.

"What you suggested in your column regarding my preferences of bedding partners has made it impossible for me to find a wife," he began.

"You're welcome. Rakes like you go to great lengths to avoid matrimony and I have solved all your problems," she said.

She idly unbuttoned her spencer, probably to keep the wet garment from clinging to her gown, and not to entice him, but for a moment he lost the direction of his thoughts.

"I would very much like to live and die a bachelor. However, circumstances dictate that I cannot. And I swear, Lady Somerset, if you tell anyone what I am about to tell—against all better judgment—I will do whatever I can to destroy the dregs of your reputation."

She visibly perked up at that. Her lips parted and her eyes sparkled. The woman did love gossip.

He purposely waited for a minute, and then another, until she was practically panting to hear his secrets. She began to fidget with the fabric of her skirts. He took pleasure in her impatience.

"I must marry within three days or else I shall be destitute. It's my father's devious plan to get his one and only son to settle down and produce an heir," he explained. In his month to find a wife, he was down to the end of the last week. Should he be so lucky as to have this bitter but beautiful auburn-haired widow say yes, a special license would certainly be in order.

"It's brilliant on his part," she said thoughtfully. "I had no idea the Earl of Carlyle was so devious and desperate for his son to settle down."

"It's evil," Roxbury said firmly.

"It's out of the question now, isn't it? I do see how my column has made this a challenge for you," she said. He exhaled slowly, surprised by the relief from her acknowledgment.

"However," she continued, "I'm sure there is some deaf and illiterate chambermaid who hasn't heard of your new reputation and would fancy being a countess."

"It must be a woman of proper birth," he said flatly.

"Well, now, that's a bit more tricky," she replied.

"It's damn near impossible. I can't even get in the door of any passably attractive female. My choices are a lifetime of poverty or shackling myself to whosoever left in town will take me," Roxbury said.

"There is always Lady Hortensia Reeves," Julianna suggested.

"Indeed. However, I'm thinking of someone else."

"She must be desperate," she mused. "Completely and utterly destitute and desperate."

"Like you?" he asked, forcing the words to sound light and suggestive and not accusative. Strangely, his heart was pounding heavily in his chest. There was no reason to be nervous, he told himself—except that everything depended upon her, in this moment.

"You are not suggesting what I think you are," she said with a little laugh. She had a pretty laugh, he noticed for the first time. It seemed she rarely laughed, and that she ought to more often.

"Earlier in this carriage ride I proposed a toast to ruining each other's lives. I have done so to yours, and you have mine."

"All right, Roxbury. Cheers to that," she said, and they clinked their bottles of brandy together. Her sip was ladylike, his was not. The quick flash of a heated gaze between them was anything but proper.

"But now, Julianna—"

"It's Lady Somerset to you," she said. Could he really stand to live with such a contrary woman? Could he afford not to?

Julianna would never bore him—she might drive him so insane that he'd be carted off to Bedlam, but life with her wouldn't be dull. The same could not be said of Lady Hortensia Reeves.

He had a feeling, too, that Edward would have approved of a spitfire like Julianna.

"Since I am about to propose marriage, Julianna, I think I'll use your given name," he replied.

Her eyes widened and her lips parted in shock—for once, the lady was speechless. He smiled and savored the moment.

"As I was saying, my dear, maddening, beautiful, terrifying Julianna. We have ruined each other's lives, but we can also set them to rights. Before you refuse me or declare me mad, hear me out . . ."

She opened her mouth, and again she was

speechless. He rushed on before she could find her words.

"If we were to marry, I would be assured of my fortune. It would repair my reputation."

"A top consideration for me," she remarked.

"If we were to marry, *your* reputation would also be restored. You would be a married peeress. One day you'll be a countess. Of course, you would also be provided for."

She appeared thoughtful as he explained this strange bargain. Except that it wasn't that unusual at all—the circumstances were different, but deals like these were made in drawing rooms every day. He, a great lover of women, was proposing a marriage of convenience.

"And if I could fix my reputation, I could get my column back," she added, after thinking about it.

"If that's what you'd want," he answered. It might be problematic to *live* with a gossip columnist, but that was a consideration for another day.

"It is," Julianna answered firmly. Her chin lifted high and her mouth set in a firm line.

"So you see that everyone wins if we are to marry," he said carefully.

"And the matter of those heirs you mentioned?" she questioned. He was relieved she asked about that—it meant she was considering it. He suspected that her considerations were different than his—more clothing involved, most likely.

"I have many cousins," he answered.

Julianna nodded thoughtfully, and then turned to look out the window. Was she considering it? She must be. Why was his heart pounding, as he waited for her answer? And what was there really to think about? Everybody would win with this marriage.

Roxbury deliberately was not thinking past the wedding, other than to consider the money and the restoration of their social status. In the vague images of married life, he pictured them attending parties together and perhaps waltzing a time or two, but otherwise keeping to themselves. What did married people do, anyway?

He'd only ever had lovers, and they were usually confined to the nighttime, with exceptions made for a few in the morning or late afternoon. He knew all about bedding, but knew nothing about building a life with someone.

Roxbury was afraid that she—who had already been married—was considering the day-to-day life of a gossip columnist living with a rake, when neither of them cared very much for the other. Any affair of his wouldn't be secret for long, and given her gun-wielding ways, his first affair as a married man would likely be his last.

This marriage had all the makings of a disaster; that much was clear as day to anyone, even him.

What was she thinking? He longed to know with an intensity that surprised him. Julianna's silence was rare; lovely as it was, there was something comforting about how she always said exactly what she thought, so he always knew where he stood with her.

Julianna's brow was slightly furrowed, and she nibbled on her lower lip. It was probably an unconscious act, and he found it decidedly erotic.

If they were to marry . . .

Roxbury forced himself to focus on their future,

and how it was in her hands—small, feminine gloved hands that grasped and released fistfuls of her red dress.

He waited as patiently as he could when his fate hung in the balance, and all depended upon the heart and mind of a most vexing woman. The temptation to down the entire bottle of brandy was great, so he put it away. This was not the time to get sodding drunk. He'd wait until after her reply. Whether yes or no, a drink would definitely be in order.

Finally, as the carriage pulled to a stop before 24 Bloomsbury Place, she spoke. Her voice was smooth like velvet as it shredded his hopes to nothing.

"Thank you for your offer, Roxbury. But the answer is no."

Chapter 29

24 Bloomsbury Place

Sophie had married and moved out months ago, and Julianna had never felt the loneliness of her absence as she did now. If she were here, they would curl up on the settee with a pot of tea and Julianna could rail against Roxbury, and all the problems he caused. Sophie would offer some insight and make her laugh.

"You would not believe the day I've had, Penny," Julianna said to her maid, hoping to engage her in a conversation. Fired by Knightly, and proposed to by Roxbury! Quite an unexpected turn of events, and Julianna needed to tell someone to make it real.

"I'll draw a hot bath," Penny answered efficiently, eyeing Julianna's wet hair and soaking garments. "There is tea in the drawing room."

Julianna poured a cup of hot tea, added sugar, and settled in. If only Sophie were here! But she was across town, snug and cozy in Hamilton House (as much as one could be, given the size of the place).

It wouldn't be long before she and Brandon had a brood of children and then Sophie would have even less time for Julianna and the other Writing Girls.

Julianna, however, lived alone. No husband or suitors—no serious ones, anyway. Roxbury was a desperate fool and did not count. The Writing Girls were true friends, but everyone else had turned their backs on her at the first hint of scandal. Aye, it was a bitter taste of her own medicine. She didn't want to complain, for that wasn't in her nature, but the fact remained that she was lonely and alone. In the far recesses of her heart and mind, she thought she might deserve it, given her line of work.

If she said yes . . .

She sighed, wishing for any distraction from her thoughts, but it was impossible not to think of Knightly's betrayal and Roxbury's proposal.

Your services are no longer needed, Knightly had told her plainly. The cold-blooded, logical part of her could understand it, but oh! It made her heart hurt. Her pride had suffered a mighty blow today. She was a Writing Girl! She was blazing a trail for history to follow. Julianna knew the satisfaction of putting a roof over her head and food in her belly. She knew, deeply, the satisfaction of being her own mistress, her own protector.

Knightly gave and Knightly took away. She thought—hoped—that he might be more supportive of the women who made his paper such a success. And now how was she supposed to pay for said roof and food?

If she said yes . . .

She stood and took a turn about the room. When

Sophie lived here, every available surface was covered with an explosion of female things: hair ribbons, Minerva Press novels, shoes, earbobs, issues of *La Belle Assemblée* and *The London Weekly*, invitations, letters, and little trinkets.

Now the surfaces were clear. Now one could see the room itself—the blue-and-white-striped upholstered chair next to the black-and-white *etoile* chair. The walls were pale blue, and the curtains were always tied back so Julianna might spy upon the neighbors.

If she said yes . . .

It would solve all of their problems, wouldn't it? A marriage certificate and a little time did go a long way toward soothing any social crisis. Even Sophie and Brandon, who had quite possibly the most scandalous marriage and wedding ceremony in recent history were welcomed everywhere. Of course, it didn't hurt that the man in question was a double duke.

Roxbury was a viscount, and would inherit an earldom. That had to count for something, she thought, as she took another turn about the room, with a long pause before the fireplace.

Yes, marriage and a title and a little time could change things significantly, but it couldn't change everything. Old dogs didn't learn new tricks, and tigers didn't change their stripes and everyone knew it was foolhardy to attempt to change a man.

Perhaps another woman might be able to accomplish such a herculean feat, but Julianna had already tried and failed at that particular challenge.

Julianna remembered a particular afternoon just a few months ago, in which she gossiped

with Sophie about a rumor she'd heard and sub-
sequently printed. It was about Roxbury carrying
on an affair with two mortal enemies simultaneously—they were the best of friends now, of course.
Two women at once—and that was just what was
known. Lord only knew what he really did get up
to in the dark of the night. Or perhaps, she thought,
still pacing, it was better if the Lord did not know.

Roxbury loved women—many women. The
thought of Roxbury remaining faithful to her was
ludicrous. In the marriage he had proposed—one
purely of convenience that would likely outlive its
need—she could not reasonably expect his fidelity,
especially if she would not go to his bed.

Or perhaps she would.

She was hotly, wildly attracted to him. She re-
lived that moonlit kiss more often than was seemly.
She could join the legions of Roxbury's women—
loved quickly, intensely, and then forgotten. Which
would be one thing if she weren't bound to him
for life.

Julianna ceased her pacing and returned to the
settee, collapsing upon it and pulling a pillow to
her chest. *Oh, Somerset,* she thought.

Somehow, this was his fault. If he hadn't swept
her off her feet when she was just seventeen. If he
hadn't gone and made her fall in love with him. If
he hadn't fallen in love with her! If she'd only been
enough for him so that he wouldn't need to satiate
his desires with all manner of questionable women.

Penny knocked upon the drawing room door.
"Ma'am, your bath is ready."

As she was passing through the foyer, Julianna
noticed that there was no post awaiting her. Not

even an offer of a suppression fee (as if she could afford it) or even a missive from her mother.

A short while later, she sank into a steaming bath. Outside, the rain was as cold, wet and relentless as ever.

It was inevitable that her thoughts would turn to Roxbury.

His offer was shocking. Gentlemanly, in an odd way, when so little about him was. His kiss was not that of a gentleman, oh no. She could still taste him—like brandy, anger, adventure, and passion. She could still smell the hothouse flowers and see the silver light of the moon.

Such an unexpected, passionate encounter contrasted sharply with the marriage proposal that was nothing more than a business transaction. It made a measure of sense—except that her heart rebelled and her stomach ached at the thought. Like how she felt on the dueling field. *As if he might be lost to her.*

But what did she care if she lost him? Or did her heart know something her head did not?

Roxbury was handsome. Charming. Wealthy. He had an immeasurable talent for kissing. He was insufferable and infuriating, but he definitely was not dull.

That kiss . . .

Oh, it was too dangerous! Heartbreak was too likely. He'd likely tire of her, and would turn to other women, and it would be like being married to Somerset all over again.

She could not foresee a happy marriage with him, yet the alternative seemed bleak, too. Sophie would naturally provide for her, but she didn't want to be the poor auntie living on charity for the rest of her days.

Upon the demise of her first marriage, Julianna turned to writing. She wrote for money. She wrote for her dignity. She wrote to keep a roof over her head, to feed her belly, and fire up her soul. She wrote to pay for her late husband's indiscretions. She wrote so that she would be beholden to no one.

She wanted to be *The London Weekly*'s Lady of Distinction. But would she become Lady Roxbury to do so?

Part II

The Gentleman's Wife

Chapter 30

St. Bride's Church

The first time Julianna married, it had been for love. The second time, she married for money, security, and a desperate attempt to salvage her reputation. In short, all the typical reasons a member of the ton betrothed themselves. She was not hopeless, but she wasn't exactly optimistic, either.

"Are you certain of this?" Sophie asked. They were waiting in a small room off the main room of St. Bride's Church. Julianna had wanted to wear a dove gray gown, the color of half morning but Sophie talked her out of it, saying that if the new couple could pass themselves off as a love match, they might have a chance at a quicker welcome from society.

Thus, Julianna wore a fawn-colored silk gown from Madame Auteuil's. It set off her auburn hair and green eyes rather nicely, she thought. Her bonnet had a veil of white lace; a stark contrast to the veil of black net that had covered her face that evening at Drury Lane when this whole debacle began.

"Of course I'm not certain of this," Julianna replied, in her typically forthright manner. How on earth could she be certain of marriage to a man whose sole aim in life had been to live and die a wealthy bachelor?

"You needn't go through with this. You're always welcome with us," Sophie offered. "Lord knows we have the space."

They exchanged faint smiles. Hamilton House was the size of a small village.

"Thank you," Julianna answered. Knowing she had a refuge of last resort meant the world to her, but Julianna was the kind of woman who, for better or worse, needed a challenge. Eloping at seventeen. Moving to London. Staying in London as a single woman, and writing. Aye, she couldn't fall back on the convenience of a room with her friend. Besides, Sophie deserved a home and husband and a family of her own—without her widowed, penniless friend moping through the endless expanse of marble-floored halls.

"Besides," Julianna continued, "as Roxbury's wife, I shall have infinite opportunities to make him regret ruining my reputation."

"Or will he regret salvaging it?" Sophie asked with a lift of her eyebrow.

"He gets something out of this, too," Julianna added, as she smoothed her skirts and adjusted her veil.

"Yes. You!"

"Among other things, yes," she said. He got his fortune and put an end to those rumors. She got her reputation back, and security, until she got her column back.

In the end, that was why she had written to him

saying, "Very well, I accept." Because it was her best shot at getting what she truly wanted—her column, and the sense of independence that she craved.

"Roxbury's not a bad man. And he's not like Somerset," Sophie said.

"How do you know it won't be the same thing all over again?" Julianna asked.

With Sophie she didn't have to explain anything, from the heartache of being left by one's love, to the terror of walking down the aisle, she just *knew*.

"They are two very different men, and you are not the same girl you were at seventeen. And if my so good and so proper husband has been friends with Roxbury for over a decade, he can't be completely irredeemable."

"It's a marriage of convenience. As long as I keep that in mind and don't let my heart get involved, it will be just fine," Julianna said resolutely.

As expected, Sophie snorted with laughter.

"You don't seem to be suffering your usual pre-wedding jitters," Julianna remarked in an effort to change the subject.

Sophie had been jilted at the altar, and then had become the author of Miss Harlow's Marriage in High Life for *The Weekly*. Weddings made her very nervous and quite ill. The situation had noticeably improved since her own wedding to the Duke of Hamilton and Brandon.

"Surprisingly, I feel quite all right. It must be a good sign," Sophie said, reaching out and giving Julianna's hand one last squeeze before she left to join the other guests.

Julianna was left alone, and very aware that this was her last chance to make a mad dash out of the church, to get lost in the crowded London streets and then to . . . well, she didn't quite know what else to do.

Fate was waiting for her.

The first notes of the organ sounded, loud and strong in the cavernous church, and she took a deep breath and held on tightly to her orange blossom bouquet. The scent reminded her of that night when he had kissed her against the orange tree in the Walmslys' conservatory.

This was a bit different from a jaunt to Gretna Green.

At the end of the aisle, Roxbury was waiting for her with his hands clasped behind his back. His hair was dark and as tousled as it ever was. His eyes were large, velvety brown, and looking only at her. His mouth was neither smiling nor frowning. It was plain from his expression that this was as surreal and unexpected for him as it was for her. That they possibly had some common ground brought her a measure of comfort.

On her way to his side, she passed her fellow Writing Girls: Annabelle was dabbing her eyes with a handkerchief. Eliza and Sophie smiled on. Alistair sat nearby, smiling as well. Knightly was with them, because she wanted him to see that she was becoming respectable.

The Earl and Countess Carlyle, Roxbury's parents, had arrived from Bath earlier that week. In a show of optimism they had previously scheduled their journey to conclude in time for their son's possible nuptials. Julianna had met them fleetingly the other day. How two such sober, upstanding individuals had produced a wild, passionate man like Roxbury was a mystery to her.

They had not quite approved of her, and she saw quickly that Roxbury enjoyed it. Once upon a time, part of Somerset's appeal had been that her parents disapproved of him. So, she understood.

And then, before she knew it, she was standing next to Roxbury at the altar. Just as she considered running away, he took hold of her hand.

There was something about a man who knew when a woman needed some comfort, and strength, and then provided it. Because of that small gesture, she thought they might have a fighting chance. And so, perhaps, she would stay.

The vicar began. "Dearly beloved, we are gathered here today . . ."

Roxbury looked at Julianna gazing at him from behind a white lace veil.

It went without saying that he had never imagined that he would marry. He certainly hadn't pictured this moment—holding hands with his bride before his parents, close friends, a vicar. God. No wonder he felt ill.

His bride was not some missish, biddable thing. No, he did not make this easy on himself. Entranced, he watched as Julianna looked scared, then scowled, or smiled faintly, or schooled her features into an oh-so-determined expression.

Life with her was not going to be boring. That much he was sure of.

If he was not bored, then it logically followed he might not need to seek diversion elsewhere. If *that* happened, he would be a faithful husband, which is to say he was at this very moment promising to be the one thing he never thought he'd be.

He glanced at their guests—his smug parents, her weepy friends. Where was her family, he wondered? There was so much about her he didn't know. But, oh dear God above, they had the rest of their lives together to discover it.

"Do you take this woman to be your lawfully wedded wife?" the vicar intoned.

This was it, then. Roxbury rocked back on his heels, contemplating making a run for it. The woman in question squeezed his hand as if she could read his mind. Hell, knowing her, she probably could.

Edward always swore he'd never marry. *A man's life is his own,* he'd said—before he enlisted in the army, was assigned to France, and died in battle. It logically followed that a man's life wasn't his own anymore if a wife and then brats entered the picture. This moment was the end of so many wide-open horizons and endless possibilities.

One of the guests coughed loudly. Brandon, his best man, elbowed him in the back. Julianna appeared to be considering a swift kick to his shins.

For a second time, the vicar asked, "Do you take this woman to be your lawfully wedded wife?"

Chapter 31

In the end, Roxbury managed to say, "I do."

He also survived the wedding breakfast hosted by his parents. The toasts were awkward, as the bride and groom at best managed civility toward each other. Julianna appeared far too interested in the family portrait, including Edward, for Roxbury's comfort. It was obvious that later there would be questions he did not care to answer.

He took no small measure of delight that his oh-so-proper restrained and uptight parents were hosting the four most scandalous women in London, and one of them as a daughter-in-law.

To have Derek Knightly, a lowborn, self-made man there was also a small triumph, though also quite unexpected since their last encounter was on a dueling field and Knightly's arm was still in his sling. Underneath his jacket, Roxbury's arm was still bandaged. They were quite a pair.

His parents acquitted themselves with the utmost politeness. His mother took the women for tea. His father smoked cigars with the gentlemen.

Roxbury had married by their schedule (without

a day to spare), but he had done it on his terms—which just happened to be a desperate bargain with his she-devil bride.

Getting his new wife to agree to his terms was another battle entirely.

After a long day, and after all their goodbyes were said, they finally climbed into the carriage to return home. Julianna smoothed her silk skirts and loosened her bonnet strings.

He wished she'd remove the thing entirely. He wanted to see her face without the veil, and he wanted to see her luscious auburn hair instead of a stupid bonnet. He wanted to see Julianna bare, pure, without adornment.

"To 24 Bloomsbury Place, please," she told the driver. Peter looked warily over at Simon. He knew who paid his wages, but he also knew the lady was capable of wielding a firearm with frightening accuracy.

"Home, Peter, to Bruton Street," Simon confirmed.

"What do you mean, home?" Julianna queried.

"We are going to our new home, Lady Roxbury, which is at 28 Bruton Street."

"I cannot. I need my things."

"Your maid packed them and brought them over during the ceremony and breakfast," he answered evenly. He had seen this conversation coming a mile away. While she was focused on negotiating the most intricate, generous, and favorable marriage settlement any solicitor had ever created, he was busy ensuring that she actually did marry him.

He also made plans for her to reside with him in his garishly decorated bachelor's residence because in order for this whole scheme to work, the ton had to believe the marriage was real and that they were in love. They could not just tie the knot and live separate lives across town.

Thus, they would reside under the same roof.

"I did not order her to pack my things," Julianna said.

"I'm sure you didn't tell the sun to rise, either, but it did," Roxbury remarked. "And I asked your maid to do so."

"This will never work. I cannot have you going behind my back and making plans for me without my knowledge or consent. I am my own person, an adult, and I will not be treated as a child or a servant."

"Lady Roxbury, if you will be calm and listen to reason . . ." he began, purposely to provoke her.

"Be calm? Listen to reason? *Lady Roxbury?*"

Her cheeks were pink, her eyes were blazing, and she was utterly adorable. It was a delight to watch Julianna practically choking on her fury. Nothing was surer to agitate a woman than to tell her to be calm and listen to reason.

"As I was saying," he carried on, trying very hard not to break into a grin, "this marriage is for the sake of appearances. So you will stay at my home, not because I wish to claim my marital rights, but because we need to dispel rumors that I enjoy bed sport with other men, that you do *not* enjoy bed sport with *many* men, and to convince the ton that this is a passionate love match and not the mercenary scam that it is."

"I want a separate room," Julianna said.

"They're preparing two chambers right now," he replied.

"With locks."

"That will not be necessary," he said, and then she surprised him by blushing, and turning away. Had he offended her modesty or was she embarrassed that he would not be seeking access to her bedchamber?

His intentions regarding bedding a female were, for the first time, pure. While his body was demanding that he claim her as his own by kissing, caressing, and loving every inch of her, his head and—dare he say it—his heart wasn't in it. He'd had enough experience with women to know that a kiss too soon could be the end of everything.

Julianna infuriated him. She also amused him. They were married now and he wasn't quite ready to ruin it all. He ought to give it a week, at least.

"I hope Penny brought my pistols," Julianna muttered.

"I specifically told her not to," he said. Because, being a red-blooded, passionate male married to a stunning beauty meant that at some point, he was going to bed her. He'd rather not risk her gunfire—again—to do so. The wrath of Julianna was sufficient to keep him at bay. For now.

She sighed, ever vexed, and he was ever entranced by the glorious rise and fall of her breasts. Perhaps it might just be worth the risk after all.

"I do not care for this," she said with a sniff. He assumed she was referring to everything. He could not blame her. His own feelings were mixed—terror, a sort of excitement, a sense of adventure, and did he mention he was terrified?

But then there was always the great pleasure

of discovering and learning a woman for the first time. To notice when she sighed, or to learn that she smoothed her skirts when she was nervous, or to discover just how she liked to be kissed.

"An excellent start for our marriage," he remarked.

"Are you going to be faithful, Roxbury?" she asked. He fought the urge to shift uncomfortably in his seat, for had he not just entertained the thought, a few hours earlier, that he might be able to do it? Or was that just delusional? Or was that how he felt at the start of every love affair? Was this even a love affair? He thought it was a bargain with the devil.

"Do you want the honest answer, Julianna, or are you having a vulnerable moment and need to be consoled?"

"Honesty, please," she answered.

"For now, yes, I will be faithful to you. But ultimately it depends," he answered truthfully.

"On if I'm a true wife to you?" she asked.

"Yes, and probably a dozen other things. But for now, Julianna, I am yours and only yours." It was a line he'd said before, but it was different this time: it was *her* and they had taken vows, and because he knew, deep in his bones, that this was not just another passing affair.

"Roxbury, I have another question."

"Life with a reporter . . ." he jested.

"At your father's house, that portrait . . ."

His smile faded as her voice trailed off. She was referring to the big family portrait above the mantel in the drawing room, and he had seen her glancing at it frequently before dinner. This question was not unexpected. Nevertheless, he did not know how he wanted to answer it.

"Tell me about how you first met Somerset," he said.

"Point taken, Roxbury. We shall suffer our curiosity about the other's deep, dark secrets until a suitable degree of intimacy is established, or—"

"All in good time, darling wife," he said. They had the rest of their lives together. He swallowed hard at that realization.

Finally, the carriage rolled to a stop before his townhouse. A footman was waiting, but Simon waved him away.

"Julianna," he said, and he took her hand in his and looked her in the eye.

Her eyes were lovely—bright green, with dark lashes. Her gaze was, as always, strong and honest. Her mouth, however, was another story entirely— here she showed her every emotion. Did she bite her lip in fear or vexation? Smile mysteriously or pout? Now, he found her lips were just so . . . kissable.

There was definitely a very significant chance that he would not be bored.

"Neither of us wanted this marriage," he began, "but now we're in it and there is no getting out of it. We have already demonstrated our capacity to utterly devastate the other. I am suggesting we endeavor to make a success of it; I only ask for a truce."

"Complete honesty and practicality. My favorite kind of romance," she remarked, sighing, and the smile she offered him could only be described as shy. Such a strange thought—Julianna, shy.

"A truce, Roxbury," she said, holding out her hand to him.

He lifted her palm to his lips for a kiss, pausing to savor the warmth from her hand and this moment of tenderness. And then he escorted his bride into the horribly decorated bachelor's abode that was now, suddenly, the newlyweds' home.

Chapter 32

In the lady's bedchamber . . .

Once upon a time, Julianna had thought that Roxbury possessed plain brown eyes like anyone else. She never understood the sighs and raptures from other women about his chocolate-colored eyes with their sparks of mischief and desire and all that rot. The legions had fanned their hot cheeks at the merest mention of his tall, lean, muscled physique. What hogwash, she had thought.

She was beginning to understand. When he held her hand and looked at her with beautiful, warm brown eyes, she noticed that he really looked at her. He really saw her.

Somerset had stopped seeing her after a while. She'd forgotten what it was like to be noticed, and that it was lovely.

"You're awfully quiet tonight, my lady," Penny said. Julianna stood in the center of her new bedroom—a very pink room—awaiting her maid's assistance in removing her gown.

"It's been a big day," Julianna replied.

"And now a big night . . ." Penny said, and Julianna caught her maid's grin in the gold-framed full-length mirror.

"No, not exactly," Julianna said. But she was very aware that he was just across the hall, and at this very moment he was probably undressing that tall, lean, muscled physique of his. A blush stole across her cheeks.

"But he's your husband now, and so handsome," Penny went on. Her maid had been completely charmed. Wonderful.

"And the last time I had had a handsome husband . . . you know how that turned out, Penny."

"Just fine," she said briskly, tucking a stray strand of red hair out of her eyes before beginning to unlace Julianna's corset.

"Just fine? Whatever do you mean?" Julianna asked.

"He conveniently removed himself from your life. He got out of your way so you could be happy," Penny said. Julianna had been thinking more along the lines of utter calamity, but the point was taken. The worst was after the love had gone, but the marriage remained.

"You make it sound as if he did me a favor, when in fact he was merely an idiot. He was killed because he was trying to make love to an actress while driving a carriage. While drunk," Julianna said. Every so often she had to repeat it aloud to confirm it. What a stupid way to go.

By the end, Somerset liked his vices in pairs, at the minimum. Alcohol and women, opium and fornication, gaming and smoking.

"But the point is he is no longer around to hurt

and embarrass you with his infidelities," Penny added.

"I have Roxbury for that now," Julianna said forlornly—and yet glancing at the bedchamber door as if he might knock at any second. Would he knock? Why wouldn't he?

"Oh, my lady," Penny said with a laugh. "He'll never get away with it! You have a network of spies and informants, starting with my six sisters and me. We'll watch out for you."

Penny spoke brightly as she worked efficiently to remove all the hairpins. She didn't seem quite aware of the revelations she had just shared.

With her network of information gatherers, Julianna would know about any infidelities of Roxbury's before they even happened. And if he were the promiscuous rogue that she feared he could be, it would be different this time because she would not be in love with him.

This marriage might have a chance after all.

In the bedroom across the hall . . .

"She's a stunner, my lord. Well done," Timson said. Roxbury removed his jacket and handed it to his valet.

"That is my wife you're talking about. And she's the devil in disguise."

"Aren't all women?" Timson asked with a shrug of his shoulders.

"I have to live with this one. I cannot just leave before morning light and be done with it," said Roxbury.

This part, in particular, worried him. He fell

easily into love, and easily out of it. Because he did not engage in long-lasting binding affairs, it was of little to no consequence at all to walk away whenever he felt like it.

Though he knew little about marriages, Roxbury knew that he could not just walk away and be done with it once he was bored.

"A wife, Timson. My wife."

"Never thought you'd say that, did you?" Timson asked with a grin. Roxbury handed his waistcoat and cravat to him and wondered what his valet did besides collect clothing and offer his unsolicited opinions. Certainly not tend to his own slovenly attire.

"No, Timson, I did not."

"So now what? We all know this marriage is a sham. How long does she stay for?" Timson asked, leaning against the armoire.

There was something about the way Timson spoke of his wife, and his marriage that struck Roxbury as troubling.

Just because it was a marriage of convenience didn't make it any less valid. Just because he did not love his wife did not mean that he wouldn't act as a husband ought to—loyal, caring, protecting.

Until now, Roxbury had not considered these things. His only focus had been on the papers—the marriage license, the contract, and the settlements. But now that Julianna was the lady of the house, Timson could not ask, in so many words, how long he had to tolerate her for.

In that instant Roxbury saw that if he treated her, and the relationship, lightly then the rest of the world would, too. She did not deserve that. Apparently, a gentleman's work wasn't concluded after the proposal, either. It was a relentless display of decency, righteousness, responsibility, and command. Roxbury empathized with Brandon in that moment more than he had in any of the years of their friendship.

"That's my wife you're talking about, Timson." There was a heavy dose of warning in his tone.

His wife, who was terrifying and lovely and likely in some state of undress just across the hall.

That image was one he dwelled on. At first, he suspected that her state of undress compromised some spinsterish nightgown covering every inch. But then Roxbury recalled the infamous night of the serenade. According to his blurred vision and hazy memory, she wore something cut low across the bodice and perfectly fitted everywhere else. And silky—he could tell by the way the fabric caressed her skin, propelled by the wind.

His mouth went dry imagining it. He glanced at the door, and considered knocking on hers.

The pistols, though. He recalled that part with stunning clarity. But those had been left in Bloomsbury at his explicit instructions to her very flirtatious maid.

How on earth had he acquired a wife, and such a dangerous one at that? What the bloody hell was he doing standing in his shirtsleeves, alternating between lusty thoughts and talking to his valet on his wedding night?

Roxbury had half a mind to go knock on her door this minute.

He would not, though, because he was an experienced rake and he knew a thing or two (or twenty) about women. For example, they did not like to be rushed. A successful seduction was a slow waltz, a long walk, and a prolonged courtship. A patient man was a lucky man.

When Roxbury decided he wanted to win her heart and a place in her bed, it would be his for the taking—it would not be forced or hurried. Hell, they were married! They had all the time in the world to tumble into bed and maybe even fall in love.

Chapter 33

For the second day in a row—and the second day since the wedding—Julianna woke up experiencing an intense wave of homesickness. Roxbury's house was nice (though the decor left much to be desired), but it wasn't *hers*. She missed her own bed and the view of Bloomsbury Square from her window.

Pink was the color of choice for her bedchamber: a dark magenta carpet with matching velvet drapes. The walls were papered in a pattern that consisted of pink roses over pink stripes. The chair was pink, the blankets were pink. There were ruffles on everything, too. It was an explosion of femininity and it was utterly strange that such a room should exist in the house of a rake.

The decoration in the rest of the house, that she had seen, was horrifying.

She wondered who had inflicted such damage. An angry former mistress? A blind person? His mother? Someone on his staff?

Never one to complain when something could be done, Julianna rang for Penny. After a short conversation about their plans to cure her homesickness, Julianna dressed and went downstairs (skipping the stair that creaked). She shuddered passing through the foyer, and cringed upon viewing the dining room in daylight. The particular shade of green on the walls was alarmingly similar to some bodily fluids that a lady dare not mention.

Then she sat down to breakfast with the company of *The London Times*. It was important to keep track of her rival.

She was halfway through reading all about England's news in the column "Domestic Intelligence" when Roxbury joined her.

She managed a slight smile and a "Good morning" before she returned to the paper. Well, she looked at it, but read nary a word. His mere presence had set her heart racing. With his mussed up hair, unshaven jaw and brown eyes that were still heavy-lidded from sleep, there was something dangerously attractive about him.

Yet it was just so bizarre to see her former nemesis across from her at the breakfast table. How had this happened? Stranger things had happened, but Julianna could not think of any.

She turned the page on her newspaper and arrived at the Man About Town's column. It was no surprise to see that news of their marriage had made its way into print.

"I swear, that if I do one thing before I die, it will be to discover and expose the Man About Town," she muttered when she concluded reading.

"You do not care for him?" Roxbury asked. He was drinking coffee after having devoured a large plate of eggs, ham, and bread generously slathered with butter.

"I think I might despise him more than you," she replied, sipping her tea.

"What did he write this morning?"

Julianna read the following aloud:

"The Man About Town reports: This just in . . . the two people least likely to marry have done just that. I am, of course, talking about Lord R—and Lady S—. By all accounts, they had never even met until last month. No one will own to introducing them. After his midnight serenade and subsequent visit to her home, a marriage was all but assured—eventually. We wonder what finally drove R—to come up to scratch and make an honest woman out of the gossiping widow."

It was almost the perfect picture of domesticity: the lady reading the paper aloud to her husband at the breakfast table. Except that they were reading the gossip column, in which they were the principle subjects, and their new marriage was already labeled suspicious.

It was a slight change from *before*. Somerset's antics were frequently reported—it's how she kept track of him. If she had a coin for every time a gossip column had concluded another one of her late husband's exploits with "Poor Lady Somerset" she'd have no need of Roxbury's money.

At least now she was an equal partner in scandal. She sipped her tea and took a small measure of comfort in that.

Roxbury's gaze met her own. His eyes were very beautiful. She was beginning to understand, Lord help her, all those ladies sighing about "getting lost in his eyes and the depth of his gaze" and other such stuff she had dismissed as utter cork-brained nonsense.

Oh Lord, what was happening to her?

She noticed more, too. This morning, he hadn't yet shaved, so he looked more rugged and less refined. He did not wear a jacket, either—only his shirt and waistcoat. This was not how society saw him. Only her—and however many women there had been before.

The thought of them brought on a rush of jealousy, even though she told herself she couldn't possibly care.

"Sophie is breaking the news in her column," Julianna said. "She will have all the details the Man About Town does not. It will be a *London Weekly* exclusive."

"And your column?" he asked, and she heard the hesitation in his voice.

"One of the other staff writers will take it over, with help from Sophie and the penny-a-liners," she answered. She frowned; it felt like giving the care of her child over to another.

"Who are they?" he asked.

"Penny-a-liners provide news about all sorts of things for a penny per line of text," she answered, always eager to talk about her favorite subject—gossip, the news, and secrets. "They give reports of fires, or arrests, or deaths and other crimes. They often weasel their way into the best houses so I rely on them for my work. Jem Jones—he's one of the best—and his crew usually come in once or twice a week with all sorts of delicious information."

"I had no idea," Roxbury said, and he looked genuinely interested.

She enjoyed a warm, pleasant feeling at being able to share this part of her life with someone new. Given that her identity was supposed to be unconfirmed, she could not speak of her work with *The Weekly*. There was nothing she hated like keeping a secret.

"You didn't think Knightly—or anyone else— would pay actual reporters when poor youths will volunteer the information for next to nothing, did you?" she asked.

"Now that I think about it, no," Roxbury said, and then he leaned in across the table in the manner one does when they wish to gossip. It made her grin and lean in closer, too, so she might meet him halfway.

"So," he asked, in a low voice, "how did you get all your gossip? How did you do it, Julianna?"

"Well," she said in a hushed whisper, still leaning forward. She caught him glancing at her breasts but decided not to chide him for it. "It is amazing what people would confide in me. Or what I would observe." She gave him a pointed nod, and he smiled ruefully. "There are other ways of course . . ."

"Those rumored networks of spies and informants?" he asked with a lift of his brow.

"A lady never tells," she said with a sphinxlike smile and he scowled.

"The Man About Town has his calling hours at St. Bride's, or so I've heard," Roxbury added.

"It's genius, I must admit, even though it hurts me to do so," she said, taking a sip of her tea. "Oh, what I wouldn't do to best him once and for all!"

"Why don't you?" Roxbury asked.

She opened her mouth to reply in the negative, but quickly closed it when she realized that she did not have a reason not to. She'd always wanted to, but gleaning material for her own column had always taken precedence. But now she certainly had time to spare.

What if she did try to unmask him once and for all? She took a sip of tea and pondered this.

The Man About Town's column had been running thrice weekly, continuously, for forty years. His true identity was one of the great mysteries. In all that time, no one had been able to definitively discover who he really was. Many had just accepted that it would remain a secret forever.

By now, he had to be an old man. While that did exclude most of the population, there were still many old men in London. What if the Man About Town, whoever he was, took his secret to the grave?

Then she would never know! Oh, how that would vex her! She'd never get a decent night's sleep again.

And if she succeeded—Knightly would definitely take her back. And that was what she wanted most of all.

"Roxbury, I think I just might," she said with a smile.

"Did you notice that we just had an entirely civil conversation?" he remarked.

"I can't think how to make sense of it," she said, "but it's a lovely note to end things on, really."

She gently set down her teacup in the saucer, while he slammed his coffee cup down on the table.

"End things?" he echoed.

"I've spent the wedding night, and one extra for the sake of propriety. I shall return to Bloomsbury Place this morning."

Roxbury stared at her, but she knew better than to interpret his silence as acquiescence. Did he want her to stay? She did not think he would care, now that his fortune was secure.

But his expression grew dark, and she became nervous and thought only to stand her ground and not allow him to intimidate her into changing her mind. She would not bend and mould to her husband's will.

"Penny is packing my things right now," she added defiantly.

Roxbury said nothing but stood and quit the dining room.

"Where are you going?"

"To order your maid to cease packing," he answered.

"I will not stay," she insisted, and she followed him out of the garishly painted dining room, into the black-and-white foyer and up the stairs. He stomped up each step, hitting the creaking stair particularly hard.

Once they reached the next floor, she repeated herself, "I'm not staying."

Roxbury spun around to face her. She tilted her head back, daring to look him in the eye and refusing to be bullied. He did not seem enraged, but then she noted the tension in his jaw and the fire in his eyes.

She wanted to confide in him, but found herself speechless at the intensity of his response.

He did not want her to leave. Did that mean he cared, she wondered? Why would he wish her to stay? Any other thoughts fled as he closed the distance between them.

Few men towered over her. This one did, and standing in his shadow, she experienced the rare sensation of feeling small. He took another step toward her.

Before she knew it, Julianna was backed up against the wall with Roxbury blocking her path. She could feel the heat radiating from him. It was not altogether unpleasant to be so near. She wanted to curl up against his chest, tug his arms around her, and just be still.

"Yes, you are staying," he said in a low voice that left little room for disagreement. "Two nights is not enough to repair the damage. You started those rumors about my *preferences* and now you will quiet them."

"So you can sleep with other women!"

"If not you, wife." His tone was suggestive. Shivers ran up and down her spine. She hoped he did not notice, but there was a flash of triumph in his eyes and she knew that he did.

"I'm not your wife, not really," she whispered. Couldn't he see that she had to get out before more than their reputations were on the line? Before she became his wife in truth, and before he returned to his rakish habits?

"Exactly. Do you think society will welcome either of us after a marriage that was born in scandal and ended within a week?"

Julianna looked away. He was right and she knew it, much as she was loath to admit it.

But she couldn't fathom explaining to him that she was homesick, and scared of this marriage and how it might change her. Yet she longed to be lost in his embrace. But that would be as dangerous as it would be comforting.

When he spoke again, his voice was gentler.

"For better or for worse, Julianna, we need each other. For a little while longer, at least."

And then Roxbury dared to push a strand of hair away from her face. It was such a gentle, possessive, affectionate gesture and that surprised her, especially given that she had been in the process of leaving him. It took all of her self-restraint not to pull him closer for an embrace, or to tilt up her lips for a kiss.

What utter madness. It would be delicious, but no good could come of it.

Julianna slipped away and sauntered off to her room. He followed her—not just to the threshold, but straight into her outrageously pink bedchamber. He cringed upon seeing the pink.

Penny was surrounded by an explosion of Julianna's gowns, all heaped into piles of rose, green, gray, and blue silks and satins. Two trunks were open as well, with shoes and hair ribbons and underthings spilling out.

"Your mistress will remain, so you may desist with the packing," Roxbury ordered.

Penny, bless her, looked to Julianna for approval. Reluctantly, she nodded her agreement, though anger simmered inside her because Roxbury was right and it contradicted her own desires, because her bedchamber was so damned pink, and because she craved his touch and could never indulge. If she were to succumb, it would swiftly turn to love and then devastation when her renowned rake of a husband got bored with her.

She did not want to be here and she did not want to be ordered around.

"If you leave, my lady, I will go directly to St. Bride's and inform the Man About Town who you are. Then you can really kiss your column goodbye and you'll be stuck in this marriage forever," Roxbury threatened.

Oooh! For him to come into her bedchamber, order her around, and threaten her was intolerable! Words were not sufficient to express her aggravation. Julianna picked up the nearest object, which happened to be a bejeweled satin shoe and threw it at him.

But it only hit the door closing behind him as he left.

Chapter 34

Gentleman Jack's
Later that day

That woman—his wife—was maddening. Julianna could understand logic and good sense when it was presented to her, but it did not seem to occur to her on her own. It was strange, because she was such a clever, witty, sharp woman.

Dear God, to explain to her their situation again and again . . . it made him violent. Since venting his frustration upon her was out of the question, he came here, to Gentleman Jack's.

Roxbury stripped off his jacket, waistcoat, and shirt in preparation for a fight.

Julianna had tried to leave their marriage after only two days. Even he, who was renowned for fleeting affairs, usually stuck it out longer than that, by at least a week.

Julianna was intriguing, maddening, a touch demented, stunningly beautiful, and unlike any woman he'd ever experienced.

Roxbury had nearly lost a fortune because of

her. Was it worth it? It was too soon to know, but there was something about a woman in the house. Temptation was always just within reach, just a room or two away. . . . It could be damn frustrating. Or damn satisfying.

But if he had that woman in his bed then he wouldn't need to be here, venting said frustrations in the boxing ring. Lord Brookes was there, and he raised his fists in an invitation to fight; Roxbury nodded yes. At first they just circled, fists ready. Unlike most, Roxbury had disregarded mufflers. Brookes didn't use them, either. This would be a good fight.

He grunted as he dodged one punch and then another.

Roxbury could just imagine Julianna naked between the sheets. He could see such a vision perfectly—her dark red hair against white linen sheets. Her full pink mouth and green eyes, dark with arousal. He could practically feel her soft skin and he could just about taste her kiss.

If he seduced her there was no doubt it would be one hell of a tumble. Julianna had that fire. Every word was a spark. Her glances, like smoldering embers.

And he could just tell—because he knew these things—that when she really made love, it would be akin to a long, hot roaring fire. He doubted she knew what she was missing, and what pleasure she was capable of.

He could show her. As a reward, he'd be the only one to see the great, invincible Lady Julianna with her hair down, her heart pounding and lips parted, murmuring *please*.

Roxbury's hair was falling into his eyes, obscuring his vision. Sweat was beading on his skin and he struck out, landing a blow on his opponent's abdomen.

Brookes struck back, and Roxbury dodged it, barely.

Roxbury was an expert at seduction. This was a well-known fact. If he were so inclined, he need only apply his experience and techniques to Julianna. Jewelry accomplished wonders, but an empathetic expression while listening, or a heated and suggestive glance went further toward conquering a woman's heart. And then a gentle touch here or a whisper there . . .

Did he dare seduce her? He had seduced wives before. Just not his own.

And if it all went wrong? It went without saying that he'd never kept a love affair going for very long, let alone until death did they part. With his own wife, there was no escape.

The fight continued, around and around, dodging blows and throwing punches until Roxbury was distracted, yet again, by thoughts of his own wife naked and happy in his bed. At that moment, he took a fist to his gut and doubled over, breathless, but not sure if it was the thought or the blow that did it.

Chapter 35

In the drawing room

If Julianna could not go out into the world, the world would come to her. Thus, she invited Alistair over for tea this afternoon and the Writing Girls promised to gather tomorrow. Had she been certain of her invitation being accepted, she would have thrown a dinner party.

She was desperate to avoid being alone with her husband. Or, since he was out—God only knew where—to avoid being alone with herself. When they were together she was plagued by desire to curl up in his arms, or to push his tousled hair out of his eyes. She nibbled her lip, recalling their one good kiss, and wondered what lengths she'd go to for a repeat of that experience.

When she was alone, she was plagued by thoughts of the men that vexed her: Roxbury, Knightly, the Man About Town. Her feelings toward the lot of them were a messy combination of passion, lust, violence, and intense curiosity. It was exhausting.

Later that afternoon, Alistair was officially the

first guest she'd entertained as Lady Roxbury. It was only fitting since he had also witnessed that fateful scene that ultimately brought her and Roxbury together.

"What interesting choices in décor," Alistair remarked lightly. "Who is responsible for . . ."

"For this atrocity?" Julianna supplied.

"I was going to say abomination against beauty, but atrocity works as well," Alistair said, and she laughed for the first time in days.

"I have no idea, and I suspect it was a vengeful former mistress," she replied.

"A drunk, blind, vengeful former mistress?" he questioned. His tone was polite though his question was anything but.

"Quite possibly," she murmured.

They sat on the red velvet settee in the drawing room and silently surveyed the room. The walls were papered in gold damask. The chairs were upholstered in a shade of velvet that could only be described as cherry. The artwork consisted of portraits of dogs, in heavy wooden frames. And the curtains and drapes . . . Julianna shuddered. There were no words.

"This is all my fault," Alistair lamented, and Julianna wasn't sure if he meant this room, or that she had to live in it, or something else entirely. "I never should have escorted you backstage."

"Alistair, do not be ridiculous. We both know you couldn't have stopped me," she said, handing him a cup of tea.

"A depressingly accurate fact," he replied. She sipped her tea. Thus far, Roxbury was the only one who dared—and largely succeeded—to impose his will upon her.

"Oh, let's not discuss it. Tell me some gossip, Alistair. I'm *desperate* for news of other people's problems."

"My pleasure," he said with a grin. "The latest is from last night. Lady Stewart-Wortly caught young Miss Montagu in a very delicate situation with the Duke of St. Alban's youngest, in the library at a party. They were in various states of undress, completely disheveled, etcetera, etcetera. When Lady Stewart-Wortly discovers them, she naturally launches into one of her—"

"Tirades?" Julianna supplied, resting her hand on Alistair's.

"Impassioned please for decency, she would say, but 'tirades' is certainly more accurate. So she is delivering this grand speech to a young couple, partially clothed and scared out of their wits. And in this grand speech, she mentions at least four times that if they had read her book, *Lady Stewart-Wortly's Daily Devotional for Pious and Proper Ladies*, this never would have happened. Of course, it immediately turns into a mob scene— and you know how it goes from there."

"When is the wedding?"

"Next Saturday," Alistair answered. "The highlight was Lady Charlotte Brandon asking Lady Stewart-Wortly directly—in front of the crowd that had gathered—if she could talk more about the chapter in her book about how a woman ought to be seen and not heard."

Lady Julianna burst into laughter at that. She laughed long and loud because it'd been some time since she had done so. Because she could so easily imagine the expressions—Lady Charlotte had perfectly mastered the look of feigned innocence and employed it often. Lady Stewart-Wortly probably turned beet red, pursed her lips, and narrowed her eyes to look more pinched and peevish than usual.

And then she noticed that Alistair wasn't laughing. Then she noticed it was because Roxbury had arrived and he didn't seem amused, either.

Speaking of indelicate positions! She was sitting alone with a gentleman who was not her husband, and her hand was resting affectionately on his. Her cheeks were pink with laughter.

Roxbury stood in the doorway, so handsome that her breath caught in her throat. Something about him was different.

He wore no cravat, and his shirt was open at the neck, offering her a glimpse of his bare skin. Just a hint of the wide expanse of his chest; her memory could supply the rest. He wore no waistcoat and his shirt clung to him. His fists were reddened and slightly bruised.

There was Roxbury in the evening, so very fine. There was Roxbury in the morning, tousled and imperfect and wonderful. Then there was Roxbury in the raw, as he appeared now. He'd been fighting, it seemed.

She had never seen him thus before. It was thrilling, terrifying, and reassuring all at once.

It was his expression that entranced her— Roxbury eyed Alistair with a strong, questioning glance, and then blatantly looked her up and down, as if searching for hair out of place or a stay left unlaced. No one had ever examined her thusly. If she was not mistaken, he seemed possessive and protective of her.

How bewildering. What did that all mean? Was that why her heart pounded?

It was a moment before she recovered her voice and manners and performed the introductions. The gentlemen acknowledged each other with the barest concession toward politeness.

"How kind of you to take the time to amuse my wife. If you'll excuse me," Roxbury said flatly and then he left. How impossibly rude of him to be so dismissive of her friends.

"My God, did you land a handsome one, Jules," Alistair murmured.

"I suppose," she replied casually, even though he had voiced her thoughts exactly.

"He clearly wanted to tear me from limb to limb," Alistair added.

"Do you think so?" she asked, keeping her voice light. She'd thought so, too, but wanted to confirm. It was strange and lovely that Roxbury should feel possessive of her.

But what were the implications of that? Somerset had been jealous of her conversations with other gents at first, but not long after their marriage he had ceased to care.

"I should go. But I see what your evening's entertainment will be," Alistair murmured suggestively. She gasped in shock—and it was only partially feigned.

"Lovely to see you, Alistair. Please call on me again. And one of these days we shall return to the theater."

"This time, we will stay in our seats instead of gallivanting backstage. You've had enough scandal and trouble—for now," he said with a grin.

* * *

From his position in the window at the house across the street from Lord Roxbury's residence, The Man About Town arrived just in time to watch as Lady Roxbury entertained not one, but two, gentlemen that afternoon—her husband and a flamboyantly attired unidentified man.

Or was she just the cover? Was the Lady of Distinction right about those rumors about Roxbury's preferences after all? Or was the new Lady Roxbury already embarking on an affair?

More sleuthing was required, and he had plenty of experience at that. Years of practice had honed his instincts for eavesdropping, and watching suspicious behavior. He'd been blessed—or cursed—with a face that was unremarkable and utterly forgettable. Given his practiced talents and natural attributes, it was only a matter of time before he—and the rest of London—knew all the secrets of Lord and Lady Roxbury.

Chapter 36

Supper that evening was a quiet affair. Roxbury barely tasted his food and favored the wine instead. In the absence of conversation, his thoughts strayed to the afternoon. A good fight at Gentleman Jack's had done wonders for his irritable temper. Lord knew if he hadn't gone and then had arrived home to find another man in his drawing room, things would not have gone so civilly.

That the man was obviously no danger to his wife's virtue was beside the point. For a hot, fleeting second Roxbury registered only three facts: his woman, other man, urge to kill. That had to mean something.

It was certainly a novel sensation to him.

The deep meaning and true significance of that was not something he wished to consider. But it couldn't be ignored. Was he beginning to care for her? He had not yet drunk enough wine to think about the implications of developing deep, passionate feelings for a woman he had married for only convenience.

"You're quiet this evening," Julianna remarked.

She sat at the far end of the long dining table. Until she moved in, he had never used this room. Now they were enjoying a formal dinner, complete with dozens of candles and fine china he didn't know he owned.

"I'm thinking," he said. *To bed or not to bed his wife? That was the question.*

"I shall not disturb you during such a challenging endeavor," she remarked as graciously as a devoted wife might, except for how insulting the words were.

Roxbury set down his cutlery, took a sip of wine, and paused thoughtfully. Always cranky, his wife. Which probably meant that she was in need of a good bedding. Which meant he would have to do it. Which was not, in fact, such a horrid idea anymore.

If he did it for the sole and noble purpose of improving her mood and thus to improve their quality of life, it would have nothing to do with whether he cared or not.

Roxbury took a sip of wine and then acknowledged that he did *care*. The woman was his wife, and she carried his name, was under his protection, and she was beautiful and too smart for her own good. Yes, he cared. It just wasn't *love*.

He'd fallen in love dozens of times before, and had tremendously loved those fleeting, passionate affairs. He loved the first spark, and the slow burn, the wild highs, and the crushing lows. Roxbury thrived on that; a new woman was a new adventure and he did love to explore.

But now there was no escape when that heady intoxicated state ended. When the loved faded, and his interest in her waned, then what? She'd still be here, or around, forever plaguing him. He really should not fall in love with his own wife. It would be a disaster.

Either way, Roxbury did not want to ponder that now. His only thought was making her happy so he could have some peace of mind.

There was only one problem with his plan to bed her into a better mood: she hated him.

Roxbury glanced at her. She took a sip of her wine and boldly met his gaze as if she could read his thoughts and was daring him to attempt to win her over.

Julianna had dressed for dinner, which was remarkable since it was only the two of them. Her hair was done up in some arrangement with a few curls side swept to brush against her shoulder. That was one of his favorite parts on a woman— the curve of her neck to her shoulders; the expanse of décolletage and the swell of her breasts.

He noted that her blue gown was, unfortunately, modestly cut. Instead he used his imagination, piecing together images of her in that low-cut gown upon their first meeting at Knightly's office. Or how she looked that night when he had kissed her in the moonlight. His mouth went dry, and he reached for his wine again.

Roxbury noticed that she did not wear any jewelry, save for the plain gold wedding band that Timson had been sent to acquire.

His wife didn't need adornment, but the lady ought to have some jewelry.

Julianna raised the crystal glass to her lovely lips and took another sip of her wine.

Aye, he thought, there was only one thing to do: seduction. The corners of his mouth curved into a sly grin. Fortunately, he was a master at that.

"I sense trouble," she said suspiciously. His smile was a dangerous one, and she knew it. His wife was a smart one.

"As you ought to, my lady," he replied smoothly.

She opened her mouth and closed it again. He knew she was going to say "I'm not your lady" but thought better of it. He was learning her. This was progress. It was also the first rule of seduction: Every woman was different. Observe, discover and act accordingly.

That was what distinguished him from other rakes—women, to him, were not indistinguishable specimens of the female sex, but lovely, maddening, wondrous, and unique.

"How was your day, Julianna?" he asked. Another rule: Ask her about herself. Many a man failed here, especially since ladies were often brought up to ask a gent about himself.

Roxbury also indicated to the footman to refill her wineglass. For all his noble strategies for seduction and insights into women, a little alcohol intoxication never hurt.

"Are you going to have a go at me for inviting Alistair to the house?" she asked suspiciously, and reached for her wineglass. The question unnerved him for a moment. What kind of ogre did she think he was? What the devil had her last husband been like? From everything he'd heard, Somerset was in no position to complain about his wife's companions when his own were numerous and of dubious quality.

"Of course not. My home is yours. If it were a

man who might be actual competition, that would be different," he couldn't resist adding.

"Perhaps I shall invite some competition over for tea," she replied.

"I would think you were trying to get my attention," he replied.

"Of course you would," she said witheringly. But it was fair; he did tend to flatter himself.

"I'll take my brandy in the drawing room with the lady," he told a footman.

Rather than stalk ahead and expect her to follow, he stood and offered her his arm and escorted her to the drawing room like a proper gentleman.

"You are acting strangely," she said, eying him warily.

He could only grin wryly, thinking, *I'm trying to seduce you, woman! It's a privilege most ladies in London would have given their reputations for.* But he did not mention other women; he'd long ago discovered that rarely led to a romantic conversation.

She linked her arm in his and together they proceeded all of twenty steps into the other room. Roxbury liked how tall she was. It meant that his neck probably wouldn't ache went he lowered his head to kiss her, as often happened with more petite women. That was another topic of conversation he declined to introduce.

With their arms linked, Roxbury could feel the tension in the way she carried herself. She definitely needed a good bedding or something.

"A good session at Gentleman Jack's always improves my mood. You ought to try it," he suggested.

"Honestly, Roxbury," she said with a little sigh, "I think I would like it."

The possibilities were immediately obvious to him: a boxing lesson would satisfy so many of his rules of seduction.

Rule: Do something together, be it a carriage ride, a waltz, a walk in the park together, or a boxing lesson. If the activity was fraught with danger, so much the better. Roxbury often preferred to take a lady out for a carriage ride not on a sunny day, but one with a threat of rain for that reason. A woman and a weapon—even if only her fists—certainly counted as danger.

Rule: Employ affection wherever possible— a slight caress of fingers and hands, or a discrete touch at the small of a woman's back was perfect for igniting those delicious shivers of anticipation.

With this boxing lesson, he would need to correct her form, and that would provide infinite opportunities for a quick caress, a slight touch, or standing closer than was proper. At the thought he experienced one of those shivers of anticipation himself—and that was rare indeed. He had to remind himself that this was to excite her, not him.

"Shall we?" he offered, even though he knew he was going to suffer mightily for it. He suspected she was freakishly strong and he knew she owned a deep-seated anger that was always threatening to bubble to the surface.

"Are you bamming me?" she asked. "Are you really offering to teach me, a lady, to box in our drawing room?"

"Yes, although I'm absolutely certain that I will live to regret it."

The smile that lit up her face was so pure, so bright, and so rare that he knew it would be worth the pain of every blow. She was a beautiful woman, but when her lips curved up and her eyes sparkled like that . . . radiantly happy were the words that came to mind.

Roxbury, again, had to remind himself that he was the one seducing her, and that he was not to succumb himself.

"Shall we begin this evening? Right now?" she asked eagerly.

"Why not?" he responded.

With the help of footmen, they cleared a space in the drawing room by pushing all the wretched red velvet furniture against the equally awful gold damask papered walls. In the center of it all, Julianna stood in a silky blue dress with a big smile, bright eyes and little, ladylike fists at the ready.

Roxbury couldn't help but grin, and he barely suppressed a laugh.

Rule: *Enjoy it*.

"First, it's important to maintain a strong stance. Watch," he ordered. He stood with his feet comfortably apart, and his knees slightly bent.

"Done," she said, but he couldn't discern any difference, thanks to her voluminous skirts.

"I cannot tell if you are doing it correctly with your dress in the way," he said.

"Are you just trying to catch a glimpse of my ankles?" she asked, stunning him with the flirtatiousness in her voice.

"Perhaps," he admitted with a grin. It hadn't been his intention, but he wouldn't let the opportunity pass him by.

Julianna's only response was a sly smile and to lift her skirts inch by taunting inch. He saw that she wore dark blue satin slippers, decorated with silver embroidery and a few jewels, suggesting a vanity he had not attached to her. Her ankles were lovely and shapely but most entrancing of all—Lady Julianna, his former tormentor and architect of his downfall, was flirting with him.

"Now you'll also need to put your weight on the balls of your feet," he instructed. She followed. How strange. "A good stance is important because it's the source of your strength, and so you can be steady and ready for anything that comes at you."

She dropped her skirts and lifted her little female fists.

"When do I punch you, Roxbury?" she asked, so sweetly he had to smile. This was a far cry from the rough-and-tumble world at Gentleman Jack's. This was a far cry from how she usually was.

"Not yet. First you need to make a proper fist."

"Like this?" Julianna held her hand out, all balled-up and he could only think of how tiny and delicate it was. He suspected that he'd be thankful of her small, ladylike fists when she started throwing punches.

"It's important to keep your thumb on the outside," he said, taking her fist in his hands and gently urging her fingers to open.

Had they even held hands before? He didn't think so. Her soft hands felt so fragile in his. There were a few fading ink stains on her fingertips that he dared not question now—not when they were having a pleasant time and she was about to hit him.

Roxbury glanced at Julianna and saw that she, too, was staring curiously at the sight of her hand in his.

Rule: *Affection*. Check.

Gently, Roxbury pressed her fingers into a proper fist, with her thumb on the outside.

"There. That's how to make a fist," he said. "Never keep your thumb on the inside, otherwise you'll risk breaking it."

"That would never do—I wouldn't be able to write," Julianna said. So she still hadn't given up on her column.

"On second thought . . ." he drawled.

"Oh, you devil!" she exclaimed, punching him lightly on the shoulder.

But Roxbury noticed that, she, too, was laughing.

"So you have your strong stance, and you have a fist. Now, you want to hold a steady, ready position. Like this." He demonstrated with his feet slightly apart, knees a bit bent, elbows, too, with fists out in front of him. He was an agile, strong boxer, but in the drawing room, surrounded by breakable things and a female, he felt like a clumsy giant that might inadvertently cause mass destruction merely because of his size.

Julianna studied his position, adorably nibbling on her lower lip, and then tried it herself. He burst out laughing when he saw it.

The sight of a woman—with skirts, embroidered and bejeweled satin slippers, "done" hair, and small, delicate hands—in such a bloodthirsty pose struck him as utterly unexpected, comical, and charming.

"What is so funny?" she asked, lowering her fists and straightening.

"You're adorable," he said.

Julianna scowled at him, but he saw that she

was fighting a smile. It must be damned hard to be her—scowling when she wanted to smile, biting back laughter, and Lord only knew how else she restrained herself.

"We're fighting, Roxbury," she reminded him, dropping back into position.

"Yes, dear," he replied. "When you are ready, go ahead and hit me."

"I've dreamt of this," Julianna told him. She dreamt of pummeling him and he dreamt of making love. How splendid.

"Are you ready?" she asked, waving her little fists around.

"Ready," he answered.

Julianna's fist shot out and landed squarely, but lightly, on his chest. He barely felt it, and she knew it.

"I hit you harder in my dreams." Her mouth twisted into a scowl of annoyance. It was irritating when a punch didn't hit with enough force.

When Edward taught him to fight, Roxbury had the same experience—he could never hit hard enough. To teach him, Edward taunted him by calling him a sissy, a weakling, a missish twit, a sapling. And then, by God, did he land a damn good punch in his gut. His older brother had collapsed and, lying on the ground, gasped, "Well done."

That was not a method he was going to employ with Julianna out of fear she would get frustrated and call for her pistols.

"I'm sure you did hit harder in your dreams, because that punch was nothing. Do you want to know why?"

"Yes," she answered.

"You're not using all of your strength. Right now, you're hitting from here—" And to indicate exactly where, with his fingertips, Roxbury lightly traced the length of her bare skin from her shoulder to her elbow, and then to her wrist.

She shivered under his caress, and he heard the faintest gasp from her lips. He resisted the urge to smile in triumph. He also fought to keep her pleasure from affecting him. They were fighting now, but it was a prelude to making love. He should not move too fast but slow down and deeply enjoy Julianna melting under his touch.

He carried on, tracing that same line on the soft sensitive skin inside her arm. She bit her lower lip. His voice was raspier than it usually was.

"But you have much more muscle to put behind it. When you throw a punch, it should come from here," he said, stepping closer to her and placing his hand squarely on her lower back.

He was tempted to lean in and press his lips to that secret spot on a woman's neck, just below the earlobe. And that was just to start . . .

With just his fingertips, Roxbury skimmed his palm up from the dip in her lower back, valiantly ignoring the great temptation to move his hand farther down. Gently and slowly he traced the line around her hip and up along her side, all the way up to her shoulder before going the length of her arm again. Soft, bare skin under his hot, bare hands.

A gentleman did not touch a lady thusly in a drawing room. But they were married and the hideous drapes were closed to the outside world. They were quite alone.

Julianna shivered again. She might have just been ticklish, but it could also be the shiver of pleasure from his touch. The man dared to dream.

"And a good punch should also come from your heart, from your gut and from your head," he added. The mechanics and muscles weren't everything. Without passion, it would never work. He was no longer strictly on the subject of boxing.

"With everything I've got," she said succinctly.

"Yes," he said. Her eyes met his. All the smoldering glances and delicate, secret caresses in the world couldn't match true longing. That initial spark could never be forced.

Rule: *Throw out all the rules and just feel it.*

"Now try again. Hit me here," he said, indicating his chest, right above his heart.

First, Julianna pushed a wayward strand of hair out of her eyes. Then she took a deep breath and assumed the position. She rocked on her feet for a second, with her fists up near her face. And then, so fast he barely saw it, her arm shot out, landing hard on his chest and knocking his breath away.

He gave in to the urge to double over, for her sake.

"Oh! I'm so sorry. I didn't mean to hurt you!"

Julianna fluttered over him, wrapping her arms around him. It was such a lovely feeling—that of her tending to him and embracing him—that he shamelessly added a groan to encourage her. She wrapped her arms around him and "helped" him over to the settee.

"You must lie down," she demanded. Simon resisted the urge to smile or tell her that he did not need to lie down after taking a little hit from a lady—that would definitely result in a smack that would do serious damage.

So he let her fuss about, fluffing pillows and resting her hand on his chest.

He added a new rule to his repertoire: *Act hurt; encourage their tendency to nurture.*

For the very first time, she gave a damn about him. It was hilarious and wonderful all at once.

"I'll call for the smelling salts," she said, leaving him sprawled on the settee.

"Don't be ridiculous," he said. That was taking things too damn far. He was a man, for Lord's sake!

"I didn't hurt you very badly?" Julianna asked cautiously, as she took a seat beside him. "Not that you would admit it if I did."

"No, and you did very well. Now you have another manner of defending yourself," he said.

"In the event that I do not have my pistols," she remarked, grinning.

"That, too, though I was thinking of that sharp tongue of yours," he said, with a wry smile.

At that, she laughed, and it was a pretty laugh. She really needed to do it more often.

"Thank you, Roxbury," she said genuinely. He got up from his sprawl and sat up next to her.

"You might as well call me Simon," he said. "After all, we're married and have just enjoyed a good tussle in the drawing room."

She rolled her eyes like a young girl, but she was smiling.

At this moment, he was fairly certain of a good reception if he were to kiss her. She was clearly happy and feeling fond of him—more than she'd ever done, at least. She'd exercised some of her anger, making some room for pleasure.

To test the waters, he rested his hand on hers. Julianna looked up at him, curiously, but she did not move or tug her hand away. She didn't scowl, either, or make some wisecrack about his proclivities or vast previous experience in the gentle caress of a woman's hand.

This was progress.

Nevertheless, he decided he would not try to kiss her tonight, even though her lips were luscious and slightly parted. Even though he wanted to keep feeling close to her, and even though he ached to be with a woman. More startlingly, he ached to be with this one, his wife, and no other.

No, he would not kiss her tonight because these things should not be rushed and because once they began down that road, of kisses and caresses and lovemaking there would be no going back.

"Let's call it a night, shall we?" he suggested, before he changed his mind and attempted to have his way with her on the drawing room floor.

"Very well," she said promptly, and he could not detect any regret or longing in her tone.

As he followed her up the stairs, he took tremendous pleasure of the view—she had a very shapely backside. By the time they reached the top, he was sorely regretting his suggestion to end the evening, especially when she glanced over her shoulder at him, with a little suggestive flash of her green eyes and a coy smile forming on her lips.

Chapter 37

When her fellow Writing Girls arrived for afternoon tea, Julianna reluctantly showed them to the drawing room.

"How nice," Eliza said, her voice hollow, and looking around at the harvest gold damask, and the red velvet furniture, and the horrible everything. Her expression was such that *nice* was a hyperbole—and she hadn't even taken a close look at the drapes.

"Indeed," Sophie managed. "How nice."

"It's very bright," Annabelle said, making an effort to be cheerful. "And this dog is darling," she said, standing before one of the portraits of an English bulldog. For some reason, the decorator had decked the walls with an assortment of portraits of various canines.

"The house is good, and one can understand why he was loath to give it up," Julianna said. Underneath all the rubbish, it was a good home in a fashionable neighborhood.

"But the decorating is horrific," Sophie said, surveying the room again with her hands helplessly by her side. "Tell me the rest of the house is not so bad."

"You should see my bedchamber. It's very pink," Julianna said distastefully.

"Oh dear," Annabelle said with a sigh, holding a handful of drapery.

"I wonder what angry mistress did this to him," Eliza said, now examining a row of blue-and-white porcelain Chinese vases along the mantel.

"I keep meaning to ask," Julianna said. "Unless he did this to himself?"

"When do we redecorate?" Sophie asked. "Please say today."

"I'm not planning on staying here long, and I do like the idea of leaving him with this," she said, with a sweep of her hand to indicate the drawing room. She took a seat on one of the horrible velvet chairs, and her friends joined her around the tea tray.

"I was going to ask how your marriage was faring, but if you are leaving soon, I suppose that's my answer," Sophie said. Julianna handed her a cup of tea, and then poured for the others as well.

"Was it worth it?" Eliza asked.

"That depends. Is there still talk about his preferences?" Julianna asked. "When those rumors are silent, my job here is done."

"Brandon tells me that on the whole, most gentlemen are too uncomfortable to discuss it, but some of the younger, drunker lads still enjoy jokes about it," Sophie shared.

"Oh dear," Annabelle murmured before taking a bite of a ginger biscuit.

"And the ladies of the ton?" Julianna asked, with a heavy heart.

"They're all shocked, simply shocked," Sophie declared. "They never saw any of this scandal coming. But there are a few former paramours with suspicious husbands that are fully embracing the rumor that Roxbury might have only been chatting with their wives, rather than . . ."

Annabelle blushed and sipped her tea.

"So this is all progress, I suppose," Julianna said even though it wasn't, really. She had so badly wanted to hear, "Oh, no talks about you or Roxbury anymore, except to wonder where you are."

"It will die down eventually," Sophie said. "It always does."

"And my reputation, dare I ask?" Julianna ventured.

"It's all quite confusing," Eliza said.

"Many are shocked at the marriage, for they never saw it coming," Sophie explained.

"None of us did," Annabelle said. "I still can't quite believe that you married the great rake Roxbury."

"No one believes it was a love match," Eliza said plainly.

"And they are having great fun at speculating what secret, scandalous reason drove two people to the altar, when they had so rarely been together publicly. Well, save for that serenade . . ." Sophie said.

"I'm not sure 'serenade' is the word for what happened," Annabelle mused.

"I'm not sure there is a word for it," Eliza replied.

All Julianna could think of were the missed opportunities for "Fashionable Intelligence." If she'd only written about her own scandal as Eliza advised and Knightly wished, she could have led the conversation among the ton. She could have introduced exclusive details, false leads, and fictitious stories that could have changed everything.

Julianna suffered hot, shooting pangs of regret.

But no—she'd been too stubborn. She had tried to ignore it, hoping it would go away. She was trying to protect the name of Somerset—and when had that ever done anything good for her? Now she didn't even have that anymore. Oh, how it burned.

"So my marriage is discussed," she summed up bitterly before taking a sip of her tea.

"In drawing rooms and ballrooms all over town, I'm afraid," Sophie replied breezily, and reaching for a ginger biscuit.

"That must mean that I haven't a hope of reclaiming my column anytime soon," Julianna said glumly.

"Not necessarily. It's not going so well without you, in fact. At least, not as well as Knightly had hoped."

"Grenville just doesn't have the same deft touch with society gossip as you," Annabelle added.

"Grenville! They gave my precious "Fashionable Intelligence" to that cranky old bat? *Grenville?*"

The man in question covered parliamentary reports and other *very important* but *very boring* news and business. Not only did he not love gossip, he thought it trivial, frivolous, and a tremendous waste of time.

That he should compose editions of her precious "Fashionable Intelligence" truly made her burn hot with regret. What had she done?

"Alistair and I are doing the bulk of it, but I'm afraid we just don't have the same wit, either."

"Oh, my baby . . . My poor, precious baby," Julianna lamented.

Thankfully, no one said something to the effect of "oh, it's just a newspaper column" because the Writing Girls—and only the Writing Girls—knew it was so much more. It was their identity, their livelihood, and their income. It was a point of pride and a source of deep satisfaction. It was anything but some column inches in news rag.

"I created 'Fashionable Intelligence' from nothing," Julianna began passionately. "Before I went to see him that day, Knightly was publishing 'News from Court' that was about as interesting as a schoolboy's grammar lesson and as widely read. I built up my own network of informants—Penny and her six sisters, and my favorite penny-a-liners. Within a year, I was rivaling a gossip columnist who had been at work for forty years!"

She paused in her rant only to take a breath.

"And it's not just gossip, or silly frivolous society news! Other people's business is a valuable commodity and a reflection of our deepest held values. If I write that red silk is the latest fashion of the fabulous, people will demand it and markets will shift to supply it. If I claim that jaunts to Gretna Green are all the rage, I can guarantee even among couples with parental approval and no need for the lengthy trip will elope there," Julianna said.

"You'll be back in no time," Eliza said, smiling broadly, and the others nodded resolutely.

"You never did tell us about how your marriage is faring," Sophie said again.

"Oh. That." Julianna sipped her tea. She eyed one of the ginger biscuits but found she had no appetite.

"You have spent almost a week together now," Annabelle added.

"You have every comfort available to you," Eliza said. "Except good taste in decorating."

Julianna had to crack a smile at that.

"Where is he, anyway?" Annabelle wondered, idly looking around as if Roxbury had been overlooked in a corner or something.

"I have no idea! He's not here!" Julianna exclaimed. She had woken to discover him missing. His slovenly attired valet refused to talk free of charge, and Penny still hadn't uncovered Roxbury's whereabouts. She had to wonder, did rakes go to visit their mistresses at first light? Most men probably didn't, but then again, she hadn't married most men—either the first time or the second.

It rankled that there were secrets in her marriage. It also rankled that she could have sworn he was about to kiss her last night, and he did not. Why, oh, why had he not done so? She'd been so certain that he was considering it. And, terrifyingly, she wanted him to!

Even at the best of times, Julianna's store of patience was not vast.

"He insists that I must stay here for the sake of appearances, which I know is the thing to do. But then he goes out, where I know not. He left at dawn this morning and no one will tell me where he has gone. Yesterday, he spent hours at Gentleman Jack's."

"Do you think . . ." Eliza dropped her voice ". . . that he might not be where he says he is?" Julianna knew what she was really asking—could he be with another woman, already?

"I think he was just boxing," Julianna said resolutely. "But if he's betrayed me already, I will murder him."

"Quite a vehement response," Eliza mentioned, while pouring another cup of tea.

"Especially since you don't really care for him at all," Sophie said, but she was looking again at the curtains—and not looking Julianna in the eye.

"What are you saying?" Julianna asked of her friends. She looked at Annabelle for an answer.

"I think they are remarking that you seem to care more deeply for Roxbury than previously admitted. But I could be mistaken," Annabelle hastily added.

"You are mistaken. I care not. It's my pride that I'm concerned with, that's all," Julianna said dismissively—or as much as she could manage. "And it's barely been a week since we've exchanged our vows. Really, it's too soon to start ignoring them."

"When is it acceptable, then?" Eliza wondered, sipping her tea.

"I believe it is until death do you part," Sophie said. "So, never, basically."

"It's not acceptable at all. Ever," Annabelle said resolutely.

"That's all beside the point entirely. The real issue is that he has left for no apparent reason, and without informing me. He went off yesterday, and again today," Julianna said. But then she thought of the previous evening's activity, and knew she had to tell her friends. She grinned and said, "But last night, he taught me to box."

"Really?" Sophie asked. "And I merely take tea after supper."

"What was it like?" Annabelle asked, tilting her head curiously.

"It was very . . . oh, just wonderful. I learned how to throw a punch and I got to hit him, which I had been aching to do for weeks now."

"How did it feel?" Annabelle asked. "I could never imagine striking someone."

"It was deeply satisfying. At the same time, the lesson was oddly . . . seductive."

"How so?" Eliza asked, leaning in curiously.

"Just the close proximity, the touching, the shivers. And having my urge to hit him satisfied, so now I feel . . . Oh, I can't quite explain," Julianna said. She had enjoyed herself, with him, and wished to do so again. But now he had vanished.

"We're all dying to know, if . . . you know . . ." Sophie said quietly.

"No," Julianna said, dropping her voice as well. "I thought he might try last night, but he just said good-night and went whistling on his way to his bedchamber."

"What does that mean?" Eliza wondered.

"I have no idea. Men generally do not make sense," Julianna replied.

"He's trying to seduce you," Annabelle said flatly. Three pairs of eyes widened in shock at dear, sweet, innocent Annabelle speaking so plainly about seduction.

"How do you figure?" Sophie asked.

"I read it in a Minerva Press novel . . . or twenty," Annabelle said, sighing impatiently. "Honestly, how have you not figured this out?"

"I don't follow," Julianna said. "He taught me how to box. That's all."

"No, that's not all, you ninny! He's making you want him by giving you a little bit—a gentle caress, the suggestion of more—but not going all the way. At least, that's what it sounds like. If nothing else, it's Roxbury, for heaven's sake! Before you spread those rumors, he was *legendary* for seducing women."

"And he has you captive under his roof," Eliza said with a mischievous grin.

"Oh, Jules, you don't stand a chance!" Sophie exclaimed.

"You're going to fall in love with your husband!" Annabelle said gleefully.

"I will do no such thing. I will not be seduced and I will not fall in love. And if he should try anything . . ."

"You know how to fight now," Eliza finished.

"I wish I knew how to box," Annabelle said.

"I'll teach you," Julianna offered. "Let's do it right now. First, let's move the furniture out of the way."

Annabelle sensibly rang the bell to request assistance from the footmen.

"Can we move it outside of the house entirely?" Sophie asked, once they began pushing tables and chairs aside.

"I know it's awful, but it's pointless to redecorate when I won't be staying to enjoy it," Julianna said. In another day or two she'd return to 24 Bloomsbury Place. If her legendary husband was indeed bent upon seducing her, it would be far too dangerous to stay, because . . .

She wasn't quite sure why, actually. She bit her lip, dismissed the thought, and adopted the boxing position, just as Roxbury had taught her.

"The most important thing is a strong stance," she said, raising her fists.

Chapter 38

When Brandon occasionally referred to the Writing Girls "taking over" his home, Roxbury never gave much thought to it. Brandon's home was vast, and there were only four women. Surely, it was an exaggeration.

Upon entering his foyer after a long day away, Roxbury learned that it was not an exaggeration at all. Who knew that four women could make so much noise at such an impossibly high pitch?

Pembleton, the butler, looked close to tears. Behind him stood Mrs. Keane, the housekeeper, with a handkerchief pressed to her mouth and her eyes bright with tears. It was not clear, however, if she was stifling sobs or laughter. Timson leaned against the wall, smirking. Behind them, it seemed the entire household staff was gathered around the closed drawing room doors.

The noise—God above, the noise that four women could make! Roxbury was painfully curious and terrified.

"Julianna, watch out!" someone shrieked. He—and his staff—all winced at the sound of shattering pottery. The Chinese vases. He'd never cared for them but hopefully they were not valuable antiques.

One of the girls yelled, "Use both fists, Sophie!"

Roxbury's eyes widened. A few of the footmen snickered until given a stern glance. That was a duchess they were laughing at.

Another hollered, "Harder, Annabelle."

Then even Roxbury could not contain his smirk. Pembleton gave *him* a sharp look for setting a bad example for the staff.

The girls were either boxing—a hilarious and horrifying thought—or . . . he did not dare consider what other activities they might be engaged in. Boxing. It had to be that.

Something *else* shattered. They all winced again. Mrs. Keane sobbed, "Oh, the vases!" A maid standing to his left muttered, under her breath, "Good riddance. I hate dusting the darn things."

His staff looked imploringly at him—none more so than Pembleton.

"I will take care of this," Roxbury said, squaring his shoulders and standing up straighter.

Slowly, reluctantly they dispersed. After a deep breath, he pushed open the heavy oak doors.

He saw four women, fighting. They wore their nice day dresses, like proper ladies, but their fists were flying like those of brawling boys. Elegant coiffures had not survived the melee. Julianna, he noticed, looked particularly fetching with her hair tousled and falling in disarray.

Two of the girls practiced throwing punches while Julianna and Sophie held up down pillows; little white feathers clouded the air like a winter snowfall. Mrs. Keane was not going to be laughing when she saw that—or the remnants of a teacup shattered on the floor. So it had not been any of the vases to go, to the disappointment of his maid.

But none of that compared to the fighting girls. Roxbury leaned against the doorframe, folded his arms, grinned, and watched.

They were having a ball. Rocking on their feet, dodging jabs, and ducking punches. There was much laughter, and more shrieks to "watch out" or "hit harder." He did not want to bring an end to such joy. And, oh, the blackmail possibilities!

It was Sophie who noticed him first. Her eyes widened in shock. Eliza paused in her punches to turn and look. She gave him a cheeky grin.

And Julianna . . .

She looked at him, and then she surveyed the damage to the room, as if seeing it through his eyes. The furniture shoved against the walls, shattered china, the down feathers, the destroyed pillows, the girls in utter disarray. Her lips parted and she mouthed the words "Oh damn," but then she gave in, lowered the pillow she held, and smiled.

The blonde one, however, was not attending to her surroundings. Her back was to the door and she must have been boxing with her eyes closed— a tactic not recommended. Her fist flew out and landed on Julianna's cheek.

"Ow!"

"Oh! Oh my gosh!" she exclaimed and all the girls oohed and fluttered around. A thousand apologies followed. Roxbury would have done something, but the girls formed a wall around his wife. There were calls for smelling salts and a doctor and medicine and even a surgeon. He called to one of the maids to hurry for supplies.

Julianna sat down on a chair, with her hand over her cheek. It wasn't long before she was laughing so hard that tears came to her eyes.

"I'm so sorry," Annabelle said for the thousandth time.

"It's fine, Annabelle. It was only an accident."

"Does it hurt?" Sophie asked.

"Not really. You'll have to try harder next time, Annabelle," Julianna replied. But Roxbury saw her wince when she touched the already developing bruise. It was not going to be pretty.

A maid arrived with a cold compress and the Writing Girls parted to let him close to Julianna. He knelt before her and pressed the cold towel to her bruised cheek.

"Thank you," she said softly.

"Of course," he replied. Other than the cause of her injury being so very unusual, it did feel right to be tending to her. He wanted to take her in his arms. In fact, he wanted to take her upstairs to his bedchamber.

Through it all, Julianna's gaze never wavered from his. After a moment, he realized they had all fallen silent. Being women, they were probably assigning all kinds of significance to his act of applying a cold compress to his wife's bruise. He wanted to say it was nothing of significance, simple care and concern. But that wouldn't have been the complete truth.

Instead, he stood up and surveyed the damage to the drawing room.

"At least you had the good sense to close the curtains," he remarked. Really, they were the most hideous, god-awful things he had ever seen. Given how many bedroom curtains he had made a point of closing, this was saying something. Lydia certainly had her revenge. "Just imagine if the Man About Town got word of this."

"Writing Girls engaged in fisticuffs," Sophie remarked, giggling.

"Writing Girl brawls," Annabelle said with a chuckle.

"The Brawling Girls," Julianna shouted, to much laughter.

"*The Weekly*'s wrestling wenches," Roxbury added, to all the girls' merriment.

"Skirmish in skirts," Eliza said, amidst the laughter.

"I imagine Knightly would be proud of your headlines," Annabelle said. "But how happy would he be with a cartoon of this for the front page?"

"We'll have to pose for a cartoonist!" Sophie leapt up to strike a pose, and in the process she knocked over one of the Chinese vases on the mantel.

"Oh dear," she said woefully. "I hope that wasn't a priceless family heirloom."

"I as well," Roxbury replied. Given that it had been selected by his former mistress Lydia Smythe, who had no idea about things like priceless objects and valuable heirlooms, he didn't think they were of any worth whatsoever.

"You're just trying to rush the redecorating!" Julianna exclaimed.

Sophie shrugged with a little grin, and pushed the shards of broken pottery aside with her foot.

"Redecorating?" he echoed, looking from Writing Girl to Writing Girl.

"I will not be redecorating," Julianna affirmed.

"Pity, that," Roxbury, Annabelle, Sophie, and Eliza all said at once. That set off another round of laughter.

"Would you ladies like to join us for supper this evening?" Roxbury asked. Rule: *Win over a lady's friends.*

"Oh how lovely! Thank you, but I promised Brandon . . ." Sophie said, beginning to gather her things.

"I have a column to write," Eliza explained. Simon noticed that Julianna winced at that.

"I must help my sister-in-law," Annabelle said with such a sad sigh that Simon did not get a very good opinion of her relative.

Julianna escorted them to the foyer to say good-bye, leaving him alone in the devastated drawing room. His staff was going to suffer apoplexies in droves when they saw it.

If anyone had told him that marriage would involve coming home to a skirmish in skirts with four brawling girls, he might have considered it sooner. Married life was definitely not as boring as he feared it would be.

A moment later, Julianna burst into the drawing room. "We have received an invitation! It's for Lady Mowbry's ball tomorrow night. I can wear my new cerulean blue satin and I can borrow Sophie's sapphires . . ."

It did not escape his notice that she lovingly traced the script, or how she clearly enjoyed the feeling of crisp vellum under her fingertips. If she slept with the invitation under her pillow tonight, he would not be surprised.

But he suspected that he would have a bruise to match hers when he said they could not attend. There would be no sapphires and satins of any color, or waltzes with the ton looking on.

"Oh Roxbury, do you know what this means?" she sighed. "We are no longer complete and utter social outcasts. Our reputations are on the mend and soon, darling, we shall be able to pretend this whole thing never happened."

Just imagining that happy day brought a bright smile to her face, but it hit him like a jab to the gut. She was eager to move out and move on when he was bent on seducing her. He was already losing her—and he didn't even have her.

These past few days he savored the novel sensation of someone waiting for him at home. It changed things. Where he might have lingered away from home, he did not. When he might have stopped at the club, he did not. All he could think was to return to *her*.

It wasn't something he'd ever experienced with another woman. Naturally, he had anticipated a midnight visit or a quick, illicit afternoon call. But he never experienced an urgent need to be under the same roof as a woman.

"Darling . . ." he said gently, and she looked up curiously. He would have to tell her they were stuck together for yet another evening.

Roxbury guided her to the mirror above the mantel, where he stood behind her. He watched as she looked at him with a mixture of annoyance and wonder. Then her lips parted in horror as she noticed the big, purple bruise on her cheekbone.

At first, he noticed the way she bit her lip. And

then he noticed her lovely green eyes were bright with tears. She was desperately trying not to cry.

Though he hated when women cried, Roxbury took some comfort in that Julianna probably loathed it just as much. There was one thing to do: he turned her toward him, enclosed her in his arms, and allowed her to nestle against his chest and bury her face in the crook of his shoulder and wet his shirt with her tears.

He felt rather than saw her sobs. She twined her arms around him and rested her cheek on his shoulder. Julianna Somerset Roxbury, infamous author of "Fashionable Intelligence," crying in his arms, in his horribly decorated drawing room. What had the world come to? A month ago, a week ago even, he would have scoffed had someone suggested the notion.

For better or for worse, Roxbury was fairly experienced with weeping women. All the ended affairs, or rumors about him with other women . . . these things tended to make a woman cry and they tended to make him deal with it.

This time, it was different.

"I never cry," she sobbed. He murmured his agreement, and stroked her lower back with his palm and just listened. "Not even when Somerset died. Or when Sophie left. Or when Knightly fired me. Or even when we married."

"Why are you crying now?" he asked.

"I want my life back. I want to get out of this house. I want to write and go to parties and buy my own dresses. I want to live in my own home and be my own mistress."

At least, that's what he thought she said. Between the sniffles and sobs, with her face now buried in his cravat, everything was a bit muffled and barely audible.

What he did understand made him burst out laughing.

She stood back, affronted.

"What is so humorous about this? I pour my heart out to you and you laugh? You are utterly heartless, Roxbury," she said, with her mouth forming into a perfect, kissable pout.

"So many women have schemed, plotted, and begged to become my wife, or mistress, or to reside here. They wanted me to buy them dresses and take them to parties. Of all the women in the world, I end up with the one who doesn't want any of that."

"Women can be idiots when it comes to rich, handsome, and charming men. Marriage. Dresses," she scoffed. "As if any of that matters."

It didn't matter at all, and she knew it. The pace of his heart quickened, because he'd never been with a woman who cared so little for those things. What could he provide her, then? Love, or something like it—but would that be enough?

To ponder that was to venture into uncharted emotional depths and he wasn't equipped for such an expedition at the moment.

Instead, he said with the classic Roxbury grin, "So you think I'm handsome and charming?"

"Occasionally," Julianna admitted. She took a few steps and collapsed onto the settee. He followed and sat beside her. "But it doesn't count for anything. Somerset was handsome and charming and a horrible husband."

"How so?" Though he would never admit it

aloud, Roxbury was tremendously curious. What had gone so wrong with her first marriage?

Usually, he couldn't muster up much interest in the husbands of his lovers. But in this instance, it was different. He was desperate for a glimpse of the girl so in love she eloped at seventeen. How had she ended up here in his arms, in his drawing room?

"Does it matter now what made him so terrible?" she asked with a shrug.

"I'll probably be a horrible husband whether you tell me or not, but I'd at least like to be horrible in my own unique way," he answered truthfully.

Julianna assessed him frankly with her lovely green eyes.

"Very well," she said matter-of-factly. After a deep breath, she told him. "His death involved alcohol, a prostitute, and a moving carriage—and he was attempting to manage all three himself. He died doing what he loved best—drinking and whoring and generally behaving like a halfwit. His will included provisions for three former mistresses and their bastards. I was left the house in an unfashionable neighborhood and a pittance of an annuity."

"That explains our extremely detailed marriage contract and settlement requirements for you," he remarked, when really he was confounded by what she described. How could one manage a woman and drive a carriage, whilst drunk? Apparently, one could not.

His wife had been married to a man who thought that was a suitable combination of companions and activities. Idiot.

No wonder she was such a shrew.

"That's exactly why," she said. "I'm not making that mistake twice."

"Smart girl," he answered. "Did your family not help you?"

"I foolishly eloped with a man they disapproved of. My mother, bless her, has never ceased writing to me thrice weekly, so I wasn't disowned. But while they might have helped me, I would be damned before I asked."

"Of course," he said, shifting uncomfortably. When he had been faced with poverty he had raged about it, but he had not done anything. Only at the end, when compliance with the ultimatum seemed hopeless did he think about going alone. Shameful.

He had become one of those people that married for money. Granted, she had, too, but it wasn't the same.

"I wrote, Roxbury, so I could have a roof over my head. So I could have my dignity." She spoke with a bone-deep certainty, and her voice carried a sad note of longing. Writing for Julianna wasn't just the glamour of a gossip column in a popular newspaper, or being a Writing Girl. She wrote to live, with the world knocking at her door, and a hunger in her belly. Her soul, her pride, her dignity, her livelihood were on the line with every stroke of pen on paper. She was a Lady but she was no idle society girl.

Somewhere along the line Roxbury had begun to fall in love with her—perhaps the first seed was sown with the first kiss, or during their first waltz. It might have been what he was trying to tell her the night he sang "Country John" outside her window. His decision to seduce her had been made long before, and it wasn't a decision so much as accepting his fate.

As for the marriage, and the money . . . the truth was that he married her for the money. But equally true was the undeniable fact that he had gone and fallen in love with his wife.

If hell froze over, he couldn't quite tell.

The planet did not seem to shift, and he didn't know if the stars had realigned or not. His heart didn't pound and his breath did not catch. But he felt different—he felt sure and strong. And terrified. Could he be a man worthy of her love?

She was a stunning, determined, revolutionary, history-making woman. He was just some rich, idle rake who married a scandalous woman for money and to vex his parents.

"Where were you today?" she asked, and he heard the *years* in her voice. Years of strain from wondering where her husband was, who he was with, what trouble he was up to. Somerset had caused his fair share of her weariness. Roxbury resolved to stop adding to her heartache.

How well did she distinguish between him and Somerset in her head and heart? Roxbury suspected not very much. Suddenly, he could see *everything* in a different light.

So, he did not take the accusation to heart. It was clear to him now that his task was to prove he was nothing like Somerset.

"I was not with a woman today," he said, knowing that he should say something quickly. He did not wish to tell her where he really had been. Not yet.

"Were you with a man?" she asked, but he could see she was teasing. Mostly.

"No. And you know that I was not with a man that night. Or any night," he said, resting his hand over hers.

"Yes, yes, I know," she said with a little laugh. "You are a hot-blooded man, with an insatiable appetite for making love to women all through the day, and all through the night."

"Do you not believe me?" he asked. "Shall I prove it to you?"

"Oh, I believe you," she replied. "No proof necessary."

"Oh darling," he murmured, grinning, as he put his arm around her shoulders. She burst out laughing and he did, too.

Julianna did not move away.

He saw that she was stealing glances at him from behind lowered lashes.

From years of experience, he knew the moment for a kiss when he saw it. Still, he felt as nervous as a schoolboy. As if it was his first time. As if it meant something. They sat close together, with his arm around her on the settee in the drawing room with the curtains closed and a few candles burning slowly.

Logic and reason had not left him. He knew very well he was nervous because he loved her, they were married, and he was uncertain of her feelings for him.

His heart began to pound because he was about to kiss the woman he loved. Already, he didn't want it to end.

Julianna, her full lips slightly parted, looked at him curiously, nervously. He saw uncertainty in her eyes. He had to take her in his arms and show her the passionate love of a reformed rake.

This was the perfect moment.

It was also the moment that Pembleton knocked on the door to say that supper was ready at their convenience and that the small matter of the attempted burglary had been resolved.

Chapter 39

The next morning

"Attempted burglaries, violent ladies, mysterious disappearances . . . So much excitement and drama yesterday," Julianna mused to Roxbury at the breakfast table. Beginning with boxing with her friends (most unusual) and ending with . . . that deeply personal conversation with her husband (also a novelty).

Julianna sipped her tea and marveled at that.

She and Somerset had a wild passion; there was little conversation and none of it had been deeply personal. To her shock, it seemed Roxbury might not be another Somerset after all. Apparently one rake was not the same as another. This was a revelation to her, the implications of which had kept her up tossing and turning quite late. She still wasn't entirely sure of what to make of it all.

If Roxbury was not some run-of-the-mill, garden-variety rake, then who was he?

She eyed him as he drank his coffee and read the paper. Roxbury was handsome. He was by all

accounts a very good-natured, charming man—
except he was often angry with her. Admittedly,
she provoked him. He liked boxing, he liked his
club, and he liked singing ballads. He loved women.

But what else did she know of him? His family?
There was that brother in the portrait, but Roxbury never spoke of him, which meant that some
sleuthing was in order.

"What disappeared?" he asked, looking through
the paper.

"You did. Yesterday. I still do not know where
you had gone," Julianna said.

"Funny, that," he responded evasively. There
was a spark of mischief in his eyes.

"Yes, it's hilarious," she said dryly. But there
was a spark of mischief in her eyes, too. She might
like him, after all. Certainly not love—that was
another mistake she would not make twice. But
it turned out that Roxbury wasn't so awful. He
taught her to box, held her when she sobbed, and
inspired all sorts of naughty thoughts.

"You don't like having secrets kept from you, do
you?" he asked.

"I'm a gossip columnist. It's torture," Julianna
answered. Honestly, she was like a dog with a bone
when it came to secrets. Until she knew where he
had gone, she would think of nothing else.

Except, perhaps, kissing him.

Well, she would also wonder incessantly about
that attempted burglary last night. One of the scul-
lery maids had heard a racket and found an open
window, a fallen pile of boxes, and a general muck
of things that had been carelessly stacked in his
way. Roxbury and the staff concluded that the bur-

glar had knocked over the boxes while attempting to enter, then become scared and fled without bothering to close the window.

It was probably just someone hungry from the streets, and attempting to break in for a bite to eat. She could not fault that, and hoped they got what they wanted.

Roxbury had been about to kiss her last night, she was sure of it. She glanced at him again, and he looked up to catch her eye. She smiled slightly. He winked and returned to the newspaper. She smiled more broadly.

Yes, he had been about to kiss her. Even thinking about it now made her feel giddy and nervous all at once. She became warm as she thought about it more—and at the breakfast table nonetheless! It was not the place for a lady to have such thoughts.

"What wicked things are you thinking?" Roxbury asked, having finished with the paper and clearly taking note of her blush.

"Secret ones," she responded. Suddenly she didn't loathe him anymore. She said it suddenly, but over the course of days or weeks that anger had faded. Now she lived with a handsome, charming man who was not, in fact, a typical rake, and she was glad he had been about to kiss her and disappointed that he hadn't.

"I'd suggest an outing for today, except for that bruise. The last thing I need the ton to do is add wife abuse to my list of sins."

"Oh, please let's go out. We don't need to get ices at Gunther's. We can do something where they might not notice." Getting out of this house and escaping her plaguing, wicked thoughts would be just the thing. She might even engage him in a conversation in which he would reveal where he'd been yesterday.

After a short, heated debate it was settled that they would go for a drive in Hyde Park and she would keep her bonnet low to cover the purple bruise on her cheek. In fact, they would venture to join the promenade of the high and mighty of society out for a drive on Rotten Row. As long as Julianna kept her head ducked low.

They took Roxbury's shiny black phaeton instead of the enclosed carriage with the bullet hole through the family crest still awaiting repairs.

"You know it is a ruled case in all romances that when a lover and his mistress go out riding together, some adventure must befall them," Julianna recited as they drove away from the house.

"Who says that?" Roxbury asked.

"It's from *Belinda* by Maria Edgeworth."

"I didn't read that one," said Roxbury.

"I'm not surprised," she remarked. It was an incredibly popular women's novel that she had enjoyed once upon a time. She wondered how true it was. Would an adventure befall them today?

She always did enjoy a spot of excitement.

They proceeded to the park without incident and joined the promenade of other carriages along Rotten Row.

"They are all watching us," Roxbury remarked. They were not subtle about it, either. Many a carriage slowed down as they passed the unfathomable sight of Lord and Lady Roxbury in public, together.

Lady Drawling Rawlings was traveling with

Lady Stewart-Wortly and neither lady acknowledged the Roxburys, though Lady Rawlings demanded the carriage to slow as they drove by. Carriages full of their former friends and acquaintances passed by, but no one condescended to even wave hello.

"They are waiting for us to cause another scandal," Julianna said softly. Those who snubbed them now had once fallen all over themselves to associate with them both. God, if she still had her column the revenge she could enact . . .

"I am sorely tempted to provide a scandal," Roxbury replied tightly. Her skin tingled with a sense of delightful anticipation.

"What would you do?" she asked curiously.

"Oh, darling. Where to begin?" Roxbury said with a laugh. "I could kiss you right now. Deeply and passionately kiss you. It would give Lady Stewart-Wortly an apoplexy and for that reason alone, I'm considering it."

"While driving the carriage?" Julianna asked, slightly wary.

"No, I would stop so that everyone could jostle around for the perfect view," he answered, and she knew he had really listened when she told him about Somerset.

More carriages slowed to ascertain that yes, Lord and Lady Roxbury were indeed out and about. She could practically hear the old matrons exclaiming "Oh the horrors!" and Lady Stewart-Wortly was probably preparing a harangue about their violation of all decency.

But she was with a devilishly handsome man who listened to her, taught her to box, and who, any day now, was going to kiss her senseless, so she couldn't quite care that an old bat like Lady Stewart-Wortly stuck up her nose as she drove past them.

"For a scandal, I was thinking more along the lines of removing my bonnet, exposing my bruise, and you could lose your cravat," she said.

"Publicly in a state of undress. Now you're talking," he replied, grinning.

"If you had a cheroot I could smoke it," Julianna said, a note of glee creeping into her voice. It was quite fun to think of all the naughty things she could do. Her reputation couldn't sink much lower, so there was really no reason not to remove her bonnet to feel the sun on her face and light up a cheroot for a smoke while on a leisurely drive on Rotten Row with her equally scandalous husband.

"If I had a cheroot *I* would smoke it—in front of a lady," he dared.

"Shocking. Do you have the brandy in this carriage, as well?"

"Darling, it's not yet noon," Roxbury chided.

"The purpose is to cause a scandal, mind you," she lectured.

"Then why don't you prop up your feet and give the ton a glimpse of your lovely ankles."

She burst out laughing, loudly. Heads turned to look, with mouths open and eyebrows raised. Not only had Lord and Lady Roxbury left the house, but they were enjoying themselves, too! Socially ostracized people were not supposed to be out laughing in the sunshine. Everyone knew that.

"Oh! My modesty!" she exclaimed, still laughing.

The picture she was imagining was just delightful: A lady without her bonnet and the sun on her face, bruised from boxing, smoking a cheroot, and sipping a brandy with her feet propped up on the carriage and ankles exposed. Of course, it wasn't complete without the rakish husband beside her, also smoking, drinking, and lacking articles of clothing.

"If I have so shocked your gentle sensibilities, you might also pretend to swoon," Roxbury suggested. "Though, unfortunately, I am not in the habit of carrying smelling salts."

"I am not the sort of woman who needs them."

"My kind of woman," he said. "Though a well-timed faint can be used to great effect."

"And if I were to do so now?" she asked coyly.

Roxbury turned to look at her, and her breath caught in her throat. He was so handsome and charming, and he was looking at her with a little bit of mischief and lust and something like adoration. Most of all he seemed happy to be with her. That was what took her breath away and made her heart pound.

"If you fainted, I would catch you, my Lady Scandalous," he murmured.

"Lord and Lady Scandalous. The name suits us," she remarked softly.

"It does," he agreed. And for the first time, it felt like they were an "us," a pair, a couple, united. There would be other Roxburys and Somersets but this was a name that was theirs alone.

She added a feeling of warmth to the breathlessness and the heart pounding. It wasn't just the weather, either. It was a feeling of something like safety, or the comfort that came from knowing one was not alone in the world.

"It's quite warm out today," Julianna remarked.

"Indeed," Roxbury agreed.

"My garments are rather confining," she stated.

"Then I suggest you remove them," he replied evenly.

"Honestly, my Lord Scandalous! Shocking!" she exclaimed, feigning prudery and propriety.

And with that, like a proper young miss who had been upset by an offense to decency, Julianna fainted into Roxbury's arms.

He dropped the reins to catch her. The horses stopped trotting, and wandered to the edge of the path to graze on the grass. Carriages swerved around them, drivers hollered, horses whinnied.

And people gawked at the sight of Lady Julianna in the arms of her husband. *Perhaps it was a love match after all . . .*

Lord Scandalous held his lady, and she indulged in the sensation of a man's arms around her, supporting and protecting her. She'd forgotten about this. But then again, it hadn't quite been like this before. This was something spectacular.

Roxbury gazed at her warmly. His smile was for her, and her alone.

When had things changed that he smiled at her like that—genuinely, warmly, adoringly—and that she liked it? In fact, she probably had a similarly gushing expression as well.

What had happened? Had they fallen in l—? No, that was ridiculous. She just didn't loathe him anymore, that was all. Any woman would enjoy being held by him; in fact, many had.

Most of all, though, Julianna ached for him to

kiss her deeply and passionately, right here and now. Lady Stewart-Wortly had nothing to do with it.

"This is quite romantic, darling," Roxbury said softly.

"No one has ever called me darling before. I like it."

"My darling Lady Scandalous," he murmured. "Let's go home."

Was this marriage a love match or was it a sham? That was the subject hotly debated in a carriage comprising the Man About Town and his companions. They had joined the throngs along Rotten Row, and it became more crowded by the minute as word spread that the scandalous couple of the moment was out and about.

Generally, he was able to maintain a certain detachment from his subjects. But this story, with its twists and turns, had the Man About Town just as captivated as the rest of London.

"But what does Lord Roxbury stand to gain by a marriage to a widow who was, by all accounts, not very wealthy?" Lady Gilbert asked.

"Especially when he is decidedly not the marrying kind," Lady Walmsly added, and Lady Gilbert blushed and murmured her agreement.

Usually, the Man About Town knew these things and it burned that he did not.

"To look at them, though, they seem very much in love," Lord Walpole pointed out. He held up his monocle to the approaching spectacle. They all turned and peered quite blatantly as their carriage slowed to pass Lord and Lady Roxbury's.

Lord Roxbury said something to make Lady Roxbury laugh rather loudly.

"It must be love," Lord Walpole said confidently and Lord Brookes rolled his eyes.

"But what is so humorous about a marriage of convenience?" Lord Brookes asked.

What really concerned the Man About Town about this whole Lord and Lady Roxbury business was that it concerned his number one suspect for his potential rival, the Lady of Distinction.

The column was undoubtedly written by someone else lately—someone with a heavy hand who clearly took no joy in the subject matter. The switch occurred at approximately the same time as the lady's marriage. She hadn't been sending out any messages to *The Weekly* offices, either (he followed).

In fact, she sat at home and entertained a few callers and Lord only knew what Lord and Lady Roxbury got up to when those terrible curtains of theirs were occasionally drawn tightly shut.

Too many questions. Not enough answers.

Again, his thoughts returned to retiring. But not tonight . . .

Chapter 40

Later that evening, just after midnight

Roxbury had been enjoying all sorts of wanton, shameless, and very naked fantasies about his wife when he heard the noise. In fact, he'd been considering getting out of bed and going to her bedchamber to enact said wanton, shameless, and very naked fantasies. It was wrong that she lay in her bed, alone, and that he lay in his bed, alone.

But that unusual sound made him pause, and after a few seconds he was able to place it as the sound of someone stepping on the creaky stair. It was not the sound of a servant, who would be using the backstairs anyway. It was too clumsy, too hesitant. It also sounded like someone sneaking up the stairs—or down and out.

Oh, that woman was not going to leave him now! Not after everything they'd been through together, and not after today. He had held her and called her darling. She had smiled and said she liked it. It was all the more amazing, given that just a month or so earlier they'd been at each other's throats like cat and dog.

His ambition had been to seduce her, but now it wasn't just about bedding. It was about love, and a marriage, and not ruining everything. There were no words to describe the terror this inspired in him and, he was beginning to understand, in her, too. But terrifying as it may be, he was determined to stand his ground and stick it out. He would not tolerate her walking out on him now.

Across the hall . . .

He had not kissed her during the remainder of their carriage ride. Nor did he kiss her upon their return to the house. Not before supper, and definitely not during. He did not kiss her after supper, either, or while he took his brandy in the drawing room with her as she had her tea. Not even at her bedchamber door after they'd walked up the stairs together.

It was maddening and she was worked up into an intolerable state of frustrated longing. He was affectionate with her—touching her hand, or brushing wayward strands of hair away from her face, or pressing his hand against her lower back and hinting at going lower. Thus, she concluded that he did not find her repulsive. Given his reputed enormous sexual appetites . . .

Why had he not kissed her?

Julianna lay wide-awake and alone in her bed. The room was dark and the house was quiet. She was keenly aware that he was only just across the hall. Nothing but some walls and horrible wallpaper and carved oak doors separated them.

Roxbury had to know that she desired him now, yes? He saw her shiver with pleasure at his slightest touch. He had to know that she tossed and turned late in the night imagining him and her together. She knew what to expect and she had an idea what it would be like. Julianna also knew that their coupling would defy all expectations and be unlike anything she'd ever experienced.

She kicked off some of the covers. It was rather warm in her bedchamber.

But did he feel the same as her? She suspected he did, but the uncertainty tormented her. Julianna could easily go knock on his door and ask, except that would be asking for all kinds of trouble.

Perhaps he would knock on her door?

Because she was wide-awake, and listening in the event that her husband should come to her room in the dead of the night to potentially consummate their marriage, she heard something very disturbing.

She heard a thud, like someone falling. It was surely nothing more than her imagination running away from her. When it occurred to her that something might have happened to Roxbury, she sat up in bed, about to go to him.

When she heard footsteps on the stairs, though, she paused. Her heart began to pound with fear and she lay back down and pulled the covers up high—after pulling out her pistol from the bedside table. Thank the lord she had disobeyed and sent Penny back to Bloomsbury Place to fetch it.

When she heard the sound of a heavy footstep on the creaky stair, she bit back a scream.

On the stairs . . .

The Man About Town existed in a league of his own because he did not merely wait for news and gossip to come to him—though he did accept his callers every week at St. Bride's. No, he sought it out as well. Such were his thoughts as he climbed through the kitchen window of Lord Roxbury's townhouse and proceeded up the stairs. This was daring, dangerous, and illegal—but it was also glorious, and what made him the best.

He had a hunch about this marriage—as did most of the ton—that it was an absolute sham. Unlike most of the ton, he—the renowned Man About Town—was going to discover if so. If it were the love match the couple tried to pass it off as, they would surely be found in bed together.

If not . . . well, he'd find out in just a second.

The stair creaked under his boot and he swore under his breath.

He winced and kept going because of another rumor he longed to prove once and for all: that Lady Somerset—Lady Roxbury now—was the Lady of Distinction that wrote "Fashionable Intelligence." Of all the gossips in London, she was the one that kept him up at night. If he could confirm and expose her identity—he'd be the greatest Man About Town that ever was or would be.

How he would confirm that, he knew not. His best hope was to find drafts of the column among her papers, which he intended to search, if given the opportunity.

At the top of the stairs, he saw two doors. Selecting one at random, the Man About Town's hand closed over the knob and slowly twisted it and pushed the door open. The curtains had been left open and he could see, just barely, by the light of the moon.

There was a bed, with someone in it—a woman, he saw, owing to the long, dark hair spread across the pillow. But was it Lady Roxbury or a paramour?

Pulse racing, he dared to go closer. She was asleep, after all.

Chapter 41

She was not asleep. Julianna's eyes were wide open, watching the door open slowly. She could barely see by the moonlight and slow burning embers in the grate, but she saw enough. She saw the large, shadowy form of a man enter her bedchamber.

He moved toward her bed. Her heart was pounding so hard that she felt it up in her throat, which made it impossible to scream, which increased her panic tenfold.

Was it an intruder? Or her husband? And if it wasn't Roxbury but some nefarious jackanapes, where the devil was her blasted husband? How could he leave her alone for this? There was an intruder in her bedroom, for Lord's sake! In Mayfair!

She could wait until he came closer, when she could surprise him with the pistol in her hand. Thank goodness for her disobedience in sending Penny back to 24 Bloomsbury Place to collect it.

She held it in her sweaty palms, waiting for the right moment.

Where the hell was Roxbury? He should be here! Of course, if her husband were here, she wouldn't have to lie in bed with a pistol in her clammy hand. Wasn't having a husband to protect one in instances like this one of the benefits of marriage? If she wanted to deal with intruders all by her lonesome, she could have just stayed at Bloomsbury Place. Honestly, as soon as she dealt with this intruder, she was going to give her husband a piece of her mind.

But, oh, for the love of God, the man was creeping closer and closer, gingerly taking steps in the moonlight, all in the direction of her bed!

Waiting to be rescued was no longer an option.

Julianna sat up quickly, propelled by an intense mixture of rage and terror.

"Don't come closer," she said coldly. "Or I will shoot." The intruder stopped. She hoped he did not see how her hands were shaking.

He didn't take another step. In fact, the next thing she knew, the intruder hit the ground with a thud. Had she fired? Or had she scared him to death?

There was little light, other than that from the moon and the last of the fire in the grate. Still, she saw that Roxbury had tackled him to the oh-so-pink carpet. Julianna could see little, but she heard the thuds, cracks, grunts, and smacks of fists against skin and bone.

Julianna kept her pistol poised, ready to shoot, but aware that she had a single shot, and that she might hit the wrong man.

She winced at the sound of a particularly forceful blow. This could not continue. With the pistol pointed at the ceiling, she pulled the trigger.

The scuffle stopped, the intruder ran, and Roxbury followed.

Chapter 42

After what seemed like an eternity, Roxbury returned to her room. His shirt clung tightly to his torso, and she could discern a sheen of sweat on his muscled chest. Even in the moonlight she could see that his fists were bruised and raw. He had not escaped unscathed—there was a small cut on his cheek and one of his eyes would surely have a bruise in the morning. She was sure the intruder suffered far worse, though she felt no sympathy for him.

Roxbury sat beside her on the bed. When she'd been imagining this moment, it was without the drama of a midnight burglary, or without his injuries. Her heart was supposed to have been pounding with desire, not fear. But nevertheless, she and her husband sat side by side on her bed—after he had just rescued her.

"Are you all right?" he asked, his voice sounding rough and out of breath.

"Don't worry about me," she whispered, pushing a lock of his hair off his forehead. "How are you?"

"Don't worry about you?" Roxbury echoed. His shock that she would suggest this was heartwarming. "My god, woman, I almost killed a man for you—and not for lack of trying." He flexed his hands, wincing as he did so. She could see they were swollen and bruised. Those hands, she thought, had fought for her. It was profoundly humbling.

Somerset had never fought for her. Somerset had never done a lot of things Roxbury did, as a matter of course. Like talk to her, or teach her things, or make her laugh rather than seethe in anger at being ignored. Or spend the night under the same roof, even if not the same bed.

This might just work after all. . . .

"It's best that you did not kill him, for that would have made a dreadful mess," she said. Meanwhile, her heart was pounding because she *liked* her husband. In fact, given his heroics this evening, her emotions were swiftly moving from like to love.

That was even scarier than the intruder. Her heart beat quickly and heavily accordingly.

"At least your sense of humor has survived intact," he remarked, and she saw a faint grin. "And the rest of you?"

"I was terrified," she told him. "Thank goodness for my pistol. Penny had gone back to Bloomsbury Place for it."

"I was afraid of that, just in case I made an uninvited midnight visit to your bedchamber," he confessed. Ah, so he had been thinking of her . . . and lovemaking . . . and he thought she would not welcome his advances. So that was why he never made any. And here she had been wondering . . .

All of a sudden, it made sense to her. Even better,

the truth—as she understood it—was lovely. If Roxbury wanted her, but was not sure of her feelings. All she needed to do was let them be known. And then, they might be married in truth.

Was she ready for that? Was he? Was now the moment? She did not know.

"I'm glad you were here," she said softly, because that she was certain of and she wanted him to know it. "Thank you."

"Of course I was there, Julianna," he said. "Why wouldn't I be there?"

"Somerset wasn't always there," she replied. In her first marriage, she would have had to deal with an intruder all by herself because Somerset would have been out at a club or a gaming hell or drunk and unconscious in the corridor.

"I'm not him," Roxbury said firmly. "I'm not the same man. At all."

"I know . . ." she replied. She was discovering all the ways in which Roxbury was different. Good ways, too. He was not what she had feared.

"And you are not the same girl that you were when you married him," he added.

"I know," she said, even though she didn't really. She wasn't seventeen anymore. In the ways of the world, she was far more intelligent. When it came to men, and love, however, she felt she didn't know much more than she did on the hot summer night she had decided to run away with Somerset.

She knew the dark side. But perhaps with Roxbury things might be different, or good, or happy. Perhaps they might live happily ever after, after all.

Such were her thoughts when Roxbury whispered her name.

When she turned to face him, he gently cupped her cheeks in his palms.

This was the moment he was going to kiss her; she just knew it. And because she knew it, Julianna could savor it. So she drank in his gorgeous face—the slanting cheekbones and the almond-shaped eyes that made women swoon. His mouth had kissed hundreds but her lips would be the last—she just knew that, too.

Julianna smiled so that he would know she wanted him. And then, *finally*, Roxbury lowered his mouth to hers for a kiss that swept away all memories of other kisses.

His lips were so light upon hers, and that drove her wild, right from the start. They'd waited so long for this moment—both of them standing on the verge of falling utterly in love—and he was feathering the lightest, softest kisses upon her mouth. She parted her lips, desperate for more—already!

But though it was just a few seconds from that first contact of his mouth to hers, it was only the latest move in a seduction that had started weeks ago, in Knightly's office when Roxbury rakishly and brazenly looked her over and a hot, pink flush swept across her skin.

And so she suffered the impatience of weeks of slow, mounting pressure and the intense longing for a man's heated, passionate touch that had been building in her for years.

Gently, he held her—as if she would dash off, or try to escape. She grasped his shirt, damp with his sweat, and tugged it over his head and tossed it on the floor.

His eyes widened in surprise; she grinned.

Roxbury's mouth came crashing down on hers for the passionate, overheated, frustrated, fervent kiss she'd been waiting for. His tongue teased and tasted and tangled with hers. She nibbled gently on his lower lip. There were gasps, and there were groans of pleasure, and relief.

Julianna wrapped her arms around him, tracing the muscles of his back with her fingertips. Her breath hitched in her throat when his hands rakishly and a little bit roughly caressed her, from just below her breasts, along her side and down to her hips . . . and down farther to the hem of her nightgown.

Julianna quickly discovered that there was nothing, *nothing*, like the sensation of silk slowly sliding along one's skin. Especially when it was propelled by the knowing hands of an accomplished lover, and when she was on the verge of complete abandon, and falling in love and . . .

Roxbury pressed a warm kiss in the delightful spot where her shoulder curved to her neck. Julianna couldn't restrain a moan, nor could she help arching her back and moving to make it easier for him to give her more of that exquisite sensation.

Meanwhile, he was slowly pushing the silk straps of her nightgown off her shoulders and leaving her exposed to his dark, heated gaze.

In a flash, she was suddenly acutely conscious of all the other women he'd seen thusly. She moved to cover herself, but he shook his head no, and looked at her as if she was the first, last, and loveliest woman in the world. So she let him look, even though it made her blush and even though it made heat pool in her belly.

Julianna took a good, long, leisurely look at

him, too—with his hair falling into his eyes, his gaze wild and dark, his lips parted. She traced the contours of all the muscles on his chest before resting her palm over his pounding heart.

He began to tug up her nightgown, before pulling it off entirely. It joined his shirt on the floor. She closed her eyes, having forgotten about how this made one's heart race, and how it was possible to be so damned warm from the inside out, even though one was utterly naked. Julianna had also forgotten about the shivers of anticipation and the curious, intense throbbing between her legs. She'd forgotten about her own desire.

Or had she never known it?

The wicked rake gave her a grin that promised all kinds of unimaginable pleasure. At his gentle urging, she leaned back against the pillows, completely at his mercy. Thus far, she'd been enjoying herself, but thanks to his dangerous, roguish smile, she knew it was only just beginning.

He began with his hand clasped around her ankle, which didn't seem like very much at all, until he began to move his grasp higher. The gentle, slow caress was lovely; the anticipation and suspicions of just where he was going with his wicked touch was quite another. That was what had her lips parting in an "o" of shock and excitement and nervousness.

The man knew it, too.

And just when he was about to touch her in that most intimate place, he stopped. Instead, he lowered himself over her, adding another layer of heat. Roxbury kissed her as if he had all night. And then he began to feather kisses along her neck. And then just when she was starting to writhe with the pleasure from that, he began to feather kisses lower still.

Roxbury covered her breast with his palm, and she arched her back for more. It was involuntary, of course. When he closed his mouth around the dusky pink center and a genuine moan escaped her lips, there was no way on earth she could have stopped it. And then when he began to give his attentions to her other breast . . . she knew she could enjoy this all night long and then even longer.

She knew Roxbury was an accomplished lover. Everyone knew it. But to experience it—that was quite another thing entirely. And Julianna knew that for all of his practice and experience this lovemaking meant something to him. It was there in the darkness of his gaze, or the way his caress wasn't always smooth and perfect, but a little rough, or when he groaned in pleasure from her touch. She could tell in the way that their mouths occasionally fumbled, searching, and tasting.

She knew because she had done this before with her previous husband, and it had never been like this. So every imperfect kiss was exquisite. Every time their limbs became tangled or they laughed softly at a little bit of clumsiness—they were still learning each other, after all—well, that made it all the more real, and theirs alone. And that was what allowed Julianna to let go.

At first, she surrendered just a little bit, giving in to those sighs and moans. And then when he did begin to touch her, there, she gave in a lot more. And when those hot, loving kisses went lower and lower and found her, there, she let go even more.

And then after a few seconds, or a few moments of sheer, unbridled bliss, there was no way she could hold on any longer.

Julianna never cried—but dear God did she cry out with pleasure and sob with relief. She could not move, nor could she breathe; she just barely registered that something earth-shattering had occurred, and it had happened to her. And Roxbury, the man that had just shown her heaven, tucked her into his arms and held her close.

Roxbury had spent hours, days, fantasizing about Julianna's kiss. Now that it was possible for him to enjoy it, he could not stop. What if she came to her senses? Or what if she changed her mind? Or what if she fell asleep? That was what he always did after he climaxed and dear God was he aching to do so now. Climax, not sleep, that is. He could barely contain himself and sleep was the last thing his body wanted at the moment.

"More?" she asked, or mumbled rather. He nibbled her earlobe and she giggled.

"If you can handle it," he murmured and by that he meant, *For the love of God please*.

"If you insist," she said lazily, stretching out beneath him. He bit back a groan because as she arched her back, she brushed against his hard arousal. He was beyond desperate for a release. But still . . .

"Whatever the lady wishes," he said, but what he really meant was, *In the name of everything sacred, please say yes*.

"Your lady says hurry up," Julianna murmured. She barely finished the sentence before he was tugging off his breeches.

He kissed her again. And then she relaxed and melted into his embrace. He kissed away her worries, and soon they both forgot, so lost in a mad, hot rush of pent-up desire on the verge of release.

He was an experienced lover, but tonight everything felt like an expedition into uncharted territory. He'd made love to women, but he'd never made love to this woman. Roxbury knew her, too, in a way he'd never before experienced. He knew of her anger and her fears and her past and he knew that there was a damn good chance that he was her future, too.

All this knowledge made the experience of making love seem utterly different—and its own kind of wonderful. It had to be perfect, and it had to be true. Above all, it had to be magical and exquisite and . . . he wanted her to enjoy it. Lord knew he was reveling in the pleasure of her full breasts in his hands, and her soft skin hot against his, and the delicate sound of her sighs, and the passion of her kiss.

They'd barely begun, and already he didn't want it to end. But he could ignore his needs no longer.

Any semblance of rational thought was swiftly evaporating, and he was completely overtaken by the primal urge to claim her as his own. He lowered himself above her, with his arousal nestled between her thighs and straining to be inside of her.

Julianna writhed beneath him, mercifully making room for him. Roxbury claimed her mouth with his, because he had to have all of her all at once. He urged in slowly, achingly aware that this was his last first time with a woman. It was just something he knew, and he wanted to remember every vivid detail. Deeper and deeper he moved within her, and for all the obstacles she'd thrown in his path before, there were none now. She wrapped her arms around him and kissed him like a loving wife.

He pushed in farther, all the way, groaning in pleasure while still managing, barely, to keep kissing her. And then he began to move inside her, slowly at first, before everything was utterly beyond his control.

It hadn't been like this before . . . that was the only thought he could manage. His mind was otherwise blank. His heart was pounding, though, like never before. And by God . . . her hands pressed into his back, urging him deeper. He buried his face in her neck, and his hands roughly caressed her. She held him tighter.

When she murmured, "Oh, Simon," he was lost. Completely. He cried out her name—or some mumbled version of it—as he reached his own climax, burying himself as deep inside of her as he could while holding her as tightly as he could.

He had meant to claim her as his own, and she had claimed him, too.

Chapter 43

The following morning

If one wanted sweet reassurances from a friend, Annabelle was their girl. If one wanted humorous conversation, Sophie was the one. But when a friend was needed to embark on dangerous adventures, Eliza was just the person to turn to.

"What is the plan for today?" she asked with a devilish grin as they climbed into a hired hackney.

"We are going to St. Bride's to visit the Man About Town during his calling hours," Julianna said with a hint of excitement in her voice. She had never gone before because, given her previous work, she did not want to risk providing any information to her rival that might expose her. Now, she had nothing to lose.

Now, she had something to protect. Almost everything had changed late last night, and it wasn't the intruder that she was thinking of. She ought not to think of that rapturous lovemaking with Simon, lest she begin to blush. Nothing escaped Eliza and Julianna wanted to keep this budding romance with her husband to herself. For now.

"And then what are we going to do?" Eliza asked. "Murder? Feed him false information? Follow him?"

"One of the above. Mainly, I'd love to see his face," Julianna said. Having seen the face of the intruder last night, she wanted to investigate her hunch that it was the Man About Town. She explained the incident of the previous evening to a very rapt audience of one. After expressing her shock and horror, Eliza said, "Good luck with getting a glimpse of his face. He might not have gone himself, you know. He could have sent some minion. Although, I would never leave such important work to just anybody."

"That is what I am counting on. But really, there is just no way of knowing. And we might not discover anything today. But I must do *something*," Julianna said. Specifically, she needed to do something out of the house. Memories of last night flooded her with loving, lusty feelings. But then . . .

"And what does your husband have to say about this?" Eliza asked with a suggestive lift of her brow.

"He is not aware of it," Julianna said, vexation creeping into her tone.

"Ah. I see," Eliza said crisply.

"Do you know why he doesn't know?" Julianna asked, her voice involuntarily rising.

"No, but I suspect you are about to tell me," Eliza replied.

"Oh, indeed I am, Eliza. He doesn't know because he left shortly after breakfast this morning and has not yet returned," Julianna said. They had woken up together. They made love again first thing—a luxury she'd never before experienced and ached for again. They finally made their way down to breakfast where they read the newspapers. Then Roxbury said he was going out and that he would return later. In spite of her pleas and promises, he would not reveal his destination.

"Where did he go?" Eliza asked.

"I would guess to Gentleman Jack's, or White's or someplace I can't get to him. But that is just a guess. The truth is that I have no idea." It burned, it stung, and it rankled. Once again, he'd gone off with nary an explanation. And he didn't need to tell her his whereabouts at any given moment, but it would be considerate. He knew how she felt about secrets being kept from her.

"Are you merely upset that he's gone off, or done so in light of the break-in last evening, or is there something else?" Eliza was remarkably astute. Nothing escaped her.

Julianna did her best to maintain a passive expression, but her blush gave her away.

"Oh my," Eliza murmured with a sly smile. "Definitely something else."

"We made love . . . or something like it," Julianna mumbled.

"Something like it?" Eliza echoed.

"Well, there's been no mention of *love*. But we did . . ."

"And?" Eliza prompted, clearly delighting in this conversation, probably in part because the typically forthright Julianna Somerset Roxbury was tongue-tied and blushing furiously like an innocent schoolgirl.

"I know exactly," Eliza said. "This morning he is having a panic about it because he's discovered that his feelings are involved."

"Is that what it is? Is that why he's gone?" Julianna's heart sank. She did not want him to have second thoughts or doubts or to leave. She was on the verge of love—and if he left now, she'd really be ruined forever. But she recalled those kisses and those caresses, and it had to mean something beautiful, lasting, and true.

"I'd wager on it. Now, hush, we are here."

Julianna wasn't consoled in the slightest, but their mission distracted her, which had been her intention.

They alighted from the carriage and dashed through a light drizzle for the entrance. Julianna slowed considerably as she passed through the doors. It was her first time here since she'd been married.

She recalled the cold-minded and iron-hearted determination with which she'd walked down the same aisle and greeted her future. The marriage was only to salvage her reputation; it was only a matter of convenience.

And now, weeks later, it might be love.

Julianna ventured down the aisle once more, this time with Eliza by her side. Thoughts of love, Roxbury, lust, and wonder were on her mind. *Focus,* she told herself. This was why she feared falling in love, because she would forget serious matters in favor of woolgathering about romantic midnight adventures and very wicked, pleasurable things she'd only discovered last night.

Today, the man she walked toward was the ever-mysterious, ever-annoying Man About Town. It was just like the stories claimed: a man in a voluminous black cloak knelt in prayer by the altar. One by one, a few of the people milling around would take turns and kneel beside him. With their heads bowed together, secrets, lies, and scandal were exchanged.

"Look," Eliza whispered, subtly gesturing to some very thuggish-looking men lurking in the shadows and near the altar. It was likely that they were there to protect the Man About Town's identity. Lord help anyone that tried to yank back that cloak and catch a glimpse of the face underneath.

There he was, just there—her arch nemesis and sworn enemy. Why had she never come here before? Because she did not want even a chance of being discovered. Because she was too jealous or too busy accumulating her own stockpile of scandalous tidbits that she didn't have the time to share any—true or false—with her rival.

"You have to admit that this is a brilliant arrangement," Eliza said quietly.

"Yes, grudgingly. He's been at this for forty years, though," Julianna replied. She'd had only one year as an acclaimed gossip.

"Forty years . . ." Eliza remarked, adding a low whistle. "Impressive."

When it was her turn, after thirty minutes of loitering about, Julianna proceeded directly to the altar and knelt beside the only man who had vexed her more than Roxbury.

"I have a confession," she began because it seemed the thing to say. He didn't say anything, only nodded that she should continue. She bit her lip in annoyance, for she so wanted to hear his voice. Perhaps she might recognize it . . . perhaps that was exactly why he said nothing.

"Lady Rawlings and Lady Stewart-Wortly were seen acknowledging Lord and Lady Roxbury in Hyde Park yesterday," she said softly, attempting to disguise her voice as best she could. "And Lady Feversham has invited the couple to her soiree Thursday next."

Lady Feversham had done no such thing, but Sophie had mentioned the party and Julianna thought she'd like to attend. There was only one way to secure an invitation—and that was publicly, via the Man About Town.

"Really? I find that surprising," he remarked, to her annoyance. But at least she heard his voice, which was so very English, yet with an indiscernible accent.

The Man About Town lifted his head, slightly, to look at her. Julianna, keeping her own face bowed down and covered by a large bonnet and black mesh veil, dared a sideways glance. She saw a clean-shaven chin. But most of all, she noticed very bruised, very swollen hands tug his cloak back into place.

Her heart started to pound, because those hands belonged to a *young man.*

Having seen enough, she stood and walked away briskly with her excitement barely contained.

All this time she had been searching for an old man! When in fact, he was young. How had she not guessed that it hadn't been an old man writing gossip for forty years? To be fair, no one considered otherwise. Not in all those years! But that explained how he had kept his identity a secret for so long.

The Man About Town was a young man, with

bruised and swollen hands. Julianna thought of last night—not the part where she made love with her husband for the very first time, but the part where her husband engaged in a rousing, vicious bout of fisticuffs quite nearly to the death on her bedroom floor. Two gentlemen had been brawling.

Was the intruder the Man About Town?

Chapter 44

28 Bruton Street

"**W**here have you been?" Roxbury bellowed when she returned home after parting ways with Eliza. He greeted her in the foyer—yet another horrifically decorated room. This one featured black-and-white *etoile* wall coverings, black-and-white-checked marble floor, glittering chandeliers, and gold-framed paintings of utterly barren landscapes. It was bizarre, frankly.

"Hello to you, too, darling," she said breezily. One of these days she would have to hire someone to redecorate this entire house. Perhaps tomorrow.

And by golly was that bruise on his cheek a rival to hers!

"Where did you go?" he demanded. "And in a hired hack, nonetheless!"

"You took the carriage," she pointed out as she removed her hat and veil and handed them to Pembleton. "How else was I going to get to St. Bride's?"

"What the bloody hell do you need to go to St. Bride's for?" Roxbury asked, crossing his arms over his chest. He was really in quite a huff, and it was adorable. Unless she was mistaken, this probably meant that he cared for her. If he didn't care about her, he certainly wouldn't be the slightest bit interested in her whereabouts.

"I went to St. Bride's to see the Man About Town, of course," she answered.

"With that bruise on your cheek. Fantastic," he remarked dryly. As if he were one to talk, with his own violent bruise on his cheek and around his eye. His knuckles had sustained some significant damage as well . . . just like the hands of the Man About Town.

"It's fading. The light was dim. I had my veil and cloak," she answered with a shrug.

"It's a monstrosity," Roxbury said flatly, and not entirely incorrectly, though it had improved remarkably in the past few days. "Now all of London will think that I beat you."

"It's perfectly legal," she replied.

"So is kicking dogs, but that doesn't mean a gentleman does it," Roxbury retorted.

"No one will think you beat me," she repeated. He seemed to mutter something to the effect of "No one would blame me if I did," but in oddly charitable spirits, she declined to confirm it.

Like her bruise, her mood had also improved. Something like infatuation had done wonders, as had her very successful mission this afternoon. And after last night . . . the tension she held in her limbs was just plain gone.

For once he was the one in the foul mood. "What has you in such a temper, anyway?" she asked.

"Coming home to find my wife is missing,"

Roxbury answered. *My wife*. He said it again and still it made her shiver—but no longer with complete dread. In fact, she shivered with something like pleasure. *Wife. Husband.*

"I left a note," she said, removing her gloves now and handing those to Pembleton as well.

"Yes, the one that says 'Roxbury, I've gone out and will return shortly.'"

"The very one," she replied, entering the drawing room and looking at the empty salver on the mantel. She had completely lied this afternoon. They hadn't received an invitation from anyone to anywhere.

"Can you see how it is not remotely informative?" Roxbury queried.

"At least I left a note. You did not. Where have you been all day?" She whirled around to face him.

"Not skulking around Fleet Street. I went to Gentleman Jack's. To White's," he replied. She eyed him suspiciously. He returned her gaze evenly. Still, she doubted him. Why did he have to leave so secretively?

"You went to places where I can't get to you. If you're trying to get away from me, why are you so upset that I've gone out?"

"Upset? *Upset?*"

"Storming around and bellowing," she replied, as she returned to the foyer and proceeded up the stairs. He stormed and bellowed after her.

"I was concerned for your safety," he said.

"I am very safe. And I am tremendously happy because I have discovered something about the Man About Town, which leads me closer to discovering him. If there is one thing I wish for, it is to know who he really is," she said. She glanced back and saw that he was following her up the stairs and into her bedchamber.

"Oh, what lovely flowers!" she exclaimed, as she noticed the bouquets of fragrant red and pink roses, along with some other hothouse flowers he couldn't name, on the bedside table. "Is this what kept you busy all day?" she asked.

Roxbury gave her a look that said, *Silly woman, don't you know anything about romance?*

"Perhaps. I did go to the club. Drank one brandy. Spoke with Brandon before saying I couldn't stay long because I had to return to the missus. Then he smugly said he'd been waiting years to hear me say that, and—"

"I missed you, too," she replied. She was thrilled with having uncovered that clue about the Man About Town and she took no small measure of delight in the information she had given him. But Roxbury giving a damn about her whereabouts topped it all.

Once, she had left to visit her mother in the country for a week. Somerset had not seemed to notice or care. Things had changed in a strange and wonderful way.

Roxbury kissed her again and again . . . leaving no inch of her skin left untouched. That, of course, necessitated the removal of all her clothing. His were cast off as well. Together they tumbled onto the bed, and were lost for hours in an intoxicating haze of kisses and whispers, sighs and moans, cries of pleasure and murmurs of contentment.

Later, as dusk was falling and Julianna nestled against her husband, she thought that if the Man About Town could see them now, he'd definitely put his money on their marriage being a love match.

Chapter 45

After a good, strong cup of tea, Julianna turned to the Man About Town's column in *The Times*. She read it aloud to Roxbury, who quietly sipped his coffee. Breakfast could wait. Gossip came first.

"Is the R— union a love match or a marriage of convenience? The couple was recently seen taking a drive along Rotten Row seeming very much in love and acknowledged by society matrons Lady S—W—and Lady R—. In fact, word has it that the scandalous couple will even be attending Lady F—'s soiree Thursday next."

"What the devil is he talking about? Those old apes stuck their noses up at us," Roxbury said grumpily.

"I know, darling. Which is exactly why I told the Man About Town that they had greeted us," she said, delighted with her simple revenge.

"And Lady F—'s party?"

"I wish to go to Lady Feversham's ball. She has no choice but to receive us now."

"Remind me never to get on your bad side," he grumbled.

"You already did, and look at you now," she pointed out.

"Touché. Impressive social maneuvering, too, madam. Now keep reading."

"But consider this: while it is not at all unusual for upper class couples to keep separate bedrooms, in the case of the R—s it is all the more notable given those rumors that plagued his Lordship about his preferences . . . Perhaps his stunning wife is not to his liking? Is it a love match? Or a sham marriage of convenience? London, place your wagers! Only time will tell on this one."

"I'm going to kill him," Julianna said immediately upon concluding her reading. She did not like the insinuations that her husband found her unattractive.

"No, you are not because I am going to," Roxbury said darkly, probably still angry about those pesky rumors about his preferences.

"How could you deny me that satisfaction?" she asked.

"Very well, my dear wife, we shall seek and destroy the Man About Town together," Roxbury agreed.

"That's the most romantic thing anyone has ever said to me," Julianna said sweetly, and her husband grinned.

"What did you discover about him on your visit yesterday?" he asked.

"His hands are those of a young man, which is significant considering that the column has been running for forty years. All this time I've been looking for an old man . . ."

It was idiotic of her. She generally trusted nothing unless it was verified, and here she just assumed that some old man filled his days and nights in gaming hells and following young girls and rakes at parties.

Instead, he was a young man.

"It might be a few men. Or women," Roxbury pointed out.

"It's been a mystery for *forty years*," she marveled. That was one hell of a close-kept, long-held secret. "And we think we can unmask him, her or them."

"Can you stand to read rubbish like that three mornings a week?" Roxbury asked, gesturing to the paper left open between them. It had been one scathing column after another ever since they married. It would continue that way until death did they part.

"You're right. We must try," she said firmly. It was decided, then. Together, she and her husband would seek and destroy their nemesis so that they might have a better chance at happily ever after.

A few days later

Julianna had begun by hiring decorators. It would just be for the drawing room, she decided. There was no significance in redecorating one very public room in the house—or so she told herself. And really, it had to be done.

"Who had done your decorating?" she asked her husband one afternoon. She found him in his study, one of two rooms in the house that wasn't awful—the other was his bedroom. She'd been spending a lot of time there lately.

Roxbury scowled and set down his newspaper. She glanced, saw it was *The London Weekly*, and felt a pang of longing. He seemed to notice, too, by the way he shuffled the paper so she might not see the front page.

"We can thank Lydia Smythe for the drawing room and for giving the next few mistresses the idea to decorate a room with revenge in mind," he answered.

"That is exactly what I thought," Julianna said. "What did you do to irk them so?"

"It's more like what I wouldn't do, which was marry them," Roxbury said pointedly.

"How lucky for me. Well, be warned that I'm taking my turn decorating this house now," she informed him. It was her turn to put her stamp on this house . . . if it was going to be *their* house. Mostly, though, she could not tolerate living in such vile surroundings when there was no reason she had to.

"Oh dear God," Roxbury muttered, which made her grin.

There was something deeply satisfying about clearing the remnants of her husband's ex-lovers. The harvest gold damask wall coverings were stripped away. The red velvet furniture was taken out. Ronaldo, the decorator, visibly shuddered when he saw the drapes and the carpet and ordered them removed on the spot.

Anyone on the street had a perfect view into the

Roxbury home. The Man About Town reported accordingly: *Lord and Lady R— are redecorating. Love match?! Or the hobby of a bored and forgotten wife?*

That's Lord and Lady Scandalous to you, Julianna thought upon reading it.

Roxbury did his best to take the redecorating in stride. Usually when one of his lovers undertook such a task, it was the beginning of the end. Bright wallpaper and horrid curtains were their way of calling for his attention and spending his money after they had ordered enough dresses.

Thus, he was mighty nervous when he came home one afternoon to find his drawing room completely gutted. *Don't go,* he thought—of Julianna, though, not the furniture.

But then the room was completed and it wasn't the work of a scorned, irate woman in a desperate bid for attention. It was the work of a woman who planned on staying for a while. In short, it was not hideous. In fact, it was quite nice. Julianna had begun the creation of a home.

Julianna tackled the foyer next, and then he knew she was going to stay. After that, she began to renovate her own bedchamber—though she'd already been sleeping in his bed for days, and nights.

Meanwhile, he read the Man About Town's column closely for clues. And he began to plan a trap. The Feversham party would be the perfect opportunity. While he wanted to have some information that would ensure silence from the Man

About Town, Roxbury mostly wanted to give Julianna what she wished for most.

He also had a ring that he'd searched for all over London, not because of any scheme to seduce her, but because he wanted to give her a gift, a big, blazing expensive reminder that they belonged to each other and he wanted the world to know it.

Chapter 46

Madame Auteuil's
Bond Street, London

"**E**veryone is talking about you, your husband, and your rumored appearance tonight," Sophie informed Julianna.

They were in Madame Auteuil's and Julianna was splurging on a gorgeous dress for her (hopefully) triumphant return to society. Lady Feversham had not invited her and Roxbury, but the Man About Town said she had, which was just as good, if not better, than a handwritten invitation on crisp vellum paper and closed with Lord Feversham's seal.

"What is Lady Feversham saying?" Julianna asked. She had donned a blue velvet gown that was lovely, but not quite right for this evening.

"That she wanted to provide entertainment for her guests or that the invitations were composed *before*. It depends who is asking," Sophie explained frankly. Julianna scowled. If only she still had her column! Then she wouldn't have to suffer such indignities.

"And the love match rumors?" Julianna queried.

"It will all depend upon how the two of you act tonight," Sophie said.

"Besotted, long gazes, etcetera," Julianna said. A maid helped her out of the blue velvet and into a rose silk.

"Exactly," Sophie said.

Frankly, with the way they had been lately, it would be more of a challenge to hide their besotted, longing gazes. Flirtatious banter had replaced their previous sparring—but it was all still thrilling. She adored his company these days, and nights, and there was no way she could hide it.

If the ton believed her marriage was a love match, they would be so much more forgiving. That would translate into invitations, restored reputations, and then her triumphant return to *The London Weekly*.

The redecorating was all well and good, as was conspiring and scheming about how to entrap the Man About Town. But more than anything she wanted to write.

She loved to feel the paper under her palm, and to fill up a page with her inky scrawl with stories of ladies and rakes and high society. She had even taken to writing editions of "Fashionable Intelligence" that went into the fire as soon as they were written. The desire to have her column back was no longer purely to support herself, or to feel useful, or to chronicle the happenings of the ton. Julianna wanted to write for the pure joy of putting pen to paper and stringing words together into a story.

"I'm sure you two will manage admirably," Sophie said.

"At what?" Julianna asked, lost in her thoughts.

"Besotted, longing gazes, small gestures of affection, and generally acting like a couple in the first blush of romance."

"Oh, that," she said with a laugh. The maid finished buttoning the silk dress, and Julianna turned around to show Sophie.

"Oh Jules, that dress is lovely!" Sophie gushed.

"Are you sure it's not too . . . much?" Julianna asked nervously. It was a dusky rose-colored satin gown, cut low and simply tailored. There was an overlay of pale tulle and some extremely delicate embroidery around the bodice. The sleeves were naught but wisps of tulle. The whole creation was like dew on a rose.

"Not for this occasion," Sophie said firmly.

"It is lovely . . . I think Simon will like it," Julianna said. She knew he would like taking it off; he tended to prefer her dresses on the floor rather than on her person.

"Oh, it's Simon now?" Sophie asked with a smirk.

"Roxbury was too many syllables to say all the time," Julianna said, offering an excuse other than intimacy for calling her husband by his given name.

"You are ridiculous!" Sophie exclaimed, her brown curls shaking with her exuberance. That was the thing about dear friends—one could not lie to them.

"You are falling for him, are you not?" Sophie persisted. That was the other thing about dear friends—they would not let you avoid the truth.

"I wouldn't say that," Julianna said evasively. She was, but she wasn't ready to say it aloud. That would make it real and if she was the woman who fell for a rake, for a man, for her husband, then she was not the woman she thought she was. In her head, she was still Lady Somerset of *The London Weekly*.

In her heart, though, she was Lady Scandalous.

"Oh really? You're *not* falling for him?" Sophie queried. "How many rooms of his house have you tastefully redecorated?"

"Seven," she mumbled. It was the majority of the rooms in the house.

"And where do you sleep at night?" Sophie asked. That was another thing about dear friends—they felt no shame in asking deeply personal questions that no one else would dream of giving voice to.

"In his bedroom. But really, it's just because of the renovations to my bedchamber, which—"

"Which concluded over a week ago," Sophie said, cutting her off, which was just as well since Julianna had no reason to stay in Simon's bed other than that she wanted to be there.

"Admit it," Sophie continued, with a broad grin. "You have fallen in love with your husband."

Chapter 47

Lady Feversham's Ball

Though Roxbury had left numerous parties with a woman on his arm more times than he could count, he could not recall ever *arriving* with one. That was new. So, too, was their reception: He and Julianna were treated to stares, sidelong glances, whispers, and benignly polite faces masking rabid curiosity.

He quickly whisked Julianna into a waltz. They could be watched and potentially squash some love match or marriage of convenience rumors—all without speaking to anyone. Perfect.

It was easy to ignore them all, and focus upon his lovely Julianna.

"You look especially beautiful tonight, my lady," he said softly and she smiled, lovingly looking into his eyes. "Ah, you no longer declare that you are not my lady," he couldn't resist pointing out.

"I think that argument was retired when I signed the marriage certificate," she murmured. He loved her mouth—luscious and mostly tart, though occasionally sweet.

Yes, she was a beauty. Her dress was very fine, and very flattering. Her auburn hair was done up in some sort of intricate coiffure with tendrils here and there. And then there was all that lovely, soft skin that he now knew so well.

She was beautiful now, all proud and dignified at a party. Later, he would be the lucky one to see how beautiful she was with her hair down and dress discarded on the floor. His breath hitched just thinking about it.

Unlike all of his other love affairs, this one didn't need to end. In fact, he didn't want it to. And that was a first.

And that was why . . . no, he did not want to think of that now. He'd made his plans, and he would follow through with them. Besides, there were some aspects that he was keenly anticipating.

"How does it feel to return to the social whirl?" he asked. "Is it everything you hoped and dreamt it would be?"

"I'm quite content at the moment," she replied. There was a spark in her eyes, and he knew that she was happy. The joy he felt was indescribable.

"Then let's keep waltzing," he suggested with a happy grin. That suited his purposes perfectly. He would take any excuse to hold her.

And . . .

If all were to go according to his plan, it was essential that they look utterly besotted and madly in love—all the better to get the attention of the Man About Town. It was inconceivable that that rascal wouldn't be here tonight; not with the rumors and wagers flying about the ever-scandalous and always shocking Lord and Lady Roxbury. Nothing was sure to gain attention like the scandalized conversations that would erupt all over the ballroom when he and his missus embarked on their third consecutive waltz.

At the conclusion of the waltz Roxbury led his bride away from the other dancers, through the buzzing, humming crowds in the ballroom and off to a secluded portion of the house.

The Man About Town watched them from the sidelines of the ballroom. Love match or not, he was beyond caring. But if he had to put money down at this moment, he'd say it was a love match. He took a sip of his drink and eavesdropped on the conversations around him.

"Look at the way he makes her laugh," one woman said with a sigh to another.

"Aye, he looked at me like that once," a different, bitter, woman muttered to her friends.

"It might be love, but will it last?" another lady wondered aloud.

The men did not bother discussing it—not when the topics of wenches, hunting, cards, parliament, carriages, and brandy had yet to be exhausted.

The Man About Town sipped his own drink and watched as Roxbury linked arms with the missus and led them through the crowded ballroom—and not in the direction of the lemonade or card room or terrace, either.

In fact, they were coming his way. Instinctively, the Man About Town flexed his fist—and winced. Roxbury had given him quite the drubbing the other night. He was deserving of it, and he was not eager to repeat it. But still . . . he knew what filled his column and paid his wages, and it wasn't privacy or decency. So when Lord and Lady Roxbury sauntered past him, and down a dimly lit corridor, the Man About Town followed.

Chapter 48

"Where are we going?" Julianna asked. It was a fair question, she thought. She'd gone to great lengths to attend this party and after only an hour, Roxbury was leading her through the crowded ballroom, and beyond that to the private section of the house. In other words, away from the party.

"It's a secret," he replied, grinning. She loved his grin, and she was not at all averse to skulking about—it was always the most interesting part of any ball—but he was being so mysterious about it.

"I hate secrets," she told him.

"You love them," he countered.

"Yes, I love them when I know them, not when they are kept from me."

"Here, my darling—" he said, tugging her close to him against a wall. He kissed her deeply and passionately and threatened to damage her very elaborate coiffure. But how could a woman care about that when she had a hot, wanton kiss from a devilishly handsome and—dare she say it—loving husband? The waltzing was lovely, but this was amazing. Would she ever tire of kissing him? She didn't think so.

And then, after just a moment—one that was far too quick—he was leading her along again. She glanced at their surroundings—a long hallway, large ornately framed paintings on the wall, and a few candles in sconces to provide some dim light. She heard their footsteps on the marble-tiled floor: Roxbury's thudding steps, her quicker steps and . . .

"Shh," she said, pausing. "Do you hear footsteps? Is someone following us?"

She was suspicious by nature, and especially so after that intruder.

"I doubt there is anyone else," he said, taking her hand in his. "If so, it's probably another couple in search of privacy. Like us."

"If you say so," Julianna said. The gossip inside of her didn't quite believe it. And, given all the times she'd followed people in search of a story, it was very plausible that someone could be following them just to glean some information to regale friends with it—or newspaper readers. Perhaps it was the Man About Town? No, that was too easy.

"Do you trust me, Julianna?" Roxbury asked suddenly as they walked along, hand-in-hand, to Lord only knew where.

Julianna was surprised by the question—here, now—and how earnest he was. She took a moment to think about it. But most of that time was spent marveling at how quickly the answer—yes—leapt to her lips. Yes, he had saved her in a midnight display of heroics. But since their marriage, he'd been loyal and stood by her, whether she was angry or sad or happy or utterly naked and completely ravished. She'd taken his name, moved into his house, had him on her mind constantly, and had given her body to him. The only question was of her heart . . .

"I do," she whispered.

And with that, they rushed along again down the long dark hall. Where on earth were they going? And why?

She was sure there was another set of footsteps . . . or was it their own, echoing in the marble-floored hallway? No, no, it had to be the sound of someone following them, so she was glad when Roxbury opened a door to a private room and closed them in.

"What is happening?" she asked, a little vexed, a little excited, and definitely breathless.

"I want to steal a moment alone with my lovely bride," he said, sliding his arm around her waist and pulling her close to him.

When he looked at her with lust in his eyes, she became heatedly excited. She couldn't help but respond to his touch. When he kissed her, she couldn't say no.

Julianna closed her eyes and Roxbury's mouth met hers, and her lips parted to deepen the kiss. He ran his fingers through her hair, and she said goodbye to her elaborate style, but what did that matter? Everything was just right—her man holding her, kissing her in a stolen moment. It might even be love.

But it didn't quite feel right. She heard the sound of a door opening, and then closing, followed by footsteps echoing on the marble floor. Then Julianna heard it again: open, shut, steps. Open, shut, steps.

Roxbury feathered kisses along her neck, and began to tug down her bodice and explore her breasts. She sighed in pleasure, but she was nervous, too.

It was as if someone was systematically looking in every room. As if they were looking for them. Her belly began to ache with fear. Why would anyone be looking for them?

It was only a matter of time before whoever it was opened the door to the room in which they were currently engaged in very private behavior. Would it still be compromising and scandalous since they were married? She did not care to discover it.

Dear God, her hair was a wreck but even worse, her bodice was not where it ought to be and much more than her ankles was showing. It wasn't just scandal she was worried about, but basic decency.

"Roxbury," she said to get his attention.

"Oh, darling," he murmured as he kissed her.

Open, shut, steps. She heard it again. Someone was definitely on a mission. The door to their room would be coming soon.

"Simon, stop," she urged. He held her closer and she writhed in his embrace.

Open, shut, steps. Louder now.

She tightly grasped the fabric of his unopened shirt in her fists, trying to hold him at bay. For the first time, she turned her head to avoid his kiss and it broke her heart to do.

"Let me go," she urged. She did not want to be seen by a stranger in this state of disarray, and in this private moment with her new husband.

"Juli—" he murmured, holding her tight and holding her close.

The footsteps stopped outside of their door. She watched the knob turn as Roxbury kissed her neck. There was no way he could be oblivious to this—not when he had previously been so attentive to every sigh, to every moan.

She pushed hard against him. He tightened his grasp upon her.

Tears stung her eyes as she realized what betrayal was unfolding. And she wasn't even fully, properly dressed—adding another level of indignity to a plan made without her, and one that involved her participation.

The door opened, as she had expected. Roxbury carried on feathering kisses along her neck and shoulder, each one landing on her skin like a poison dart.

She writhed for release, but he kept her close. At the very least, he kept her from being utterly exposed when the door opened a crack and the light flooded in.

All she could see was the silhouette of a man, and Julianna just knew that she was absolutely caught in a compromising position by the one who could only be the Man About Town. Because of the lighting, she could not see his face.

"Oh, I do apologize for the interruption," he said smoothly. The bounder wasn't at all sorry, and they all knew it. And with that, the intruder gave a short bow and shut the door.

Roxbury started toward him, obviously intent upon giving chase, brawling, and generally causing another raucous scene that would have the ton talking for years. Lord Scandalous, indeed.

Lord Dead Man, she thought as she grabbed his coattails.

"Julianna, that's him. The Man About Town," he said urgently, straining to go after him. She held fast to his coat.

Later, she might fully indulge in the feelings of betrayal and heartache. Was it on the scale of Somerset's indiscretions? No. Did it hurt any less? God no. For some reason it hurt more, because she was in the first throes of a new love.

"Darling," he echoed. He took a step back. Apparently, he had his moments of not being a fool. Unfortunately, that moment was now and not five minutes earlier.

"You are a terrible actor," Julianna said witheringly. She began to tug her bodice back into place.

"Julianna, I can explain," he said, reaching out to assist putting her dress back to rights. That didn't stop her from lecturing.

"You brushed off my concerns that someone was following us—as if you knew. Or expected it! And yet you claimed it was silly for me to think someone was following us. And you lead me here . . . to this dark, quiet room with an unlocked door, you hold me close, you kiss me passionately, you deliberately muss up my hair and my clothes and you won't let me go when someone was coming . . ."

"Darling—"

"Forgive me, *darling,* if I think this is a setup," she said, and tears were stinging her eyes, which was ridiculous because she never cried.

"Julianna . . ." Roxbury reached for her, but she stepped aside. It was all starting to make sense to her now.

"You have everything to gain from being seen in a compromising position with a woman. With your wife. The Man About Town can put to bed the rumors about your inclinations, once and for all. The Lady of Distinction cannot."

"Julianna . . ." he murmured her name again. She wiped the tears away from her eyes.

"Are you going to deny it?" she questioned. "Because the evidence is quite damning to me."

For a moment, they both fell silent. She bit her tongue to give him a chance to say what she wanted to hear: That she was a ridiculous woman letting her imagination get away with her. That she was suspicious and really ought to be more trusting. For the first time in her life, she prayed. *Please tell me I'm wrong.*

"The truth, Julianna," Roxbury said quietly, "is that I did it for us."

"For us?" she echoed softly.

"For you, my wife, and for our marriage. So that we may be left in peace and not have to prove our feelings to the world or constantly defend our relationship to the lowlife Grub Street hack writers."

"Might I remind you that I am—in my heart, if not in fact—one of those Grub Street hack gossip writers," she said coldly.

"Julianna, you know what I mean," he said softly, but firmly.

"Yes, I do. I know that you care more about what the world thinks of us than how I may feel in this relationship, or what I may think of you!" She resisted the urge to stamp her foot on the floor.

"That's not true. I did this for *us*. For you—to show you . . ."

"And you didn't even let me in on the secret, when you know how I feel about secrets being kept from me," she said. Not that she gave a damn about secrets, per se, but she did care about not being consulted about a matter that concerned them both. She was not some child or little miss that would tolerate having decisions made for her. He knew that!

"I made a mistake, Julianna," Roxbury said frankly. He took her hands in his, looked her in the eye and said, "I am sorry. My intentions were pure."

She could see the pain etched in his features. It was made all the more worse because she could see that this was not at all how he had planned it. That he expected to be triumphant and now . . .

Her heart ached for him, because she wanted to make him happy but she could not tolerate what had just happened. She had trusted him, loved him, against all better judgment.

"I want to go home," she said. And then she walked out.

It was a strange thing, Julianna thought, that the Man About Town had been just right there, and she was more consumed and concerned with the *other* man in the room. Surely, that signified something. Unmasking her nemesis no longer seemed like the most important thing. In fact, nothing seemed to matter at all because she had been betrayed by her lover, her husband, and her friend.

"Julianna." Roxbury was calling her now, and she could hear his heavy footsteps following. She turned a corner. She needed to be alone.

"Julianna." She missed him already. But if

they spoke now, they would fight more. Quickly, she turned and opened the first door she saw and slipped inside. Her eyes widened in shock, and her lips parted to gasp but no sound came out.

The scene within was so improbable, so outrageous, and so wildly unexpected that Julianna actually pinched herself. The scene she had stumbled upon actually made her completely and utterly forget that her marriage had just collapsed. The sight before her eyes was indeed for real.

There was scandal and then there was hot, salacious, you-will-*never*-believe-this, dear God above SCANDAL. This was the latter.

Julianna turned to tell Simon—to share her joy, her triumph, her excitement—and he wasn't there. The moment was utterly ruined.

Chapter 49

Home, it turned out, was 24 Bloomsbury Place. Roxbury woke the next morning to find his wife and all her belongings long gone.

When other women had moved out or moved on, he'd felt nothing but relief. If he was tempted to miss them, he need only take one look at a horribly decorated dining room or drawing room to remind himself of just what he'd escaped.

But now he felt hollow, incomplete, lonely, and all sorts of pathetically morose feelings.

His home was hers now—from the drawing room to the guest bedroom—and it was just wrong that she wasn't there. What really made his gut ache was the realization that she had been planning on staying—Why else would she have redecorated the whole place from top to bottom, tastefully, and to her liking?

He had meant to seduce her, and had fallen in love with her. She'd been planning on staying so perhaps she had fallen in love with him, too.

He had completely, utterly cocked up.

As a gentleman does, he sought refuge in his club.

What ought to be a man's haven no longer was for Roxbury. He could only imagine Julianna skulking through the rooms, dressed as a man, with a sly smile of triumph on her mouth. He thought of their one afternoon together here, when he'd had a lovely time with the last woman he'd expected to, in the last place on earth he'd expected.

He ordered a drink. Brandy might provide an escape.

But then Roxbury thought of clinking brandy bottles, toasting to ruined lives in his carriage. Or watching her first sputtering sip.

"When she said she wanted to go home," Roxbury told Brandon, "I thought she'd go back to our house and sulk for a day or two. But no, she's packed everything up and returned to Bloomsbury Place."

He took another sip of his second brandy.

"Shocking," Brandon replied dryly. He'd been reading the newspaper, *The Weekly*—damn him—while Roxbury rambled.

"You're not at all shocked, I can tell," he replied.

"Roxbury, you deliberately exposed the woman, which is one thing. Far worse than that, *you made a plan without consulting her.* I cannot stress enough how this is one of the worst things you can do," Brandon told him.

"Why has marriage made you wise and I've stayed a fool?" Roxbury grumbled.

"I grew up with three sisters. I was born with an advantage," Brandon said. Roxbury had only one wild and reckless brother who died in an attempt to avoid matrimony.

"Since you're so wise to the ways of women, tell me what to do," he muttered.

"Why don't you try serenading her outside her window," Brandon suggested, smirking. Roxbury scowled.

"Might I remind you that the last time I did that, I was shot."

"Jewelry. Flowers," Brandon said, suggesting the obvious. Flowers were not sufficient for a sin of this magnitude.

But jewelry . . . Roxbury thought of the ring he had locked in his desk drawer. He'd spent days away from her in search of it. He could give her that, if he could only get time with her.

However, the ring was still in his possession because—as he had been about to give it to her—she had said, "If there is one thing I want it's to uncover the real identity of the Man About Town."

He had tried that. If only diamonds and rubies were sufficient. Given the rift between them now, he would need both and more.

"I should finish this business with the Man About Town," Roxbury said.

"Whatever you do, you should definitely not be seen talking to, looking at, or breathing in the direction of another woman," Brandon counseled.

"Shockingly, the idea never even occurred to me," Roxbury remarked. Brandon looked at him wide-eyed and then broke into a grin.

"Inchbald! This man needs another drink. He has just realized that he's in love with his wife."

Chapter 50

The offices of The London Weekly

"**G**ood afternoon, Knightly," Julianna said as she strolled into his office unannounced much as she had done a little over a year ago. She was in search of a position then, and she was now.

Then: She'd been desperate and quaking in her boots as she tried to act calm and collected.

Now: The need for this job was just as raw and urgent as ever. Having survived two failed marriages, one firing, and the backside of society, it took more than Knightly to make her nervous.

This time, however, Knightly was not surprised to see her.

"Good afternoon, Julianna. I'd ask what brings you here, but I'm certain I already know," he said, setting down his pencil and pages and leaning back in his chair. He always leaned back, as if he were open and at ease. She knew him, though, and that he was sharp and forever on the lookout. He was not to be underestimated.

"I've come to submit my latest column," she

said, pulling the folded sheet out of her reticule. His blue eyes flashed interest and she smiled slyly.

She spent the morning at 24 Bloomsbury Place with her quill, her paper, and some delicious gossip. She had longed to be writing her column in her own home, and was dismayed to find it not as satisfying at she had imagined. She missed Roxbury.

She missed him with an intensity that continually surprised her. In the morning, in the afternoon, and at night. She missed kissing and sparring. She missed just knowing he was under the same roof. It didn't make any sense to her at all, but nevertheless, she felt his absence like a hole in her soul and she ached with longing for him.

He had to go and muck it all up. How could he do that when he knew how stubborn, suspicious, and proud she was? Honestly, men were such idiots.

Julianna had bullied through her maudlin emotions and composed a stellar edition of "Fashionable Intelligence." Knightly reached for it; she waved it away with a smile that said, *Not so fast or easy, Mister.*

"*A few of the guests at Lady F—'s ball were up to no good,*" she began to read. "*Rumors are circulating that Lord R—and his new bride were discovered in one of the drawing rooms in a most delicate and intimate position. Is it a love match? The Man About Town and the rest of London are eager to know. Has Lord R—been reformed? Or is it a case of once a rake, always a rake?*

Consider this, London—the new Lady R—has returned to her bachelorette lodgings. What this means for this stormy, mysterious, scandalous marriage we can only speculate."

Here she dared a glance at Knightly, and his expression made her want to cry. Knightly occasionally grinned, but mostly his expression was inscrutable. Half the time he was clearly woolgathering about the only thing he ever talked or thought about: *The Weekly*.

Now, though, he had not only registered what she was saying—that her marriage of convenience was over, and that it wasn't a simple, amicable parting. Somewhere along the lines it had become a love match. And then it was over.

She knew that the other columns would report on the love, for that was what they all saw. Feeling she had nothing left to lose or to hide, Julianna laid it all on the line—or page, rather.

Knightly understood; his expression was pained, and empathetic. And that made her want to cry.

She took a deep breath and carried on:

"But that is old news. Every few years—or every decade—something so delightfully salacious, deliciously scandalous, wonderfully outrageous occurs. I can hardly believe my pen as I write, but this author witnessed the following with her own eyes . . ."

"Care to guess?" she asked Knightly. He scowled.

"Keep reading," he ordered, leaning forward. That brought a proud smile to her lips.

"Lady S—W—, authoress of the book Lady Stewart-Wortly's Daily Devotional for Pious and Proper Ladies *and famously outspoken authority on morality, was seen in the company of Lord W—. Faithful readers will remember that his Lordship has previously graced these pages due*

to a shocking preference in undergarments. This unlikely pair was discovered in a different drawing room. Alone. Unclothed, mostly (save for women's undergarments that may or may not have been on the lady in question). In a position more fitting for a barnyard than a ballroom. This Lady of Distinction is speechless."

Upon concluding, Julianna took a bow. Knightly applauded. She grinned.

"If you think Grenville and the penny-a-liners can top this, say the word and I'll take my work to one of the hundreds of other London newspapers," she challenged.

Knightly leaned forward, resting his forearms on the desk and looking at her intensely with his vivid blue eyes. She did not wilt under the heat of his gaze.

"Why haven't you?" he asked.

"Because I love *The London Weekly*. Almost as much as you do. But there is only so much heartache a woman can take. Are you going to take me back or send me on my way once and for all?"

She acted as calm as she could, but her heart was pounding and she held her breath, waiting for Knightly to decide her fate.

Chapter 51

St. Bride's Church
Two weeks later

When it was her turn, Julianna—in her disguise as a boy—knelt by the side of the Man About Town and confessed her secret to him.

"Lady Roxbury is going abroad," she said softly.

It was a fiction, just like the last thing she had confided in him. And just like the next few things she—or someone on her behalf—would tell him. The plan was simple—systematically feeding him false information to discredit him as a reputable authority of high-society gossip. She, on the other hand, would have the pure, sterling, verified truth in her column.

Julianna thrived on the competition. Part of her wanted to expose him. She also wanted to know his true identity, and for the Man About Town to be aware that she knew. And then there was a small bit of her heart that wanted Roxbury and didn't give a damn about anyone or anything else.

She sighed. It always came back to Roxbury.

It had been a fortnight since she moved back to Bloomsbury Place. The ache didn't fade, as she had hoped it would. Her longing for him was like that for water or air—as if she needed him in order to survive. But he did not come back for her, and she was still too stubborn to go to him.

She was beginning to hate being stubborn, but old habits and lifelong traits died hard. So she was telling the Man About Town that she was going abroad, with the vain hope that it would be just the thing to set Roxbury on fire, and running after her.

Dusk was settling over London when the Man About Town concluded his calling hours. He quit St. Bride's and headed north.

Julianna followed him from Fleet Street to High Holborn, dodging pedestrians, merchants, horses, and carriages all the way. More than once she nearly lost sight of her quarry, but thanks to the ease with which she could move in breeches, she was never too far behind.

He entered a coffeehouse called Griswold's. So did she. However, by the time she arrived, a few steps behind, she had lost him in the dark, smoky recesses of the crowded space.

"Curses," she muttered. And then, "Oh hell and damnation."

She'd come too far to have lost him now. Pulling her cap low, she sauntered through the room, glancing about. She had half a mind to take a seat, order coffee, light up a cheroot, and read a paper.

A faint smile played upon her lips at the memory of her scandalous drive on Rotten Row with Roxbury. They had laughed over a woman smoking, ankles showing. All things proper ladies did not do. Proper ladies did not fall in love with rakes when they knew better, but look at her now.

Far from proper, and having fallen in love.

The men around her chatted about stock performances at The 'Change, horses, boxing, and they placed stupid wagers. They drank. They smoked. They spit. It was definitely no place for a lady.

But before she left, she looked again for her archrival. It was too dark, and too many men had horrible slouching postures, and too many of them had neglected to remove their hats. What manners! Then she reminded herself that no one went to a coffeehouse for well-mannered company.

She did not notice a certain gentleman until it was too late.

He firmly and discretely grabbed her arm and ushered her forward. No one seemed to notice or care.

"Sir, what are you—!" she hissed, not wanting to cause a scene in case she revealed herself. Then she might be in even more trouble—as if this wasn't bad enough.

"*Shh!*" he said sharply. Perhaps she should call for help. What was worse: being kidnapped or discovered in a coffeehouse? Her reputation had certainly seen worse than either.

She squirmed around, hoping to catch a glimpse of her abductor. She also squirmed in an attempt to escape. He held firm. Her heart began to pound.

"Damn it, Jules, hold still," he urged.

"Oh, it's you," she muttered. It was her husband, coming to rescue her when she did not need rescuing. Well, she might, but that was beside the point. He was here—with her! What was he doing here?

"Yes, it's me. And if you know what's good for you, you'll come quietly," he said. His voice was low and firm and it sent shivers sparkling up and down her spine. Things had gone from dire to dramatic.

"Are you kidnapping me? I will not go home with you. Not now. What are you doing here anyway?" She was asking a million questions all at once. As glad as she was to see him, she did not want to leave just yet. Not when she was so close to solving that vexing mystery. With an equal fervor, she wished to throw herself into Roxbury's arms and kiss him passionately.

While Roxbury's presence was addling her brain and sending her thoughts spinning in a thousand different directions, the Man About Town was getting away. She squirmed again, trying to get away.

"Jules, be quiet and be still," Roxbury ordered. "You are causing a scene. I am not taking you home. If you want the information you've been seeking, you will come quietly with me."

"How do you know what I'm seeking?" she retorted.

"Don't be obtuse. I know you, Julianna. I know your thoughts before they occur to you, your quick retorts before they cross your lovely lips. I know what you look like unclothed and I know that you *think* you are perfectly disguised as you search for the Man About Town."

"How did you find me?"

"I followed you from St. Bride's, sweating bullets all the while."

"Yes, but where are you taking me?"

"I am going to see the Man About Town. You

can wait here, if you'd like. Alone. With all these drunken men who don't give a damn if you're a lady. I taught you how to box, so you can defend yourself."

"I'm coming with you," she said in a rush.

"I thought so," he said smugly.

Roxbury led her up the stairs, past a few doors that were open to decently sized bedrooms. And then he opened one that led to a closet.

"In you go," he said, nudging her in the back. To be fair, it was a large closet, but still. It was a closet. It was a small, dark, dank enclosure above a coffeehouse in High Holborn. This was certainly on the list of places ladies did not go, and definitely not with rakes.

She merely lifted one brow, questioningly.

"I know," Roxbury replied dryly. "I'm so romantic."

Chapter 52

Roxbury exhaled impatiently. The maddening woman had once declared that if there was one thing she wished for, it was to know the identity of the Man About Town.

If there was one thing Roxbury wished for, it was his wife. He was going to win her back, and he was going to do so by revealing the Man About Town to her. Julianna was writing her column again—he knew her voice, her wit—and if she knew her rival's secrets then she would have a certain measure of security.

She wouldn't need Roxbury. But, God above, he would make her want him. He loved her, like no other woman. And so he knew, really knew, that she, Julianna Somerset Roxbury otherwise known as the Lady of Distinction or, more affectionately, his Lady Scandalous, was beyond a shadow of a doubt the woman for him. Forever.

A man's life was his own. The last words of his beloved brother had been a rallying cry for all sorts of selfish and rakish behavior. Now, however, a revision was in order. Roxbury's life was his own, but he wanted to share it with his wife.

He'd explain all that to Julianna later; she'd delight in stories of Edward's outrageous exploits. Roxbury was sure Edward would have approved of a spitfire like her. In fact, he would have been rolling with laughter at the predicament they were in now.

At the end of the day, his plan to win her was just some plan that was nothing more than the workings of a desperate man. And it involved a tiny, dark closet above a coffeehouse in a less than fashionable neighborhood.

Thinking it too bad he didn't fall for a woman who would be happy with merely jewelry or flowers, Roxbury leveled a stern look at her.

"After you, madam."

"Are you demented? We'll never both fit in there."

"My dear Julianna, for the past month I've been following the Man About Town from St. Bride's to this place. I've watched him go upstairs, come back down an hour or so later, and then I've followed him to the offices of *The Times*. In that time, I've found this spot that will enable you to stay hidden and watch everything unfold," Roxbury told her, with impatience seeping into his voice.

He heard footsteps thudding up the stairs.

Julianna ducked in, and pulled him with her. He tugged the door shut, and then they were enveloped in darkness.

"This is lovely. Cozy, private," she remarked. It was a prime opportunity for all manner of intimate, inadvertent touching as they shuffled around as quietly as possible in a place that was not made to accommodate two people.

"Roxbury," she gasped. His hand had just "accidentally" caressed her bottom.

"Terribly sorry," he replied with a grin.

"Indeed," she drawled, but she nestled close against him, much to his pleasure and frustration.

"I thought I would have a few more days to get this ready," Roxbury told her. "I was going to whisk you away."

"I'm still not sure what this is, other than a horrendously compromising position, should we be caught," she replied.

"We're married," he said. It didn't matter where they were caught now, or by whom. It was a benefit of marriage he had never before considered.

"I am dressed as a man," Julianna reminded him, "and you are trying to dispel rumors about your preferences, spread by some horrible shrew."

And then, so very softly, Roxbury whispered, "She's not a horrible shrew."

"Oh Roxbury . . ." Julianna sighed.

"Though she can be if she doesn't get a good bedding by her husband," he couldn't resist adding.

"And here I was about to apologize," she retorted, which was a good enough apology for him.

"I know, my dear Julianna, and I forgive you." If they had a prayer of making their marriage work, those words needed to be said.

There was noise in the hall—the sound of footsteps thudding up the stairs, and low male voices in conversation.

"Look here," Roxbury whispered, and he managed to guide Julianna's attention to two small holes carved into the wall, enabling her to see into the other room. He knew very well what she saw, and it was the revelation of a great mystery.

Chapter 53

Julianna peered into the room. When her eyes adjusted to the light, she saw a rough-hewn table with a large towering sconce full of lit candles. There were two chairs, and a window showing a periwinkle sky. Anything else was cloaked in shadows.

Julianna fumbled in the dark until she found Roxbury's hand to clasp in her own. Her heart began to beat hard with anticipation.

But her heart also beat hard with joy. This moment was just for *her*. It was a moment that he had planned and that had taken work to enact. Even after she had left him, he had still been devoted to her. Surely, Roxbury loved her. She squeezed his hand as if to say "Thank you. I love you."

There was a man seated at the rough-hewn wooden table—but not just any man. She'd seen him out and about. Lord above, she'd even had conversations with him! But what was his name?

She nearly growled in frustration.

Whoever he was, he sat down at a table with writing supplies and brandy.

"Well, well, Branson, what's the news today?" he asked, leaning back and sipping a glass of brandy.

The other one, Branson—there were two!—she recognized as the one from St. Bride's this afternoon. He carried that big, black cloak under one arm. It seemed the Man about Town had an apprentice among his vast network.

"Lord and Lady Haile are moving to a new residence," Branson answered. "There is more gossip about Lady Stewart-Wortly—her husband has sent her to a nunnery."

"I already knew that," Julianna whispered to Roxbury. She couldn't resist.

"Of course, darling," he murmured, giving her hand an affectionate squeeze.

"I'm surprised he hasn't sent her to the afterlife. What a slow week. Has no one eloped or died under suspicious circumstances?" the other man asked, bored. She knew the feeling. After a while, one felt like they'd heard it all. He could only be the Man About Town.

"Lady Mayhew has refused Lord Pershing's offer of marriage. As you know, everyone expected her to accept. Oh, and Lady Roxbury is going abroad," Branson said.

"Interesting. Was it the lady herself that told you?" the Man About Town asked.

"No, a young lad. Probably a footman," Branson said with a shrug.

"Probably the lady in disguise," the Man About Town suggested, leaning forward.

How did he know?

"I'm sure it wasn't. He was wearing breeches,

boots, and he was alone," Branson said, defending himself.

"Anyone can put on breeches and boots or a dress and speak in falsetto," he lectured. "If you're going to take on this job, Branson, you cannot believe everything you see or hear. That's one of the key lessons about being the Man About Town. I've learned it, my predecessors have learned it, and you will, too."

Julianna gasped. So that was how it was done!

It wasn't one man for forty years, but a succession, each one training his replacement. It was quite beautiful, really, how the column itself was bigger, grander, and greater than its writers. She would do well to copy this, so that if anything should happen to her—were she to be fired, again, for example—the column could live on in the hands of a trained and skilled gossip columnist.

"Right. Be skeptical," Branson said.

"Verify," the Man About Town corrected.

What was his name? He was Lord Something. But how could she not *know* this?

"And the other lessons of the Man About Town, passed down from one to the next?" the Man About Town tested his successor.

Branson clasped his hands behind his back and began to recite them.

"First, never speak of the Man About Town."

The real Man About Town nodded.

"Second, never speak of the Man About Town."

The real Man About Town nodded again, adding a grin.

"Third, nothing is sacred. Everything is fodder."

Julianna had learned that the hard way.

"Fourth, verify."

A good one, she thought. Wild speculation led to all manner of trouble. Consider Roxbury, the duel, their marriage. All sorts of wonderful trouble.

"Fifth, print anything and print everything, so long as it's gossip," the new Man About Town finished.

"Damn right. Now let's write this thing. I have a party to attend tonight," the Man About Town said as he picked up the pen, dipped it in ink, and began to scrawl on the sheet of paper before him. He spoke as he wrote.

There was no greater proof of his identity than this. She knew the tone of the writing, the turns of phrase, and here they were coming out of the man's mouth. *But what was his name?* Julianna wanted to jump with glee, and cry out in vexation.

And then he finished with a flourish, set down the pen and said, "One column closer to retirement."

"What will you do if you don't do this?" Branson asked.

"Haven't you heard?" The Man About Town leaned back in his chair, folded his arms behind his head and grinned. "I'm going to inherit."

"Oooh," Julianna said softly under her breath. Now she knew who he was! The Earl of Selborne was on his deathbed, and had been for weeks now. They all said he was holding on just because he didn't want the title and the wealth to go to his heir, his brother's son. Now she understood.

"Which reminds me of the last vow," said the future Earl of Selborne, currently known as Lord Brookes. "I am not the first Man About Town and I shall not be the last."

Chapter 54

Outside of the coffeehouse, Roxbury quickly hailed a hackney for them.

"We're going to 24 Bloomsbury Place," he told the driver.

"We are?" she asked. After all that, she thought he might take her home—to *their* home.

"Do you have an objection?" he asked.

"No," she said, and then she added, "I cannot thank you enough."

"My pleasure. I live to oblige my lady," he said gallantly. "And now if my lady will oblige me by—"

"Oh Simon, I have missed you," she burst out. She'd never been one to hold her tongue and now was really not the time to start.

"I missed you, too," he said softly, reaching out for her hand.

Why had they parted? Because of a plan she didn't like that had been put in effect with the best of intentions. Did it merit a fight? Yes. Was it worth abandoning their marriage? No.

It all seemed so silly now. She'd been overly sensitive and emotional, most likely—not that she would ever admit that aloud to anyone, especially him. Roxbury had more than made up for any mistakes. But it didn't even matter, really, because they missed each other and now they had a chance to reconcile.

"I was going to ask if you would listen to my heartfelt pleas to have you return to our home and truly be my wife," he said, smiling a bit shyly.

"I shall hear you out," she said, trying to sound like a disaffected lady. But she couldn't; tears of happiness stung her eyes and she knew that he saw them.

Somehow, Roxbury managed to kneel in the carriage. She laughed and placed her hand in his.

"My dear Julianna," he began. "We married for all the wrong reasons. For money. For reputation. For convenience. The marriage has been a disaster, and some of that has been my fault. No, don't protest, you are just as guilty as I and you know it."

"This is not very romantic, Roxbury," she chided. And yet, it was heartfelt and the truth, which was, she knew, true romance.

"Have patience, woman, I'm getting to it," he told her. Then he took a deep breath and carried on. "And yet, in the wreckage of our marriage thus far, I have fallen in love with you. The real you. The one who occasionally cries and teaches her friends boxing, the one who is fiercely proud and independent and witty. The one who has been hurt before and has dared to love again—and brave enough or mad enough to dare to love a disreputable rake like me."

"I must be mad," she said. *Madly in love.*

"Stop interrupting and let me finish," said Roxbury. "Where was I?"

"Marriage for the wrong reasons, it was a disaster, but still you love me anyway because you must be mad, etcetera," she reminded him. Then she squeezed his hands affectionately because she thought her heart would just burst with happiness.

"Ah, right. Julianna, marry me again for the right reasons. Because I love you, and you love me—don't try to deny it, I know you do. Marry me because we are so suited for each other and because I want to spend the rest of my life having adventures with you and only you."

"Oh Simon," she said, sighing like the worst sort of lovesick ninny. "I love you, too."

"Tell me you are weeping because you are so overcome with joy."

"I am. I have missed you horribly. Since our separation, I have gotten exactly what I wanted— my column, and now I know the identity of the Man About Town—but then it wasn't everything I wanted anymore. I just want you. The whole time, I missed you intensely. But still . . . I'm crying because I love you and you love me and yes, I want to marry you again, for all the right reasons."

The carriage rolled to a stop in front of her little gray townhouse with white trim at 24 Bloomsbury Place. It had been her late husband's, and then it had been hers. It all seemed like a lifetime ago. And it was a lifetime that she was ready to relinquish so that she could go forth as Lady Roxbury.

Roxbury looked out the window as well, and then at her.

"I won't give up my column," she declared.

She loved it, writing gossip suited her, and Lady Roxbury could certainly moonlight as the Lady of Distinction.

"I would never dream of asking you to," he said.

"Terribly sorry, driver. We'll be going to 28 Bruton Street," she called out. And then, softly so only he could hear, she whispered, "I love you," and there wasn't much talking for a while after that.

His lips met hers for a kiss that promised a love match, forever.

Epilogue

White's

The new Earl of Selborne, previously known as Lord Brookes, sat by the fire with a brandy in one hand and a copy of *The London Weekly* in the other. It was the first week since he inherited and since he officially retired as the Man About Town. He might have given up skulking about town at all hours, but he would not cease to follow the gossip. Thus, he opened the paper directly to page six and began to read.

FASHIONABLE INTELLIGENCE

By a Lady of Distinction

The first rule of the Man About Town is that you do not speak of the Man About Town.

The color drained from his face.

Of course, all of London breaks this regularly

and this Lady of Distinction shall be no exception because this lady has news about the gentleman— or gentlemen?—that composes that popular column in a small room in High Holborn. This lady learned the secrets of the Man About Town and might reveal them at any time.

A slick sheen of sweat beaded upon Selborne's forehead. How could she know? For forty years the secret had been secure. He drank, heavily.

There are more secrets to share, of course. We are told that Lady Stewart-Wortly is comfortably ensconced at a nunnery in France.

He already knew that, but it was a small comfort indeed.

She will be at liberty to write and one has to wonder—will she continue to publish conduct guides for ladies, or turn to writing romances?

The eminent collector, Lady Hortensia Reeves, has donated her vast collections to the British Museum and has resolved to begin collecting suitors.

All of London is saddened by the loss of the eminently respectable Earl of Selborne. His heir, Lord Brookes, is certainly less than respectable; in fact, one might say he's thoroughly disreputable. What has he been up to these past few years, we wonder?

Selborne glanced about the room, and shrank into his seat. For years he had gone undetected and now this Lady of Distinction had learned his secrets!

By the time he reached the final paragraph, his color was wan, his skin was damp, and his heart was pounding. But nevertheless, he managed a wry smile at the answer to a mystery that had plagued him. He raised his glass in salute, and downed the rest of his brandy.

In other news, Lady Roxbury is now wearing a stunning diamond and ruby ring, gifted to her by her husband. By all accounts, including their own, the marriage is indeed a love match.

Next month, don't miss these exciting new love stories only from Avon Books

The Sins of Viscount Sutherland by Samantha James
Claire Ashcroft has good reason to despise Viscount Grayson Sutherland. A reckless man with a frightening reputation, he is responsible for a death that deeply pains her. She'd kill him if she could, but instead she plans seduction that will result in a shattered heart: his. Her scheme works perfectly…too perfectly.

Devil Without a Cause by Terri Garey
Faith McFarland is so desperate to save her sick child that she's willing to make a deal with the Devil: steal a ring worn by bad-boy rock star Finn Payne and receive a miracle. Temptation and seduction become necessary evils, yet Faith's salvation means Finn's damnation… he sold his soul years ago and the ring is all that stands between him and Hell.

Guarding a Notorious Lady by Olivia Parker
She may be the sister of a duke, but Lady Rosalind Devine can't seem to stay out of trouble—which is why the duke asks his friend Nicholas Kincaid to keep an eye on her while he is away. But Rosalind will not make things easy for an unwanted guardian, and Nicholas finds himself desiring an entirely different role….one of passion and unavoidable scandal.

Too Wicked to Love by Debra Mullins
Genevieve Wallington-Willis knows better than to trust *any* man—which is why her attraction to John Ready is so disturbing. He's devilishly handsome, but far too mysterious— and a coachman, no less! John dares not reveal his true identity until he can clear his name, but being this close to the exquisite Genevieve could be the greatest risk of all.

At Avon Books, we know your passion for romance—once you finish one of our novels, you find yourself wanting more.

May we tempt you with . . .

- **Excerpts** from our upcoming releases.

- Entertaining **extras**, including authors' personal photo albums and book lists.

- Behind-the-scenes **scoop** on your favorite characters and series.

- **Sweepstakes** for the chance to win free books, romantic getaways, and other fun prizes.

- Writing **tips** from our authors and editors.

- **Blog** with our authors and find out why they love to write romance.

- **Exclusive content** that's not contained within the pages of our novels.

Join us at
www.avonbooks.com